MAYDAY MAN

MAYDAY MAN

A
NOVEL
OF
NUCLEAR
PERIL

WILLIAM BEECHER

 BRASSEY'S (US), Inc.

WASHINGTON· NEW YORK · LONDON · OXFORD · BEIJING
FRANKFURT · SÃO PAULO · SYDNEY · TOKYO · TORONTO

Copyright © 1990 Brassey's (US), Inc.

Brassey's (US), Inc.

Editorial Offices	*Order Department*
Brassey's (US), Inc.	Macmillan Publishing Co.
8000 Westpark Drive, 4th Floor	Front and Brown Streets
McLean, VA 22102	Riverside, NJ 08075

Brassey's (US), Inc., books are available at special discounts for bulk purchases for sales promotions, premiums, fund-raising, or educational use through the special Sales Director, Macmillan Publishing Company, 866 Third Avenue, New York, New York 10022.

Library of Congress Cataloging-in-Publication Data
Beecher, Bill
    Mayday man : a novel of nuclear peril / Bill Beecher.
        p.   cm.
    ISBN 0-08-036729-1
    I. Title
PS3552.E327M3   1990
813'.54—dc20   89-25262
                                                                    CIP

British Library Cataloguing in Publication Data
Beecher, Bill
    Mayday man.
    I. Title
    813'.54[F]

10 9 8 7 6 5 4 3 2 1

Published in the United States of America

To my father and mother,
Mr. and Mrs. Samuel Beecher,
who sacrificed that I might learn and grow,
and to my wife Eileen,
who encouraged me to persevere.

Acknowledgments

This book has a singular history. First, I must doff my hat to President George Bush. In a sense he's the godfather of *Mayday Man*. In 1985, as vice president, he invited five Washington correspondents to accompany him on a working trip to Western Europe. While there was a diplomatic agenda at each stop, the unacknowledged though underlying purpose was to be near Frankfurt to greet 39 hostages from a hijacked TWA aircraft when they were freed. During the long hours of waiting, I began to think what if instead of it always being an American airliner that was hijacked it was a Soviet aircraft? What if, instead of hijackers seeking publicity for a cause, it was a cunning group seeking a strategic outcome? The idea that began on a trip with then Vice President Bush gave rise to this book.

Several people helped in the process. I am grateful to the publisher, Dr. Frank Margiotta, who had the vision to see the potential of the manuscript. I owe a special note of thanks to Connie Buchanan for being a dream editor, easy to work with, patient, and full of excellent stylistic and substantive suggestions. It was a delight to work with such professionals.

1

The sun, the color of molten brass, was slowly lowering behind the ancient sand-whipped fortress wall on the western edge of San'a. The air was as hot and dry as the interior of a pottery kiln. Mohammed nudged Achmed and nodded toward the dust-covered van on the next block. The two Yemenite workmen in gray coveralls had loaded trays of food and cartons of soft drinks and slammed the rear doors. Now they were heading to the front of the van.

Achmed groped under the dashboard and found the two bare wires he was looking for. Quickly he twisted them together, creating sparks that burned his fingers. But no matter. The engine of the dark-green Volvo roared to life reassuringly. He smiled. It was a trick he had learned in the slums of Cairo, something that high-born Mohammed had to admire even if he offered no praise. The sudden engine noise made Nadia start. She was in the back seat fighting off nervous exhaustion and the day's heat. "Is it time?" she asked, brushing back her short black hair.

"It's time," Mohammed said. He slipped the Browning automatic from his belt and with his left hand carefully screwed the silencer into place. "Remember," he warned, "we're not to use our guns except as a last resort. These Shafi rarely have weapons, and the Zeidis, their enemies, nearly always carry *jambiya* daggers. Sergeant Major Samir and his men also have daggers. They'll use them and leave one behind. We want this to look like the usual squabble between rival tribesmen."

As the van passed through the western gate of the city

onto the Airport Road, it gathered speed. Achmed accelerated too, but not as much. They weren't in any rush. They only had to keep the van in view so they could block its retreat, if necessary. There was little construction outside the city limits. Not at all like Cairo, which kept racing to accommodate an exploding birth rate. And here in Yemen the buildings were of mud or stone, not reinforced concrete. The tallest were seldom over five or six stories. Rows of swaying date palms lined the road. Occasionally they passed small orchards of squat fig and walnut trees. Along one stretch Achmed breathed in the sensuous perfume of tamarisk and frankincense.

He smoothed his dark pomaded hair above his right ear. He was not nearly as handsome as light-skinned Mohammed, but had a wild look and the more spirited girls were attracted to him. Mohammed was about fifteen years older than Achmed, in his early forties, with wisps of silver in his wiry black hair that gave him a distinguished air.

Up ahead on the road, Samir was startled by the sight of two gazelles loping gracefully up a hillside. His eyes had been half closed. He always got sleepy at this time of day, when the sun was going down. He would have to stay alert. As planned, he had stopped his stolen car just beyond the blind turn. No vehicle could pass. The four commandos in his squad were hidden on both sides of the road.

Samir had the spare tire and jack out when he heard the Yemenite service van approaching. "Get ready," he warned his men. The van rounded the curve and screeched to a dusty stop when the driver saw Samir's car. He was angry—just as they had expected. He stuck his head out the window and shouted a curse. Samir responded in the Shafi dialect: "Your mother prefers camels to your father!"

At this, the doors of the van blew open and the two incensed tribesmen jumped out, the driver with a tire iron in his right hand. Samir's men rose from their hiding places beside the road, grabbed them from behind, and slit their throats. Quickly they dragged the limp bodies to one side, removing an ID pass from the Shafi driver. Under his body they left a Zeidi dagger, a short curved dirk with a bone and brass handle. That done, the stolen car was pushed to the shoulder of the road and the right front tire punctured. One commando threw the spare tire and the jack close to the car and left the trunk open. Samir and his men had been chewing qat leaves; as instructed, they spit them out beside the car and the flat tire.

The more dangerous part of the plan lay ahead.

Achmed, Mohammed, and Nadia pulled up in the Volvo. As soon as the van and Samir's stolen car were out of the way Mohammed and Nadia got out. Achmed drove ahead in the Volvo until he found a steep ravine. It only took him a minute to push the car over the edge. He grinned with pleasure as it tumbled to the bottom. So far, so good.

Samir spit as he climbed into the van. "How can they stand chewing that stuff, sir?" he said. "It gives me a stomachache."

Mohammed smiled. "It's a mild narcotic. In highland homes, there are two qat rooms, one for the men, one for the women. They chew the stuff for hours. We have televison; the Zeidis have qat."

A quarter of an hour later the van, Mohammed driving, Achmed in the passenger seat, approached the chain-link service gate at the perimeter of San'a International. The others were concealed in the back of the van. They had all changed into gray coveralls.

Mohammed barely slowed as he neared the entrance and waved the ID. A solitary guard motioned them in with a lazy nod of the head and reached for a cigarette.

"Keep your eyes open," Mohammed warned when they were beyond the gate. "We're looking for an Il-76M, a four-engine Ilyushin with a high tail. It's the weekly Soviet courier flight carrying outsize cargo and a few lower-ranking military and diplomatic personnel and their families back to Moscow." He looked at Achmed. "We need it for the drive-on loading ramp. Courier flight no. 79 has an important mission."

Achmed bristled, but said nothing. He resented not being trusted with the full details of the plan. Mohammed had insisted it was a matter of security, that if for some reason he or Nadia or Samir was picked up none of them could be forced to compromise secrets they didn't know. But they did know it was a strategic operation of great importance, that its target was Israel, and that it was being masterminded by General Rahman Hazi, the Fox of Cairo. They were a handpicked team. It was an honor to be involved.

"There it is, on the other side of the Air France plane!" Achmed cried, gesturing.

Mohammed glanced at his Rolex. It was 1950 hours. The plane was scheduled to take off at 2005. He wheeled the van to a side door of the aircraft where a metal gangway awaited their delivery, then signaled Achmed up the stairs. Just inside the gangway, Achmed ran into a fussing steward in a blue uniform with red piping. "Why are you so late?" the steward demanded in broken Arabic.

Achmed smiled and mumbled something about an accident. He brushed past, looking for additional crewmen. None in sight. When the others followed him up the stairs, the steward glanced at Achmed suspiciously. He started to say something. In response, Achmed slammed his automatic into the man's ribs, shoved him toward the lavatory, and opening the door, pushed him onto the toilet. The steward sat quivering, his hands covering his face. Achmed fired a single shot through the hands, then clapped the door shut. No one would use the facilities just now; they were buckled up for takeoff.

Achmed was proud of the fact that he had suggested specially loaded, undercharged 9mm dum-dum ammunition. The soft-nosed lead bullets would flatten out as soon as they penetrated the flesh, tearing a hole inside the body. If by chance one should pass through a body, it wouldn't have the oomph or the shape to pierce the pressurized hull of the aircraft.

Mohammed, Nadia, Samir, and three commandos had carried provisions up the gangway. Samir was the last in the plane. He pulled the door shut and secured it. The fourth commando would drive the van away from the airport

4

before abandoning it and making his way back home on a commercial flight.

Guns drawn, they fanned out quietly through the compartments. The pilots were shut up in the flight cabin; they would be left alone for now. In the forward passenger cabin Achmed came up behind the lone stewardess, a broad-bottomed, heavily rouged blonde.

"A word with you," he whispered in Russian. Startled, she turned to stare at him. He was pointing a gun at her chest.

"Who? What?"

He stopped her questions by placing a finger across her lips, gently. He didn't want a panicked woman on his hands. "Relax. Do as I say and you have nothing to fear. Now, pick up the intercom and inform the captain that the passengers are secure for takeoff."

"But we're not—"

"No buts. Do precisely as I say. Talk normally. As you can see, I speak Russian."

She nodded her flushed face and picked up the handset. "Yes, yes," she said in answer to the voice on the other end. "Once we're in the air I'll bring coffee."

In the second cabin Nadia was counting passengers. "Thirty-two," she reported to Mohammed. "And Samir says there were two loadmasters in the rear cargo area. They were knocked unconscious and tied up. The aircraft is ours."

"It may be ours, but it's still sitting on the tarmac."

As if on signal, the captain fired up the engines. Moments later he released the brakes and began to taxi for takeoff. There was no competing traffic. The vibrating airplane roared down the runway into the wind, its four Solo-viev turbofan jets lifting it gracefully aloft.

It was 2012 hours, Achmed noted. Not bad, not bad at all. He waved two bald men, low-ranking diplomats by all appearances, to seats further in the rear so he and the blonde dumpling could take the two in the front left. She was smiling at him nervously, trying to curry favor, hoping to save her life. But she was too frightened to ask questions.

He glanced out the small aircraft window. Beneath them stretched the black surface of the Red Sea and he could see occasional patches of incandescent light glowing from small trading villages along the Sudanese coast.

"Time to serve the drinks," Achmed said, smiling pleasantly. The stewardess hesitated. "Up, my girl. The crew can't wait for your wonderful coffee. Just do as you're told and you'll live to dance in the Bolshoi. I have nothing against you."

Fear showed in her small blue eyes but she complied with shaking hands, getting up and moving about the galley while periodically glancing over her shoulder at Achmed, who could watch her from his seat. The coffee had already been brewed. She poured it into plastic cups, two black, one with cream and sugar, and put them on a tray. She added a plate of cookies. She would use the cart later to serve the passengers. Then she got on the intercom and told the pilots she was coming in.

Achmed was close on her heels as she carried the tray into the flight cabin. When she was through the door he grasped her fat waist with both hands and shoved her into the cockpit, slamming the door in one smooth motion. The coffee pitched onto the cabin floor and splattered in all directions across the rubber matting, running in rivulets down its grooves.

A battleship of a woman, the stewardess wheeled around. She was angry and ready to do combat now. Achmed swung the Browning hard into her chest and fired once. Her face turned instantly from anger to puzzlement as the force of the bullet threw her on her back. The weight of crumpled flesh crushed one of the styrofoam cups and instantly her blood mingled with the rivulets of coffee, spreading over the mat in the irregular shape of a Rorschach blot. The other two cups rolled around in the mess.

The navigator reached for his sidearm. Before he was able to clear his holster Achmed leveled his automatic, squeezed once, and blew the top of the man's head off, then grabbed the navigation chart he had been studying and leaned it against the wall; they would need it later.

6

This happened within seconds. The captain's earphones and the noise of the flight made him oblivious. The copilot, however, had been waiting for his coffee and keeping an eye out for the stewardess. Having seen everything, he sat frozen in his seat, staring at the man with the Browning.

Achmed waved the long, black automatic at the copilot and motioned for him to remove his earphones. Then he rapped on the captain's shoulder and repeated the gesture.

"Put the aircraft on automatic pilot," the Arab ordered in stiff Russian, after the men had removed their headsets. "Good. You should be aware that I'm a pilot too and will know instantly if either of you try any foolish heroics."

The captain nodded; he would cooperate. But now that the copilot had come out of his stupor and realized fully what was happening, his eyes darted frantically about the cabin. Without hesitation, Achmed commanded him to unbuckle and step away from the controls. The man was slow to respond. Achmed raised the gun and swung it with terrible force against his left ear, drawing blood. The copilot rose quickly but unsteadily, his hand massaging his injury.

This must be the KGB man, Achmed thought. The guy sent along to spy on the rest of the crew. He would be trained in the martial arts. Achmed could take no chances. He gestured the man to the left and, sensing that he was about to leap, fired twice at point-blank range into his heart. The copilot crumpled into a sitting position, his soft blue flight cap sliding over his staring eyes. The captain remained obediently hunched over the flight controls.

Knocks sounded on the cabin door—three fast, one slow, then the sequence was repeated. It was Mohammed. Carefully he picked his way over the bodies, losing his balance momentarily when he stepped on the splatter of coffee, cookies, and blood. He surveyed the flight cabin, realized that Achmed had only the pilot to watch, and shoved his Browning into his belt.

"Any trouble back there?" Achmed asked, his eyes on the pilot.

"Nothing that couldn't be handled. Samir and his team

had a bit of trouble subduing the loadmasters without killing them. They still have a role to play."

Achmed glanced at his compatriot. Cool and professional, as always. The operation was extremely well planned, well practiced, well executed. And why not? Though outside the chain of command, it was a military mission. Achmed stepped over the console and climbed into the copilot's seat. It wasn't easy getting into an aircraft seat, and there was the danger the pilot might take this opportunity to act. But he was too scared. Nervous sweat had turned his collar limp. Achmed almost felt sorry for him. He would be humane; he wouldn't let the pilot suffer. Pointing with his gun, Achmed waved him out of his seat. When the man was clear of the flight controls he put one bullet through his left ear, killing him instantly.

The Arab didn't feel remorse, he felt elation. And not because of the killing, he reassured himself. It was pride over an operation pulled off like clockwork. They were soldiers, professionals.

Mohammed had been watching with what seemed an expression of disgust. What was he acting so superior for? He understood blood had to be spilled. Lots of blood. But because he was high born, he didn't like soiling his hands.

The unspoken hostility between them would have to wait its venting. They had a job to finish and only Mohammed was trained sufficiently to bring it off. If they were successful, Mohammed had assured him they could change the course of history in the Middle East, redeeming the shame of Egypt, allowing her to resume her rightful place as leader of the Arab world.

Both Mohammed and Achmed were pilots, but the older man, who had spent over three years in advanced flight training in the Soviet Union, was more comfortable at the controls. Without a word Mohammed climbed into the left seat and took over. Achmed buckled into the copilot's seat. It was 2038. Phase one, the hijacking of a Soviet military transport, had taken twenty-six minutes. And nobody was the wiser.

"Just as I expected," Mohammed said with satisfaction.

8

"When Sergei Vladimirovich Ilyushin designs an airplane he keeps the controls largely the same. Military, civilian, it doesn't matter." He had clocked his share of hours in the Il-28 twin-jet bomber.

They were now beyond the range of Soviet-monitored radar at San'a, Aden, and Asmara, and not yet within range of Syrian radar at Damascus. They might be on the scopes of certain Arab military radars, but these didn't normally track routine traffic, nor did they remain operational around the clock.

The door of the flight cabin opened slowly and the barrel of an Uzi submachine gun poked through the crack. Seconds later Nadia burst through the door with her weapon raised, ready to fire. When she saw Mohammed and Achmed at the controls she lowered it with relief. "The aircraft is secure," she reported crisply. "We're lucky the flight's not very crowded. Most of the passengers are acting like angels. I've promised them they'll be released unharmed." Surveying the carnage, she nodded her head approvingly, then closed the door and returned to the passengers.

At a sign from Mohammed, Achmed switched the radio to 243.0, the international distress frequency. "Soviet courier flight no. 79. Mayday, Mayday," Mohammed cried out in English, the international language of commercial air operations. He gave his position and added, "Losing altitude rapidly. Explosion . . ." The IFF, identification friend or foe, was set to emergency. He reduced power, put the speed brakes out, and went into a steep dive toward the dark choppy surface of the Red Sea. Just above the waves he pulled back hard on the stick and leveled off. Achmed turned off the IFF radar identifier as Mohammed held the aircraft at an altitude of 500 feet. He lowered flaps partially and slowed the aircraft to 200 knots.

That was the signal for Samir in the cargo area. The rear loading ramp opened with a shudder. He and his men heaved out several passengers and the loadmasters, unresisting due to drug injections. Pieces of luggage followed, some of it rigged with a charge of plastic explosive. Small muffled explosions sounded as they hit the water. If bodies and wreckage were found it would suggest that the plane had been sabotaged. The rest of the bodies, it would be assumed, had been trapped inside the aircraft somewhere on the ocean floor. They had thought of everything.

"Now for the hard part," Achmed said to Mohammed. They had to fly below ground-based radar, without radio contact or lights, and land safely at Wadi Natrun. "Allah be with you and with our sacred mission."

Mohammed nodded. "Remember this moment, 2108 hours, 18 February 1980. You may want to tell your grandchildren you played an important part in the history of our people."

*   *   *

The sweat on Peter Robbins' forehead was not from the heat of the Pan Am jumbo jet but from apprehension. Had his bags made it onto the connecting flight to Cairo? He shouldn't have booked a tight connection through London. Wildcat strikes at Heathrow were frequent. But it had seemed the most convenient connection, so he'd risked it. Bad choice. Very bad choice. This time it turned out to be the goddam baggage handlers. He must remember in the future not to book through London if he could avoid it. Even Athens was better. All you had to worry about there was terrorists.

Since his flight from Washington was more than an hour late, he hadn't had time to go down to the tarmac as instructed and pick out his two bags for transfer to this aircraft. If he'd done that he never would have made his connection—and he was being met in Cairo. Instead, he'd described the bags to a harried Pan Am agent, provided the tag numbers, and pleaded to have someone transfer them.

"Can't promise, mate, but do me best," the man had said.

It was distinctly possible he would find himself in Egypt, weary, dirty, and without so much as a change of shirt. Not to mention his voluminous background files, which were vital to his work.

10

To compound the problem, he didn't have a hotel reservation, and rooms in Cairo were scarce.

The Egyptian press counselor in Washington had promised to use his connections to locate something decent for him. He'd boasted of a close personal friend at the Sheraton and assured Peter that even if it was booked solid, he'd be met at the airport with word on accommodations. But could the diplomat be counted on? A gracious Arab whose intentions were good, but . . .

Peter, husband, father, and chief diplomatic correspondent for the *New York World*, was a man who abhorred loose ends. At forty-six he was an experienced traveler, had covered the war in Vietnam, a failed revolution in Panama, and some trouble in the Congo. You would have thought he'd be accustomed to loose ends. But in starting a new assignment he was always more confident when he had some idea of the challenges ahead. Uncertainties were unsettling.

It was early evening when the 747 jounced down onto the runway with a squeal of brakes. As he descended the gangway to the bus that would transport passengers to the terminal, a wall of hot dry air hit him. The humidity of Washington was far behind; now he must acclimate himself to the arid desert air.

The bus was packed like the rush-hour subway in New York, most of the passengers forced to stand, shank to shank, on the bumpy ride into the terminal. The stink of cigar smoke and travelers too long without access to shower facilities turned the close air rank.

In the terminal, passport inspection lines were long and disorderly. An obese Egyptian businessman whose every other expression had been "pardon me" on the flight now boorishly elbowed his way to the front of Peter's line without apology. Peter was tempted to grab him and thumb him to the rear. But this was the man's country, and he was obviously accustomed to privileged treatment. It was his due; foreigners such as Peter Robbins might as well learn that straight off.

Peter craned his neck searching for a placard bearing

11

his last name and identifying the foreign office functionary assigned to meet him. There were several hand-lettered signs, but none for him.

Was there anyone he might phone if he wasn't met? The *World* had lost its last stringer in Cairo months ago and hadn't yet hired another. Finding a reliable replacement was one of Peter's lesser jobs on this assignment. His major task was to write a series of stories on Egypt one year after it had signed a peace treaty with Israel.

Once leader of the Arab world, Egypt was now shunned and cut off from Persian Gulf subsidies. It was struggling to develop closer ties with the West, especially the United States. What was the shape of its economy, now that it could shift resources from the military to the civilian sector? How were the generals reacting to smaller budgets? Was Egypt having any success curbing population growth? Was there much tourist traffic between the once bitter enemies? These were some of the questions he had come to answer.

He also wanted to find out if President Anwar Sadat was firmly in power after his diplomatic triumph. He had refused to be a Russian catspaw in the East-West struggle or to be cannon fodder for Arab rulers and PLO chieftains who issued truculent rhetoric from their safe palaces and five-star hotel suites. He concluded that it was in Egypt's national interest for the repeated cycles of war between his country and its Jewish neighbor to be broken. In the eyes of the West, Sadat was a strategic visionary for having dared to travel across a historic divide, angering the entire Arab world while lecturing the Israeli parliament on the need to grant Palestinians an independent state.

But Peter needed to check out persistent rumors that Sadat, notwithstanding his sudden celebrity in the West, wasn't all that popular in Egypt.

From his place in line Peter continued to survey the crowd behind the waist-high partition. If all else failed he could phone the American embassy and ask for assistance. He only knew one man, the political counselor, but the name Robbins would be recognized from his articles and the fact that he'd been a senior Pentagon official.

When finally he got through passport control he headed for the luggage carousel. He was lucky enough to snatch a cart just before one of the passengers from his line got it, a pushy, sweaty, sallow-faced fellow. Survival of the fastest, Peter thought, making a face at the man. Now where were his bags? Perspiration soaked his shirt and the underarms of his lightweight cord suit. It was supposed to be wash and wear; without luggage, he'd have to put that to the test, he thought. His throat was parched. He loosened his sodden tie and cursed.

Most of the other passengers were collecting their bags and fast disappearing. Perhaps he should exchange some money and find a phone. He whirled around, looking for an exchange window, when he heard a distant voice calling plaintively, "Mr. Peter, Mr. Peter!"

Peter waved his arms. "You looking for Peter Robbins?" he called out.

The man, who had started tentatively toward the waving arms, ran the last few steps. He was thin and young, dressed in baggy gray polyester trousers and a rumpled shirt. "Ah, Mr. Peter! Welcome to Cairo." He bowed. His breath smelled of garlic and cumin.

"I have been calling and calling your name," he said. "I feared you had missed the airplane or changed your plans." He handed Peter a scrap of paper with the words "Nile Hilton, Rm. 610" and then, mission accomplished, scurried off.

At that moment, as if on cue, Peter's two brown bags dropped onto the carousel.

He carted them through the nothing-to-declare customs line without challenge and headed toward a foreign-exchange window. There he cashed $100 in traveler's checks for the taxi into town.

Promoters offering limousine service tried to grab his bags as he pushed his way through the crowd at the main door. No doubt their rates were exorbitant. He held out for a metered taxi. But the traffic of trucks, small cars, and donkey carts was so heavy and slow he thought it might have been better to negotiate a fixed price. Everywhere he looked the sidewalks were teeming with pedestrians. Few seemed in any hurry. Occasionally a Western businessman or a harried messenger clutching a large manila envelope would glance worriedly at his watch.

At the Hilton, he was assigned a small suite overlooking the Nile. He made a mental note to take Samieh Salem to an expense account lunch at Maison Blanche as soon as he got back to Washington.

From his balcony he saw gray freight barges and small single-masted dhows with orange sails meandering slowly down the milky-brown river. The reddish-bronze sun began its evening descent. A pleasant breeze stirred from the direction of the pyramids, which he could just barely make out on the horizon.

He felt a rush of exhilaration now that the ordeal of traveling was over. Though exhausted, he was anxious to get started on his reporting. So before he showered and took a nap he rifled through his files, looking for a folder with the name and phone number of an Egyptian general, Rahman Hazi. A military aide from Peter's Pentagon days, Colonel Ron Blackwell, a sharp West Pointer, had insisted it would be worth his while to see the general as early in the trip as possbile.

"The guy teaches at the Egyptian war college and has one of the best military minds in Egypt," Blackwell had said with enthusiasm. "I'll send him a cable that you're coming and suggest dinner. He'll give you a perspective you'll never get from a dozen Foreign Ministry lard-asses."

Peter wasn't in the mood for a stiff evening with an Egyptian martinet. He would have been happy phoning his wife and kids and then calling it a night. But he respected Blackwell's judgment and perhaps General Hazi had laid on some plans. He might as well make the call and get it over with.

The Cairo phone system lived up to its reputation as one of the world's worst. After two wrong numbers and an incessant series of loud busy signals that kicked in before all the digits had been dialed, he finally got through to Hazi's home.

The general sounded genuinely pleased to hear from him. "I cannot wait to meet you. Simply cannot wait. I've read your columns for years, reprinted in the Paris *Trib*, and Blackwell informs me you were a high-ranking Defense Department planner."

"Medium-ranking," Peter said. "Deputy assistant secretary of defense."

"Modest, too. I understand you're somewhat of an authority on nuclear strategy. I've recently published a book on the subject. We have a lot to talk about. If you're not too tired I'd like to show you some of Cairo's night life. French cuisine suit you? I assume you drink scotch; I'll bring a bottle of Johnnie Walker. Be by at nine, in a yellow Mercedes."

Peter was bushed, but the general's enthusiasm was infectious. "Should I wear a tie?"

"A tie? British colonial days are long gone," Hazi laughed. "A sports shirt and—if you insist on being formal—a jacket. Trousers would be appropriate, too, since it gets chilly at night." Again the laugh. "Should I provide a woman for you? No? I'm sure you won't mind if a couple of close friends join us. Fun-loving people, and interesting." He clicked off, not waiting for a response. There was no need.

Peter stared at the dead receiver. The general wasn't stiff at all. Sounded like a sophisticated, humorous, no-bullshit guide. This could turn out to be fun.

2

Mohammed had turned off the lights and kept the aircraft hugging the water, beneath the view of radar. The radio altimeter was essential. He had guided the big plane at an altitude just above 500 feet, skillfully skirting populated Dahlak and Farasan islands. Just south of Ras Banas, he flew westward over the Egyptian mainland. With course changes from Achmed, reading a previously prepared navigation chart overlay, he flew a dogleg around Aswan and then turned north over the desert west of the Nile.

He kept one eye on the fuel gauge. The low-altitude flying was burning a lot more gas than high cruising, but all that had been calculated in advance. He had reviewed the computations himself. Though it would be tight, they could make it to Wadi Natrun. Air currents could be tricky at such low levels, but at night the heat thermals were thankfully reduced. Even so, the aircraft wasn't designed to be flown just above the nap of the earth like a fighter-bomber. The ride was a rough one.

In the passenger cabin, a young girl clutching a black and white teddy bear was screaming. A thin white-haired old woman sobbed into her lace handkerchief. The passengers had felt the plane shudder shortly after the hijacking started. They'd been terrified when it went into a steep dive, thinking it was out of control and headed for a fiery crash. But then it had leveled off into that low, frightening, bumpy ride.

An ashen East German electronics specialist, stroking his chest with one hand and his thin mustache with another, moaned that he was suffering a heart attack. A middle-aged

Russian woman in a red cotton dress held her gagging mouth to a vomit bag. When she was finished she tried to leave her seat for the restroom, only to be ordered back.

Nadia got on the loudspeaker. "Please remain calm. No one is permitted to leave his seat, for whatever reason. No one. Please forgive the inconvenience. We will land soon. We mean you no harm. You are innocent bystanders. When we get to our destination, transportation will be waiting to transfer you to other flights so that you may resume your journey. Agents on the ground will be available to ensure your luggage is transferred to the appropriate aircraft. Please cooperate and you will soon be safe."

Several minutes later, though it seemed like a lot longer, they approached their destination. The little-used Egyptian air base at Wadi Natrun was located about fifty miles southwest of Alexandria in the Western Desert.

Mohammed did not break radio silence. Achmed pointed ahead, and after Mohammed nodded yes, he lowered the landing gear and switched on the landing lights. A parallel string of lights snapped on ahead, outlining a single runway.

Nadia got back on the loudspeaker. "We are about to land. Put your seatbacks in an upright position and extinguish all cigarettes. Remain seated until we have come to a full stop and I instruct you to deplane. Then move quickly to the waiting buses for transfer."

There were smiles of relief on nearly every face, some applause, and a few prayers of thanks when the jet thudded heavily but safely down and Mohammed brought it to a sudden lurching halt on the short runway. The East German technician made a remarkably quick recovery and the lady in the red dress seemed more concerned about getting a napkin and a glass of water than a hijacking. Mohammed taxied toward the two buses in front of base operations.

Although this was an Egyptian air force base, the men standing around the plane, all armed with automatic weapons, were not in uniform.

When the little girl started to cry again she was sternly shushed by her mother. A Ukrainian engineer asked Nadia a question in Russian; she answered by raising her Uzi and waving him brusquely out of the plane with the others. A few older noncommissioned officers grumped about the treatment. But overall the mood was one of relief and joy.

When the buses had been loaded with passengers they headed toward a distant hangar. Several minutes passed. Then from that direction came a thunderous outburst of machine-gun fire and screams.

"Was that absolutely necessary?" Mohammed asked Achmed. They were still in the cockpit.

"The general's orders. You know that. And he was absolutely right. If even one person got away, the security of the entire mission could be compromised. They die for a good cause."

As they spoke two bulldozers, headlights slicing a path through the darkness, used their giant blades to gouge a mass grave in the Western Desert for the passengers and crew of Soviet courier flight no. 79. Nearby, a tug was hooked up to tow the huge jet into a hangar, safe from the prying eyes of spy satellites.

*   *   *

The Soviet signals-intelligence detachment at Baku had intercepted a puzzling radio message from the general vicinity of Alexandria, Egypt. In Arabic it said, "The dove is in the nest." But it wasn't coded, so the sender didn't mind others listening in. The radioman, who had plans to go drinking with some friends, didn't want to work late. He gave the intercept a routine classification and logged it accordingly.

*   *   *

Captain Mordechai Tzur was perplexed. All sources confirmed that Soviet courier flight no. 79, out of San'a, North Yemen, had mysteriously exploded, and it was presumed there were no survivors. Something didn't smell right.

Tzur was sitting in the underground headquarters of Junction, a top-secret agency located at Ramat David Air Force Base between Haifa and Tel Aviv. Even the name was classified, so as not to stir speculation about its mission.

A lot of intelligence organizations around the world

had extra-sensitive facilities whose existence was never mentioned publicly. Tzur knew of one such in the United States, the National Reconnaissance Office in the Pentagon. But while the NRO operated all the spy planes and satellites for the Central Intelligence Agency, the National Security Agency, air force intelligence, and other spooky organizations, Junction's purpose was linked to Israel's paranoia. Staffed around the clock, it monitored all radio intercepts, radar trackings, and spy reports from any quarter that could conceivably pose a military threat to Israel, including all Arab countries and the Soviet bloc.

Captain Tzur, Motta to his friends, reviewed the possibilities. A malfunction in one of the engines or fuel lines could have led to an explosion. A spark in the cargo bay could have set off volatile chemicals or explosives that were known to be ferried occasionally if a mission had high-enough priority. A terrorist could have slipped a bomb on board. Or a hostile group with access to small shoulder-fired missiles—the Soviet SA-7 Strella or the American Redeye, for example—could have shot the aircraft down. A lumbering airliner with its red-hot engine exhaust would be a sitting duck for heat-seeking weapons.

By secure phone Tzur checked with a friend in another branch of air force intelligence and learned that all Soviet aircraft flying abroad, including commercial airliners, were now equipped with a sensor to warn of just such an attempt. A cockpit display flashed a warning when an enemy radar control locked on, instantly triggering the firing of flares to draw off any heat-seeking missile heading toward the aircraft. So Tzur discarded that hypothesis.

He could not so readily rule out a bomb. Soviet security was almost as tight as Israeli airport security, but for enough money a member of the cleaning crew might have secreted a powerful explosive aboard. And while the Russians would be on guard against an attempt on an Aeroflot airliner, they probably felt more secure about a military cargo plane. He made a mental note to check Mossad on that.

He lit his pipe and puffed slowly, willing himself to

concentrate harder. Surely the clue was in the data he had reviewed, but where?

The most logical explanation was an accidental explosion. The Il-76M four-engine jet had been in service for years, and although it had a decent safety record and the Russians posted maintenance supervisors wherever they operated, the Yemenites couldn't be watched every minute.

For perhaps the twentieth time Tzur replayed the intercepted tape of the plane's mayday message. The emergency radio procedure was faultless, the words appropriate to the crisis, but something wasn't kosher. He ran his fingers through his wavy blond hair and sighed deeply. He trusted his instincts. So did his superiors. That's why at twenty-nine he was a senior analyst at Junction, having been pulled out of his previous billet as a photo interpreter with air force intelligence.

And then it came to him. He realized what he'd been groping for. The words were right, the radio procedure perfect, but the accent wasn't. The voice he had played back again and again didn't sound native Russian. He was almost certain. He would have a linguistics specialist study the tape.

He lifted the secure red phone and punched a six-digit number. "Moish, this is Motta. You know about the Soviet courier flight out of San'a that exploded last night? Good. I need your expertise. I'm sending over a messenger with a recording of the mayday message. I have to know the pilot's national origin and where he learned his English. Priority Aleph. Thanks, I owe you one."

*   *   *

In PVO air defense headquarters for the southern region of the USSR, at Tashkent, Lieutenant Pavel Sokolov was studying the same problem. A Soviet aircraft had disappeared under unexplained circumstances and standard operating procedure required a thorough investigation and report within thirty-six hours.

Sokolov wasn't a magician. The information was fragmentary and inconclusive. The Soviet air traffic controller in San'a reported that courier flight no. 79 had exited his radar coverage before the explosion. The incompetents in Riyadh and Cairo had nothing to report so far. Damascus had picked up a Mayday radio signal, but the incident was beyond the range of its radar.

"Unfortunately, it was in the seam of what would have been overlapping radar coverage if our armed forces had continued their presence in Egypt," Sokolov told an inquiring Colonel Konev of GRU, Soviet military intelligence. Neither had to be reminded that Sadat had kicked the Russians out a few years before. Until then, they'd had a massive military presence.

"Moscow has been demanding a thorough search-and-rescue effort from Cairo," Sokolov went on, "but so far the wogs have been searching for nothing but excuses. First they told us the appropriate planes were busy looking for an overdue Komar missile boat in the Mediterranean. Then that they were grounded for repairs. Then the specialized crews were sick. Who knows what excuses they'll think up next? It's probably already too late to locate the exact spot. And even if they did, who would man the surface effort to look for bodies or debris?" He banged the heel of his right hand against his forehead in frustration.

Sokolov had analyzed the mayday call and it was in order. He guessed that a faulty turbine blade had broken loose and ruptured a fuel tank. That hypothesis was supported by a classified report that had crossed his desk only two weeks before recounting quality-control problems in turbine-blade production at the factory in Smolensk. The plant manager, notwithstanding the fact that he was a life-long party member, had been sent to Siberia.

A check of the passenger list showed no one of importance among the thirty-seven passengers and crew. That, at least, was a lucky break. Had there been even a distant relative of a VIP on board, Sokolov knew from experience that hot breath would have been blowing on his neck.

3

Shasta, her hazel eyes flashing, was performing a belly dance before an audience consisting of enthusiastic Persian Gulf oil sheiks, Egyptian businessmen, and a smattering of bemused Western tourists. They were in the main dining room of Mena House, a five-star hotel on the outskirts of Cairo. According to General Hazi, she was the best belly dancer in the city. At their table, fronting the dance floor, were Hazi, his petite wife Lila, and Petra Tewfik, a squat, bald, jolly man introduced simply as a close friend. Tewfik didn't have the bearing to suggest he might be a fellow officer.

"Well, Peter, what do you think?" Hazi said. "Isn't she extraordinary?"

Peter thought Shasta was about as seductive as an over-age stripper in a sailors' waterfront bar, and only smiled. Perhaps it was jet lag, but he couldn't understand why the Arabs in the audience seemed so turned on. True, there was a certain fluid grace to the ancient dance of the desert temptress. And the translucent veils were more alluring than pasties and a G-string. In cadence to the shrill, urgent music she gyrated, bumping her hips, thrusting her pendulous breasts and prominent abdomen, making eye contact with first one, then another, and then another of the men in her audience.

Perhaps you had to acquire a taste for it. Like black olives or feta cheese.

Hazi filled Peter's glass with a healthy slug of Johnnie Walker Red, using his fingers to add chunks of ice from a silver bucket. Peter was uncomfortable at the thought of ice made from Egyptian tap water but could hardly refuse without offending his host.

"Our restaurants aren't allowed to sell hard liquor," Hazi was saying, "so we bring our own and keep it in plain view. It's one of the many paradoxes in our society." He smiled, flashing a mouth full of gold teeth, his mustache stretched to a thin line. Women would find him attractive, Peter thought. Dashing.

He stood about six foot one, tall for an Arab, and had the lean, hard physique of his soldiering profession. Like his ancient forebears he was light-skinned and black-haired and his features were finely sculpted.

His friend Tewfik was some sort of engineer. In contrast to the spare, athletic general, he was heavyset, with a powerful upper torso and arms a bit long for his body. He laughed indiscriminately at all of Hazi's jokes, suggesting a need to ingratiate himself continually. But Tewfik appeared to be bright and well informed, as Peter found out when the talk occasionally turned to serious topics.

Hazi had ordered a feast in advance by phone. They started with a large platter of prawns sauteed in garlic and butter and accompanied by stuffed figs and grape leaves. This was followed by a medium-rare rack of lamb with puffs of whipped potato and artichoke hearts. Instead of wine, the food was washed down with scotch.

As Peter was draining his glass, the general leaned across the table and said with sudden intensity, "You used to be a ranking Pentagon official, maybe you can explain something. When the M-60 tanks you supply us arrive on the docks they lack machine guns. And the F-16 jets come with only a token number of air-to-air and air-to-ground missiles.

"Is this American policy? To provide first-line weapons that are good for nothing but parades? When Israel gets your weapons they're fully equipped."

Peter was no longer a Defense Department official and shouldn't have been expected to speak for the United States. And yet he was intimately aware of the thinking that

24

lay behind the go-slow policy. It would do no harm to explain. "Our new relationship is just getting off the ground, General. It wasn't long ago that Egypt was a Soviet ally. Now you've chucked out the Russians and are pursuing a more constructive strategy. It takes time for attitudes to change, particularly in Congress, where Israel has a lot of powerful friends. If the White House had moved too fast in providing arms to your country, Congress might have killed the whole thing."

Tewfik turned and put his mouth close to Peter's ear so he could be heard over the loud rhythms of the band. "Did you know that Hazi here was the brains behind our greatest modern victory, when we slipped across the Suez and smashed through the Bar Lev line?"

Peter hadn't known of Hazi's personal role, but had followed the war closely as the second-ranking member of the Middle East Task Group in the Pentagon. He was acutely aware that while Egypt lost the war, its early victories did a lot to restore its national pride, probably emboldening Sadat to break with the Russians and negotiate a peace treaty with Israel.

"You must be very proud of him. Sadat too," Peter said.

General Hazi looked as if he'd been insulted. "Sadat is a traitor," he countered, bitterly. "He may be the toast of Washington and London, but certainly not of Cairo."

"But I thought—," Peter was at a loss for words, "—I thought you Egyptians were tired of wars planned by men in Parisian cafes boasting how they'll drive Israel into the sea."

His hosts exchanged glances. "You're right about one thing," Hazi said with feeling, "Egypt should chart its own course, fight its own battles. Not serve as mercenaries for a bunch of back-stabbing hypocritical Arabs." He leaned on his elbows, moving closer to Peter and lowering his voice. "I'll concede that man for man Israeli forces are better, if you'll concede that time and demographics are on our side. We can afford to lose ten thousand to every one of theirs;

we won't be hurt, fundamentally. It might even help our overpopulation problem." He paused and winked at Tewfik, who nodded agreement.

"But the Israelis can't sustain the casualties. They're too small, they value each life too highly. You would say that's a moral strength. But from our point of view it's a basic weakness, their strategic Achilles' heel. In time they would sue for peace—on our terms. Don't you agree?"

"There are so many variables," Peter said slowly. "Even though Arab forces are acquiring more sophisticated planes and missiles, the technological edge will continue to work in Israel's favor. No offense, but it has to do with the quality of their soldiers and scientists.

"As for kill ratios, I agree they can't fight wars every five or six years without losing their best men and bankrupting their economy. On the other hand, recognizing this, they may never again give their enemies the first shot. In the most recent war they were confident until the last minute that Egyptian and Syrian ground maneuvers were feints, not the real thing. But then the air force got hard evidence from radio intercepts. Golda Meir refused to let the air force launch a surprise attack. Afraid the Americans wouldn't understand. I'm not giving away secrets when I tell you Israel appears to have learned its lesson. If it ever comes to a crunch again, the generals will remind the politicians of the differences between the wars of '67 and '73."

They could have been sitting in the Pentagon, not a Cairo club, Peter thought. This was exactly the sort of thing he'd come to Egypt for, some real insights into the thinking at senior planning levels.

"But you're basing your analysis on conventional war and weapons," Tewfik argued. "Times change, and so does weaponry."

"Poison gas has too localized an effect to be decisive," Peter said. "Unless you can achieve total surprise and deliver hundreds of weapons at critical targets simultaneously."

"What about nuclear weapons?" Hazi said. "Theoretically, of course," he added with a dry laugh.

"How many weapons are you talking about? One?

Fifty? Israel probably has at least a couple dozen nuclear weapons and could retaliate overwhelmingly. Where would Egypt get these weapons? Before you sent them packing, the Soviets even refused you long-range fighter-bombers. Too provocative. China? France? I doubt it. Anyway, how would you deliver them? Theoretically, of course. You don't have medium-range missiles and your medium-range bombers could be shot down."

Hazi stared at Peter intently. "I'll answer your question with another. China has a relatively small nuclear arsenal. If it wanted to, how would it start a nuclear war between Russia and the United States?"

"I suppose by firing a couple of missiles from submarines in such a way that the first would appear to be from the Russians against an American target and the second from the U.S. in retaliation. A triggering attack. The two sides might get so caught up in the presumption of an imminent barrage that they would fire hundreds of warheads to destroy as many of the other's missiles as possible before they could be launched."

Hazi and Tewfik nodded silently.

"But you don't have that sort of situation in the Mideast. If you could get the bomb, would you want to trigger an exchange between Israel and Syria, which has none? Even if it worked, Syria would be devastated, not Israel. I fail to see the point."

Before Hazi could respond Mrs. Hazi held up her hands. "We've known Peter for what, an hour or two? And already you two are saying things that could ruin your careers if overheard by the wrong people. How can I hold my head up in polite company if you get fired, Rahman?"

"He's a sophisticated journalist. A former top official of his government who ought to understand what we're really thinking," the general retorted. He paused. Then he smiled and patted his wife's hand. "But of course you're right, as usual, my dear. We have plenty of time for serious talk over the next few days. Let's drink, dance, and have some fun. Peter, take my wife around the dance floor." Peter hesitated, but the general insisted.

Lila, barely five feet, had her lustrous black hair piled

high atop her head, no doubt to appear taller. Her skin was olive-hued and without blemish or wrinkles, except for laugh lines around her mouth and eyes. She spoke English with a slight French accent, explaining with hauteur, on meeting Peter, that she'd spent a couple of years studying at the Sorbonne in Paris. No common desert flower, she.

As Peter swung her around the floor, he thought of his discussion with Hazi. Was the general merely demonstrating he could play strategic chess with a former Pentagon official? Or was he hinting at serious thinking in the Egyptian general staff? Was the peace a ruse? What was the status of Egypt's nuclear effort? He had a lot of heavy lifting to do on this visit. And Hazi was clearly determined to shock and provoke him into talking.

The general's wife was asking him a question. "I'm sorry, Mrs. Hazi, what was that?"

"Lila," she said into his ear. "My name is Lila. And I asked whether I'm really so boring a dance partner as all that."

"Hardly," he said. "I was just thinking that every other man in the room must be jealous of me. I'm dancing with the prettiest woman here."

She pressed a little closer to him.

*　　　*　　　*

Lila Hazi fancied herself a liberated woman, not all that common in Egypt, even among her class. Tonight was an example. Seldom would an Arab man bring his wife for a night on the town with a foreigner, and certainly not before he'd had a chance to size him up. But she'd insisted, and rather than fight about it, Rahman had let her come.

She had been born to wealth, she traveled abroad at least once every year, and she dressed in European fashions. Her royal-blue Jaguar was a gift from her doting father; her husband couldn't afford it on a general's salary.

Rahman seemed to be growing increasingly preoccupied and inattentive, not as in their early years of marriage. He was off to the war college at dawn each morning, hours before she arose. And when he came home, those

28

nights he came home at all, he usually buried himself in the study, writing those dreary military books of his.

She wondered if he had a little *hoori* on the side. Probably. But so long as he made sure he brought no disease into their bed, and was discreet, she could accept that. Didn't like it, but could accept it, like so many other wives in their circle.

In the beginning it had been different. He had been so solicitous of her every whim during courtship, and even in their first few years together. But after she'd given him two children, a son and a daughter, he repaid her with the loss of both ardor and attentiveness.

She had brought wealth and social status to this son of an obscure army major. But now that his needs had been met, her needs became irrelevant. She was relegated to little more than chief of staff at home, someone to supervise the servants and discipline the children.

"You have such a sure hand with a woman," she whispered to Peter and glanced in her husband's direction. "I'd guess you've had lots of experience. It must get lonely, traveling so far from home."

Peter also glanced at the general. "It can get tedious," he agreed, looking uncomfortable. "But I'm usually too busy to let the loneliness get to me. And I try to call my wife and kids at least once a week."

"Your wife must be a very trusting woman. I mean you're in a foreign land, with no fear of gossip, away for what—weeks at a time?"

"The average trip is about three or four weeks," he said, his tone matter-of-fact. He pulled away slightly.

Lila pulled closer. Perhaps she could steer them nearer to the table. Rahman should be made to realize that two could play at his lusty game. At the very least, her coquettish display would make him angry. His dearest possession threatened because a man looked twice at her. If she were the aggressor, it would raise questions about his manliness. There might well be a row when they got home, she knew. But if she played it right, heated words should be followed by fierce lovemaking. Rahman would have to demonstrate once again his matchless ability as a lover. Matchless he wasn't. But adequate.

*   *   *

In a windowless interior office at Mossad headquarters in Tel Aviv, Deputy Director Avraham Shavit was trying to clear out his in-box. The report of the explosion of a Soviet military aircraft over the Red Sea piqued his curiosity.

He picked up his white desk phone and punched a three-digit extension for Dov Etzion, one of his top assistants.

"What do we know about the circumstances of that downed Soviet plane? Accident? Hostile action?" Absently he scribbled a crude sketch of an airplace on a notepad, then drew a sharp arrow into its midsection.

"Still checking, sir. It appears to have been a courier flight that originated in Aden and exploded midair not long after leaving San'a, its first stop. We've alerted our assets along the route to be sure and be the first to locate debris for laboratory analysis."

"Anybody getting excited over this, Dov? The Russians? The Egyptians? The Yemenites?"

"There's been a slight increase in radio traffic from PVO Moscow to Cairo West. It appears to be a low-grade tactical military cipher. We should be able to crack it shortly. I'll let you know."

Shavit cradled the phone. He ran the side of his pencil along his long thin nose. Dov is a good man, he thought, and very thorough. He'll check out all the possibilities and get back as soon as he can. Even if he has to work through the night.

*   *   *

Captain Tzur had placed the highest priority on his request. A day later he got a response from Moshe Rabinowitz, the top linguistic specialist at Mossad. But, curiously, instead of passing his findings over a secure phone he'd insisted they meet at Mossad headquarters, a series of three-story gray stucco buildings tucked inside the well-guarded army head-quarters in Tel Aviv.

"There were good reasons for reporting in person," Rabinowitz said as soon as Tzur walked into the room. He was an owl-faced man with thick lips, heavy jowls, and a fringe of black hair around his bald crown. "The front office has been getting tight-assed lately about not disseminating sensitive stuff to other agencies unless it's cleared through channels in triplicate. Avraham Shavit's on the prowl. Wants to make an example of someone who's playing loose. I'm rather fond of my paycheck, paltry as it is." He patted his bulging stomach, no doubt to offer evidence of his need to remain gainfully employed. "For some screwy reason he's developed a particular interest in this case. Don't ask me why."

He peered over his bifocals at Tzur, then winked and broke into a grin. "But the real reason I asked you here was to see your face as I lay out my conclusions.

"I put the voiceprints through a succession of high-tech tests. And I have a special ear. It may not look special, but believe me, men have staked their lives on it."

Tzur had never met Rabinowitz before, having always dealt with him on the phone, but he knew his reputation and didn't need to be convinced. "So what did you find? Is he Russian or isn't he?"

"It's not that simple. I'm pretty sure the pilot has spent a significant amount of time in the Soviet Union and can speak the language fluently. But no, he isn't Russian. You know I was raised there, in Leningrad, before we immigrated to Israel."

"So what is he?"

Rabinowitz leaned back, grinning. "He speaks several languages, English and Arabic among them. But I think he spent his formative years—had his earliest schooling, that is—in northern Africa. Morocco, to be exact."

Tzur was startled. "I suppose his father could have been a Soviet diplomat in Morocco. Kid learned Arabic as his first language."

"I don't think so. Our fancy computers and other gadgets aren't foolproof, of course, but they suggest the man is probably an Arab. And my ear's fairly certain."

"Could he come from Moslem stock in Soviet Central Asia?"

"Trained as a pilot in the elitist Soviet air force? Shame on you. You know the Soviet General Staff doesn't trust anyone but Russians and Slavs for those jobs." A wicked grin spread across Rabinowitz's round face. He'd been holding something back. Tzur leaned forward in his chair and beckoned with both hands for him to come out with it.

"One of the reasons I didn't even trust a secure phone was because I suspect—," he paused for dramatic effect, "—that our man also speaks Hebrew."

Tzur sat upright in his chair, making no effort to hide his disbelief. Then he started to laugh. The man was obviously playing a game with him. It must be boring sitting in a windowless office all day with earphones glued to your head.

"I'm not pulling your leg," Rabinowitz went on. "The mayday message was brief, so there wasn't much to go on. But I listen to accents all day, every day, don't forget. Call it an educated guess, based partly on instinct. Our mayday man also speaks Hebrew." He placed his elbows on the desk, chubby fingers touching prayerfully. "I've done my job. Now it's up to you to do yours. What was a native-born Arab, conversant in both Russian and Hebrew, doing in the cockpit of that particular Soviet jet aircraft?"

4

General Hazi and Dr. Tewfik had been consumed by Operation Trojan Dove since August 1979, several months after Sadat signed his infamous peace treaty with Egypt's blood enemy. Both had been determined to build a nuclear bomb and use it to destroy Israel. Under their plan, not only would Egypt survive, it would also achieve unchallenged leadership of the Arab world. Some might have called them traitors for what they were conspiring to do. If discovered, they could be shot. But Hazi believed most Egyptian officers would applaud their boldness and their vision, if only they knew. Which, of course, they did not. Secrecy was everything. Without it their plan would be thwarted. Sadat loyalists were constantly sniffing around for any signs of serious challenge. And Hazi suspected that Mossad had penetrated the government and would go to any lengths to abort a nuclear program believed to have a chance of success.

Before the inception of Trojan Dove, Tewfik had been engaged as a senior scientist in a long-standing secret government program to develop nuclear weapons. But he was convinced top-level incompetence, corruption, and ambivalent attitudes from above would render the official effort a failure. His and Hazi's plan had taken shape late one night in Tewfik's study. They had been sipping one scotch after another, lamenting the fate of Egypt and the fact that two such exceptional men as they should be unable to shape events, even affect them significantly. It was Hazi who came up with the inspired concept. They would require at least one bomb of about 200 kilotons, more than ten times the potency of the weapon that destroyed Hiroshima.

"If you could handpick your own team and had the necessary funds," Hazi inquired, "could you produce a weapon within a reasonable time, say six months?"

Tewfik thought about it. "I'm fairly sure I could, yes."

"Fairly sure is not good enough. Could you do it with certainty?"

Tewfik nodded. "With the right men, recruited carefully from within the current program, with sufficient capital, and total secrecy, yes, I could do it. Or at least with a 90 percent probability of success."

Hazi was pacing back and forth across the room, punching a fist into the palm of his hand. The leather heels on his riding boots slapped the parquet floor. "How much?" he said. "How much money would you need?"

Tewfik had an enormous capacity to drink without impairing his faculties. He went to his desk and took out a small calculator. After several minutes he had the answer. "Seven million dollars. Eight million to be on the safe side."

The general didn't ask for details. He had firm confidence in Tewfik's technical expertise. Where could they get that kind of money? Tewfik had a considerable private fortune from his father, but clearly he couldn't underwrite a program of such magnitude. The Saudis and the Kuwaitis had the money but not the guts. The PLO had the guts and the money, but in all likelihood they had been penetrated by Mossad and the CIA.

"Colonel Moammar Khadafy," Hazi said presently. "What about him?"

They decided he was their best bet. After General Zia took over in Pakistan strong mutual animosity had dashed Khadafy's hopes of getting his hands on an Islamic bomb by that route. To be sure, the Libyan was probably insane, and an enemy of Egypt, having made several attempts on Sadat's life. But Hazi now hated Sadat with such passion that he secretly wished the Libyan success.

Their plan was a daunting one. First they had to con-

34

vince Khadafy to finance their effort, without filling him in on the details and risking a security breach that could foil the scheme. Then they needed to acquire either enriched uranium or plutonium. There was no way that undetected they could divert the necessary quantity of weapons-grade material from the Egyptian program. And, finally, they required a long-range Soviet jet that could deliver the bomb. Not American, French or British. It had to be Soviet.

Given the nature of his clandestine government assignment, it was fairly easy for Tewfik to travel abroad without raising eyebrows in the security services. After all, his job was to move about picking the brains of nuclear experts at seminars and conferences around the world. How else was Egypt going to join the nuclear club? And so one month later, in early September 1979, Tewfik had slipped into Tripoli with false papers on a flight from Naples, where he had been attending a three-day conference on nuclear-power-plant safety. The Egyptian weapons project was masked as a civilian nuclear-energy program.

For Hazi it had been more difficult. He had to be inventive. Seizing on a series of armed incidents along the Libyan border that had resulted in the reinforcement of Egyptian forces there, he convinced the General Staff he should do an on-site inspection to see if he could devise a plan for a commando raid across the border. That, he argued, should persuade Khadafy he was playing with fire.

To keep his visit unobtrusive he traveled not in a medium transport, with the staff and flourishes a general would normally be accorded, but in a small twin-engine Beechcraft liaison plane. He selected Mohammed, Tewfik's son, as his pilot.

After two days on the ground Hazi informed the head of the Western Forces Command, General Mustafa Zayid, that he planned a surreptitious reconnaissance across the border.

"No, General Zayid, I don't want any of your troops to accompany me," he said firmly. "I must remain undetected. I've studied the radar patterns and I'm convinced flying low my aircraft can slip through without notice. On the map I've also located several hard-pan plateaus close to the border where an aircraft like ours can land and take off. I'll be gone a day or two. You're to tell no one; I don't want my mission jeopardized by any unusual reconnaissance or air-cover flights near my position. And I don't want a buildup of mobile rescue forces on our side of the border."

Zayid didn't attempt to argue. Instead, he embraced Hazi and kissed him on both cheeks. There was a feeling among senior officers that Hazi had the potential one day to become chief of staff or defense minister. That sort of reputation engendered cooperation except among those who themselves had competing ambitions. Fortunately, Zayid didn't appear to.

With his Egyptian flank covered, at sunup the next morning Hazi directed Mohammed to fly across the border and then veer toward the Libyan air base at Oqbah ibn Nafi, on the northwest coast. The flight was uneventful. They shared the cloudless sky first with a few brown-speckled desert hawks hunting breakfast and later with white sea terns, screeching as they circled wide from the nearby Mediterranean.

Surprise was complete when their light plane landed on the main runway. An aviation fuel truck had come out to top off their gas tank before the sleepy unshaven driver noticed the Egyptian air force markings and shouted curses at the two officers climbing from the cockpit.

"Go get your commander, you young idiot!" General Hazi barked at the gesticulating driver. He left in haste, but it took a full fifteen minutes before a jeep mounting a machine gun and two troop trucks were on their way, kicking up clouds of sand as they sped toward the plane.

The base commander, a Libyan air force captain, leapt out of the jeep and, tripping, almost fell flat. When he saw Hazi's rank he stopped and started to salute, before thinking better of it and pulling his hand down in embarrassment. A couple of the soldiers tried to suppress laughter.

Hazi drew the officer out of earshot. "Captain," he said in a low voice, "I'm on a secret mission too sensitive to discuss with a man of your rank. I need a vehicle and a driver to get me to the capital without any complications at security checkpoints."

The base commander was a relatively unsophisticated officer. He had to assume it was an important mission for an Egyptian general to fly in unannounced with instructions to proceed to Tripoli. But still he hesitated. He'd received no orders.

Hazi handed him his sidearm. "I'll leave my nephew and my aircraft in your charge during my stay," Hazi said. "You will guard them with your life, Captain. You'd better wheel the plane into a hangar right away. We wouldn't want Israeli reconnaissance to spot an Egyptian liaison plane at a Libyan base."

The young officer smiled and this time gave a full salute. "I would be honored if you'd allow me to escort you to Tripoli, General. And don't worry, I'll order my second in command to take care of security here while you're gone."

Hazi returned the salute smartly. The Libyan soldiers muttered in approval. An Egyptian general was saluting a Libyan captain. This was indeed a day to tell the grandchildren about.

Hazi changed into civilian clothes for the long dusty journey into Tripoli. Emboldened by the importance of the mission he was entrusted with, the captain shouted curses at even the slightest hint of delay at any of the checkpoints, once even drawing his pistol before being waved through. He was reluctant to leave after depositing Hazi at the Tripoli Sheraton, but he did, snapping off a salute. As soon as the elevator doors closed behind Hazi, the captain was on a pay phone.

Tewfik was lingering over a second cup of breakfast coffee in his hotel suite in the Sheraton when he heard three sharp raps on the door. It was probably the waiter come to retrieve the breakfast tray. But when he opened the door there was Hazi standing nonchalantly, hands on hips. They embraced warmly. Then Tewfik phoned Dr. Wadi Hamidi, one of the two Libyan physicists running Khadafy's nuclear program. Tewfik and Hamidi had been close friends as

37

graduate students in India. They'd corresponded over the years and occasionally renewed their friendship at international conferences. Tewfik realized the hotel phones were likely monitored by Libyan security. If not, Hamidi's home phone certainly would be. But they weren't trying to hide their mission from the Libyans; quite the contrary, they wanted an audience with their leader.

*   *   *

Libyan security forces, responding to the captain's report and the call to Hamidi, quietly sealed off the hotel and the floor on which Tewfik was staying.

*   *   *

When Hamidi showed up at the Sheraton, the Egyptian scientist minced no words. "General Hazi and I have come here at great risk. Were our government to discover our mission . . ." He snapped his fingers to demonstrate how quickly they would be eliminated.

Hamidi, a squat compact man with a receding chin, looked at his friend, then at the Egyptian general. "Do you realize the risk I run by being here now? It's only because of our long-standing friendship that I would even consider such a dangerous summons." He glanced nervously at the door.

"We have a proposition," Tewfik said, "that must be outlined personally to Colonel Khadafy and no one else. It's in the interests of both our countries: the destruction of Israel. But we must meet soon—tonight—otherwise too many questions will be raised over our absence. Can you arrange it?"

Hamidi took off his spectacles and wiped them slowly with a handkerchief. When he had checked the lens against the ceiling light and put them back on, he said, "Petra, I would trust you with my life, just as you say you trust me. But I need more information if you want me to set up a meeting. Are you offering to come work for us? I don't know about the general, but you'd be welcome. If not that, what?"

Tewfik exchanged glances with Hazi. They had agreed

to reveal a portion of their scheme to one man only, Khadafy. They couldn't risk a leak. Hazi spoke. "We're in need of resources for a top-secret effort that we're convinced Colonel Khadafy will support. At the very least he'll want the opportunity to hear us out. You know we're not confidence men; we're two of the most senior people in our fields in Egypt. We've risked everything to come this far.

"Tomorrow we must leave, whether we succeed or fail. But you have my word, our word, that Colonel Khadafy will thank you for having urged him to hear us out."

The Libyan scientist rose from the couch. "I know you're men of stature and I believe you're sincere. But I can make no promises. I'm not even sure Khadafy's in the country or that I can get through to him if he is." Disappointment showed in the faces of the Egyptians. Hamidi looked away from them, out the window. A stiff wind had risen and was thrashing the palm fronds along the hotel's curved drive. He rubbed the back of his neck and shifted from foot to foot. He thought for a few moments and then, having made a decision, turned back toward the center of the room.

"I may live to regret this, but I'll try to help you. You know I could do no less for you, Petra. Don't leave this room, at any time, for any reason. Order your food sent up. If I'm not successful by the time you feel you must leave . . ." He shrugged his shoulders and walked out of the room, closing the door quietly behind him.

That night Hazi, always a light sleeper, heard a key in the lock and froze. He glanced at the luminous dial on his watch. Two-thirty. If only he hadn't left his service revolver at the air base. Quietly he eased out of bed and grabbed the metal lamp on the bedside table. If it was a thief he'd be sorry he came to this room.

Someone jiggled the key again, then several men burst into the room. One of them snapped on the lights and pointed his pistol at Hazi's chest until he dropped the lamp. The others were carrying submachine guns. Tewfik sat up suddenly, jerked from a deep sleep. "What's going on?"

"Both of you," the leader said, gesticulating with his

gun, "get dressed, pack your bags, and be quick about it."
His cohorts kept their own guns at the ready.

After the Egyptians had dressed and packed they were
frisked for weapons and blindfolded tightly. "What's this all
about?" Tewfik protested.

"No questions. Come with us." They were hustled to
an elevator, through what must have been a kitchen judging
from the smell of baking bread, and outside to a waiting car.
Their heads were pushed down and they were thrust into
the back seat. The multiple screech of tires suggested at
least three cars, one in front, one behind.

After a jouncing high-speed ride lasting about half an
hour, they stopped. Hazi heard a window being rolled
open. "Open the gate, we're coming through," the leader
said.

The smell of jet fuel mingled with the salty sea air.
Hazi guessed from that and the length of the ride that they
were back at Oqbah ibn Nafi, formerly Wheelus Air Force
Base, where he'd left his plane and Mohammed the day
before.

Were they to be expelled on his plane? Had the grandi-
ose mission on which so many dreams depended failed? At
least they would escape with their lives.

Then a new voice addressed them, respectfully this
time. "Please excuse the rude awakening and the blindfolds, gentlemen. We're about to take a helicopter ride, and
when we get to our destination everything will become
clear. Now, if you'll step out of the car and allow your
escorts to guide you to the chopper."

They stumbled their way to the helicopter. The powerful engine gave a sputtering roar and the *whoomp-whoomp-
whoomp* of accelerating blades created a strong downdraft.
Hazi was pretty sure he recognized the sound of the engine—a Soviet MI-8, which his own air force also used.
After they had boarded, the chopper lurched off the
ground. The side door had been left open; Hazi could feel
the rush of wind. The tangy salt air receded. We must be
heading inland, he thought, away from the sea.

They had been flying for nearly an hour when the

aircraft began struggling to a higher altitude. A mountain range? Sudden downdrafts, which caused a yawing motion, confirmed Hazi's judgment. About a quarter hour later the helicopter settled on the ground and their blindfolds were removed.

"Where in the world are we?" Tewfik asked, rubbing his eyes. Except for the stars, it was pitch dark.

Hazi shushed him. He was now fairly certain they were going to get an audience with a ranking official, perhaps Abdel Salem Jalloud, the number-two man. Their mission still had a chance. He glanced at his watch. A few minutes after five. He steeled himself to be calm, as if he were going into battle. This would probably be the most important encounter of his life.

They were driven by Land Rover a short distance into the desert. The night air was biting cold and they wore no jackets. At quarter-mile intervals along the highway, squatting pairs of heavily armed soldiers maintained a drowsy vigil.

Eventually they pulled up at a collection of multicolored tents and were ushered into one of the smaller ones, red and white striped like a circus tent. The uneven sand floor was covered with an overlay of bright Persian rugs. Colorful oversized pillows were scattered in a semicircle around the single piece of furniture, a custom director's chair, the wood of black ebony, the seat and back not canvas but soft brown leather. Off to one side was a charcoal brazier, which held a long-handled copper pot of Turkish coffee. Above them a ceiling fan turned lazily.

The aide, wearing the rank of captain, poured them demitasse cups of what tasted like sweetened diesel fuel. He didn't utter a word, but kept glancing at the flapped entrance.

It was much warmer inside the tent than outside. The heat stored during the day lingered at night. At sunrise, breezes off the desert would be allowed to cool the interior, a sort of natural air conditioning.

Without warning Khadafy strutted in, accompanied by three heavily armed bodyguards. Though he continued to call himself colonel, the rank he'd held when he swept to power in a 1973 coup, he didn't wear a military uniform. He had on a blood-red silk shirt, matching cobalt-blue slacks and open vest, a gold cape, and black leather boots. In his right hand, held flush against his right leg, was a thin, black swagger stick.

The Libyan leader sank into his director's chair, inspecting them intently with a slight, supercilious smile. Addressing Hazi, he spoke slowly, deliberately. "I know who you are. And Dr. Hamidi vouches for your companion. But that doesn't excuse you for sneaking into my country and demanding an immediate audience. Your arrogance is typically Egyptian." He whipped the air with his swagger stick, just as suddenly rested its tip in the palm of his hand. "But, to be frank, you intrigue me. I've been bored. So I'll indulge you. For a few moments.

"Now tell me, General, by what brilliant stratagem do you propose we liquidate the damned Israelis?"

Hazi rose, and as he did, the three burly guards moved out of the shadows toward him. Khadafy raised his swagger stick. They stopped but didn't retreat.

"According to our intelligence," Hazi responded, hands clasped behind his back, "the Libyan nuclear program, although run by competent men and employing a number of foreign specialists, is getting nowhere. No one is going to sell you a bomb. And since Zia came to power you've lost access to Pakistan's program. Notwithstanding the $370 million you provided him or the 250 tons of high-grade yellowcake uranium ore from Niger."

Khadafy looked intrigued. "Your information, if correct, would not be widely known." He indicated with a wave of his stick that the Egyptian should go on.

"I figure we're now in the vicinity of Sebha, south of the Djebel al-Sawda Mountains and north of the Fezzan Plateau," Hazi continued. "What makes this an interesting spot is that it's part of a test range where the West German company Ibex has been secretly developing and testing medium-range ballistic missiles for you."

Khadafy's expression turned sour.

"I'm sorry, Colonel, but that's known to a number of intelligence services, including our own. I'm saying this to demonstrate that you're dealing with well-informed men." Hazi stood before the Libyan, feet apart, gesturing with his hands for emphasis. It was as if he was back lecturing at the war college in Cairo and Colonel Khadafy was an attentive student. "Egypt also has a nuclear-weapons program, which like yours, is not going well. Dr. Tewfik here has the knowledge to design and build nuclear weapons. He could do so if it weren't for the incompetent, corrupt bureaucracy in our country and if he had the funds to assemble a small team." He paused.

"We've come up with an ingenious strategy for employing a nuclear weapon to ensure the destruction of Israel."

"We have no nuclear material to spare," Khadafy said dismissively.

"We're not asking for nuclear material, only a modest investment of capital." Tewfik had said eight million, but Hazi knew as a military planner there were always unexpected contingencies, ones that a little extra cash might overcome. "We estimate $10 million will do it."

"Ah, finally it's on the table," Khadafy said, his voice rising. "You want our money, nothing more."

"No, sir. How could we be so foolish as to try and swindle you? Neither Tewfik nor I travel with bodyguards. We know you could have us killed easily."

Khadafy nodded with satisfaction. It was true. His assassins could operate anywhere, even in the United States. With a gesture he indicated that their cups be refilled. But he wasn't convinced. "Do you take me for an innocent goatherd? Ten million can't purchase a nuclear-weapons capability."

"You're quite right," Tewfik agreed. "If we were talking of starting a program from scratch and doing everything ourselves— a 1,000-megawatt power plant, a chemical separation plant to extract plutonium-239 from spent fuel, a weapons factory, a modern delivery system. That would take several hundred million dollars at the very least. More likely a billion."

"Two or three billion," Khadafy sighed. "Believe me, I know."

"But we plan to leapfrog several steps. We have one plan to acquire plutonium virtually free, and another plan for a free delivery system."

Again the Libyan leader looked annoyed. Hazi held up his hand and spoke. "Not exactly free, but almost. Our plans are realistic, if daring. We plan to liberate the plutonium from South Africa. We need a modest amount of seed money to do that. Perhaps you could provide us with, say $1 million, the remainder to be transferred after we acquire the plutonium. If you'll have Dr. Hamidi designate someone who is technically competent, mutually acceptable, and able to move around in Egypt without raising suspicion, we'll arrange for him to inspect the plutonium after we secure it."

"Are you offering to manufacture nuclear weapons and provide them to me?"

This is what Hazi had dreaded. Riding on his answer was the success or failure of their mission to Libya. The success and failure of Operation Trojan Dove. "No, sir, we are not," he said softly but firmly. "We're offering much more than that. We're offering to destroy Israel. We're offering the final solution to Zionist imperialism. We're offering to do this in a way where neither of our countries will be blamed or retaliated against.

"As a military strategist, you understand the details can't be shared. I'm sure your security is tight. But who can be certain one of your guards isn't in the pay of a foreign power?"

One of the bodyguards lunged forward. Khadafy flicked his swagger stick and the man retreated sullenly.

Hazi paused and squared his shoulders. "The Christians, the Jews, and the Hindus have nuclear weapons," he declared. "Even the nonbelievers in the Soviet Union and China have them. While the Islamic nations sit like beggars

44

outside their tents. We have the capacity to transform this situation. And to transform history in our part of the world. But we need your help, which we humbly beseech."

Khadafy stood up majestically, adjusting his gold cape with a dramatic flick of the shoulders like a stallion shaking his mane, and stared intently at Hazi as if to unnerve him. A sardonic smile played across his lips and disappeared. Then he strode from one side of the tent to the other, back and forth, hands behind his back. Suddenly he whirled around and fixed his gaze on Hazi once again. "By the grace of Allah, you shall have it!" he thundered, slashing the air with his thin black stick.

*   *   *

Peter was handicapped by the fact that his newspaper lacked an Egyptian stringer. The last guy had been lured away by a well-paying public relations job with a hotel in Dubai. Had a local reporter been in place, Peter would have been spared considerable time and trouble and hit the ground running. Before leaving Washington he could have telexed a list of people he wanted to see. The stringer, with office and home numbers at his fingertips, speaking the language and knowing how to work the Egyptian bureaucracy, would have been able to set up several appointments in advance.

As it was, Peter had no choice but to make his own appointments through the Nile Hilton switchboard. He had to search out appropriate numbers, endure the impossible phone system, when he got through ask for someone who spoke English, leave messages, wait by the telephone endlessly for answers.

Still, he'd been able to arrange some solid, useful interviews. He'd seen an official of the Egyptian National Bank and the economic counselor at the American embassy who painted a comprehensive picture of the country's financial woes and how it intended to improve things. A planner for the Ministry of Health and Culture ran through the many efforts underway to persuade the people to practice birth control, but admitted frankly the campaign was not working. Foreign Ministry officials detailed various strategies to

45

get Egypt readmitted into the Arab camp, one of which was for Sadat to broker an understanding between Jordan and the PLO to open the way for a second peace treaty with Israel. Finally, a number of Egyptian officers spoke frankly of their difficulties in switching the entire armed forces from Soviet to American weaponry. There was grist for several anniversary pieces.

Hazi and Tewfik had informed Peter they were making him their special project. Through his reporting, they said, they could begin to modify widespread misperceptions in the United States about Arabs as uncultured and bloodthirsty.

"The stereotype is spread by your grade-B movies and cheap novels," the general said. "I know firsthand. I've been to the States a lot. In addition, judging from your writing and your time in the Pentagon, I look upon you as a fellow military strategist who can provide a rare perspective. There's much to talk about. We will learn from one another."

One night his hosts had arranged a charcoal-grilled-chicken dinner at a Greek restaurant, Andreas, near the pyramids. They sat out back, on a wide flagstone veranda, at a table covered with a faded green-and-red-checked cloth. The desert air was stagnant as the sun dipped slowly below the horizon, still shimmering from the late afternoon heat. Hazi and Tewfik pretended not to notice the swarms of voracious mosquitoes.

They had also entertained him at the Giza Sporting Club, where they ran into a group of boisterous senior Egyptian officers; at a French-Swiss restaurant near the heavily guarded Soviet embassy; and at a jam-packed dance hall where Hazi tried to fix Peter up with a girl who had big dark eyes and seemed to know the general well. Peter declined, politely. It didn't seem to bother Hazi that Peter was married.

But despite the generous display of Arab hospitality, despite all of Peter's failed attempts to pick up the tab, he was troubled. Hazi and his engineer friend were trying subtly, but persistently—usually late in the evening after lots of wine and Johnnie Walker Red—to extract all he knew about Israel's nuclear-weapons program and military doctrine.

Peter shouldn't have been surprised. It was he, after all, who several years before had broken the story that Israel was thought to have secretly built about a dozen nuclear weapons and was working hard on both aircraft and missile-delivery systems. Subsequently, as head of the policy plans shop in the Defense Department, he'd had access to extremely sensitive intelligence on the subject. Not that he would divulge secrets, of course, but when asked his opinions about various Mideast scenarios he was candid. And both he and they were aware his judgments had been formed against a background of closely held intelligence.

The Egyptians' insatiable interest in the subject itself was not cause for concern. Why shouldn't they try to get a window on Israeli thinking through a former Pentagon official who'd peeked in? But the whole thing took on an entirely new and troubling dimension with Peter's discovery of a trove of books on nuclear-weapons manufacture in Tewfik's office.

The discovery had come about by accident. Unexpectedly delayed by a late interview at the Foreign Ministry, Peter called the hotel switchboard for messages and found that Hazi had been trying to reach him all afternoon. The general was out when Peter returned the calls, but an aide said Hazi would meet him in the waiting room of Tewfik's office since the restaurant they'd picked out for that evening was in the neighborhood.

The office was located in fashionable Zamalak, a high-priced commercial/residential district of Cairo across the river from the main tourist hotels. When he arrived at the door of the fourth floor office and knocked, no one answered. It wasn't locked so he went inside. The secretary seemed to have wandered away. "Anyone here? Dr. Tewfik? General Hazi?" No response.

Cairo traffic, normally jammed until at least seven, had been unaccountably light that evening and he was twenty minutes early. He figured the secretary was in a back office arranging files or something and that Tewfik and Hazi would show up any moment. He started to sit down in an easy chair in the outer office, but decided instead to find the secretary in the main office to see if there had been any last-minute change in their plans.

Tewfik's office was spacious and well appointed with a large window overlooking the Nile. "Hello? Anybody around?" No answer. Perhaps the secretary had gone to the ladies' room or nearby on some other brief errand. To kill time he browsed among the books. No novels here. This was clearly a working office, not a home library.

Then he noticed that several shelves were devoted to a single subject: nuclear-weapons technology. Most were in English, a few in French and German. It was not the collection of an idle intellectual. He recalled all the recent conversations when his hosts had grilled him on Israel's nuclear program and presumed strategy. He remembered Tewfik's evasive joking whenever Peter asked him what sort of engineering work he did. "Somebody has got to design a better toilet," his typical answer went. "And it keeps me flush with money."

But it was not a plumbing engineer's reference library he stood there surveying. There was something ominous about this discovery. On second thought, it might turn out to be one hell of a good story. If he could flesh it out.

He hurried out of the private office and took a seat back in the waiting room before someone saw him. He picked up an Arabic-language photo magazine and flipped through it without seeing the pictures. The more he thought about it, the angrier he grew. Were his new friends who claimed only to want to correct an unfair stereotype confident that a few dinners and drinks would unlock the Pentagon's secrets? Did they think him so easily manipulated? Much of his adult life had been spent prying information from reluctant sources. Now the roles had been reversed. He didn't like it one bit.

Peter had intended to be a lawyer, but midway through his undergraduate years at Harvard he concluded a career in law would bore the hell out of him. As an editor of the *Harvard Crimson* he discovered a world promising a broad range of intellectual challenges. There were different issues every day, interesting people, the need to exercise ingenuity to learn things some folks were determined should remain undisclosed. He did a year of graduate study in journalism at Columbia, earning room and board as an emergency oxygen therapist at St. Luke's Hospital a few blocks from the campus. Which meant he didn't get much sleep that year.

Following that, he spent three years in Cleveland covering everything from a fire at a candle factory, a serial killer who turned out to be a prominent mortician, and meetings of the local school board. His editors at the *Plain Dealer*, seeing him growing bored, had subsequently made him second man in their Washington bureau.

Two years later, the *New York World* needed a Pentagon correspondent and Peter fast-talked his way into the job. A wonderfully full and varied career followed, including stints covering Vietnam, the Congo, Panama, and Central America. But in between those overseas assignments he'd spent a lot of time in Washington writing about the U.S.-Soviet confrontation, national security policy, and arms control. He became known in the small community of academics, think-tank analysts, and government officials who concentrated on strategy as a clear and imaginative thinker.

Nonetheless, he was surprised and not a little flattered when Senator Arleigh Hempstone, picked to become secretary of defense, asked him to come to the Pentagon for a couple of years to head its policy-planning shop. "The place is too inbred, Peter," Hempstone insisted. "I want you to come in and breathe some new life into long-range planning. Shake 'em up. Challenge their premises. Kick 'em in their intellectual pants. I want some creative, unconventional thinking in this musty old fudge factory."

The *World* agreed to give Peter a two-year leave of absence. Although he had enjoyed his time in the Pentagon, he longed to return to his calling. When he did, so there would be no appearance of conflict, the newspaper let him switch from defense to foreign affairs. Before long he became the paper's chief diplomatic correspondent with unlimited license to roam the globe in search of answers to a wide variety of questions. And now he was in Cairo, in the anteroom of a nuclear-weapons reference library.

5

Khadafy had stood by his word. Two weeks to the day after the desert meeting, in early October 1979, $1 million had been deposited in a numbered Swiss account. Tewfik received an innocuous picture postcard of an Alpine winter scene. The return address in Zurich was composed to reveal both the bank and the account number. The Dove was launched.

With their daring project partially funded, it was time to discuss how to get the plutonium.

"Well, Mohammed, how useful was your first day in the Code Orange vault?" General Hazi had asked. It was a bit after six—about three hours before dinner—and the two had joined Dr. Tewfik in his Cairo office. Mohammed was Tewfik's adopted son. He had been orphaned by an automobile accident at the age of thirteen.

Mohammed poured himself a cup of the hot pungent coffee his father's secretary had prepared before leaving for the day. He lifted the pale-blue Wedgewood cup to his nose and inhaled with pleasure; it was a fine Colombian blend his father sometimes had ground for him at a gourmet shop near the antiquities museum, and one of the small reminders that his family was different, had wealth. He set the cup on the corner of his father's rosewood desk, removed his jacket, loosened his tie. This was going to take some time.

"I had no idea how much detailed intelligence the security services have on the South African–Israeli nuclear connection," he said. "Very impressive. There was also an intriguing report from a cryptonymous source suggesting

51

South Korea and Taiwan are involved, too. But a hand-written notation in the margin questioned the lack of corroboration. It's damn hard for someone untrained in intelligence to evaluate a lot of this stuff."

Hazi walked to the window and looked out before speaking. The Nile at sunset shimmered as multicolored lights from adjacent buildings skittered across its slow-flowing water. "One thing you should understand about intelligence people," he said, turning to face father and son, "two-thirds of their output is pure camel shit. They're masters at turning coffeehouse rumors, scraps from obscure publications, and plausible garbage from low-level agents into what sounds like first-class intelligence. Believe me, I know. I have a second cousin in internal security."

"All well and good," Tewfik retorted, "but don't forget the Code Orange material includes intelligence that the KGB and GRU provided before they were expelled." That was why it was so important for Mohammed to get access. To get him through security, Tewfik had to pass him off as his research assistant.

Mohammed was glum. "You know, I feel rotten about the masquerade, the false papers, the lies. It's necessary, but . . ."

Tewfik circled the desk and patted his son on the shoulder. "Of course you do. We all do. Because we're true nationalists and patriots. But remember—there are men who wouldn't hesitate to have our heads if they knew what we were up to."

The general slammed a book onto the table alongside the window. "Enough. We all understand the importance of our project. There are no sentimental schoolboys among us. Let's get on with the damn report."

Mohammed looked pained. Hazi was his father's closest friend. It was Hazi who had taught Mohammed to ride and to shoot as an adolescent. Mohammed called him uncle.

The younger man unzipped a well-worn leather case and extracted a yellow legal pad full of notes. "Israel and South Africa are in nuclear bed together," he began. "It's a division-of-labor relationship. South Africa mines the uranium and reprocesses it at a facility near Pretoria into high-grade U-238. This is shipped to Israel, where it's fed into the reactor at Dimona, producing plutonium-239. Israel then shares a portion of its fissionable plutonium production with South Africa so that both can manufacture and stockpile nuclear weapons. About 30 percent is the estimate."

"Why does South Africa need plutonium?" Hazi asked. "I thought you could make atomic bombs directly from enriched uranium."

"A matter of efficiency," Tewfik explained. "It takes three times as much U-235 or U-238 as plutonium to make a bomb. Depending on a variety of factors, 5 to 10 kilograms of plutonium are needed to make a weapon that would require 15 to 30 kilograms of weapons-grade uranium. So with the same amount of material you can turn out three times as many bombs."

Mohammed flipped a page and continued. "According to the uncorroborated report I mentioned a moment ago there's a cooperative arrangement among South Korea, Taiwan, South Africa, and Israel on nuclear technology, special metals, and delivery systems.

"Korea has the money and the technology but was forced to abandon most of its secret program because of threats of an aid cutoff from the United States. But it's paranoid about North Korea and wants to join the nuclear club through the basement. Besides capital, it manufactures maraging steel, which South Africa needs for high-speed centrifuges.

"Taiwan has a supply of beryllium which is apparently vital—"

"Beryllium," Tewfik interrupted, "is employed to coat the core of plutonium that's compressed by high explosives to detonate the bomb. As the nuclear explosion initiates, the beryllium reflects neutrons back into the central core, enhancing the efficiency of the chain reaction."

"Will we need a supply of beryllium?" Hazi asked.

"I've already obtained a small quantity. Diverted it from the official program," Tewfik said, smiling smugly. "It won't be missed."

"According to the same report," Mohammed resumed, "South Africa contributes the enriched uranium while Israel produces plutonium. Israel has also offered to sell solid-fuel missile technology and inertial guidance systems to the others. Apparently the only thing they don't share is the technology for making bombs and warheads."

"Let's not waste any more time," General Hazi interjected, kicking a metal wastebasket for emphasis. "South Africa and Israel are nuclear partners. Now, what about the setup in South Africa? Where do they enrich the uranium? Where do they store the plutonium? Where is their weapons stockpile? How tight is their security?"

"Right." He flipped a couple of pages and reviewed his notes. "Most of their nuclear effort is concentrated in and around Pelinbada, west of Pretoria. The actual enrichment plant is nearby at Valinbada, which I understand in Zulu means 'that which we don't talk about.' "

Hazi made an exasperated gesture. "No language lessons, please!"

"Of course. Sorry. For our purposes, the key thing is that the Pelinbada area is the most heavily guarded in South Africa. It's off limits to commercial overflights. The security zone is enforced by Mirage jets that stand round-the-clock strip alert to chase away or destroy any aircraft that penetrate the airspace.

"There's also a commando brigade stationed in the area to prevent snooping or infiltration on the ground. It's equipped with helicopter gunships, advanced radar and acoustic anti-intrusion devices, excellent communications, and the best weapons in the South African armed forces."

"Unfortunately we don't have Egyptian forces to draw on," Hazi said. "We have to mount a small, fast, clever operation. Any ideas?"

"Possibly. I've been analyzing my notes and so far as I can see the only potential gap in their defense is when the plutonium is turned over to the South Africans at Durban for transportation to Valinbada. The plutonium's shipped under heavy guard by the Israelis.

"It's not vulnerable in Israel. According to the GRU,

54

the supply freighter's crawling with Israeli guards and it's shadowed by an Israeli submarine all the way to South African waters and back."

Mohammed referred again to his notes. "Once the freighter reaches port and the cargo is turned over to the South Africans, they transport the plutonium containers in a specially configured tractor trailer equipped with some sort of chemical foam dispenser. If the truck is broken into, the dispensers fill the cargo area with a quick-hardening cementlike substance. En route, the convoys are protected by advance and rear guards with helicopter gunships overhead."

General Hazi began to pace, his hands folded behind his back. "It sounds hopeless," he said dismally. "I had Khadafy in the palm of my hand and I asked for a measly million. He tosses small change like that to Latin American leftists just to stir up mischief.

"Why did I say he didn't have to put up the rest of the money until later? If we had enough cash now we might be able to buy a fast patrol boat with deck guns and depth charges. We could use piracy. Or organize a mobile commando raid from the air to snatch plutonium inside South Africa. But not with just a million."

"As I mentioned," Mohammed said, "there could be an exploitable gap. We'll have to check this out carefully on the ground, of course, but the stuff might be vulnerable when it's transferred from ship to shore, on the docks. The Israelis probably let their guard down at that point and start thinking about shore leave in Durban. With luck, the South Africans will feel complacent about security until the plutonium is inside the transport van. The transfer time is short, but there might be an opportunity to strike."

*　　　*　　　*

And so Nadia, Mohammed, and Achmed had traveled to Durban in late October 1979. That's where Nadia and Mohammed met Kenneth Hani.

They were sitting in a rear booth at Magoos, a popular art-deco bar along the Golden Mile beachfront in Durban.

Mohammed and Nadia were on one side of the stainless steel table, Hani, a tall thin intent black, on the other.

A KGB report that Mohammed had read in the Code Orange file identified Hani as a rising leader in the black labor movement. More importantly, he was a lieutenant in Umkhonto we Sizwe, the Spear of the Nation, the military wing of the outlawed African National Congress.

Nadia had phoned Hani at union headquarters and asked for an interview, posing as a correspondent for Cairo's *Al Ahram* newspaper. But for reasons he wouldn't explain, he'd declined to have her come to his office.

"How about a drink?" she asked in desperation. "My hotel or any place else you care to suggest. That way we can meet and you can decide whether I'm a serious journalist."

Mohammed had praised her quick thinking. Hani was cautious and presumably felt the authorities would not view a meeting with a foreign reporter in public as suspicious. The privacy of his office at union headquarters was another matter. But it would look suspicious for a light-skinned non-African woman to be seen having a cocktail alone with a black African, so Mohammed had decided to come along.

"You know, a few years ago I would have been turned away at the front door of this place," Hani was saying, shortly after they'd taken seats and been served. "And both of you might have as well, since you're not ivory white." He made overlapping circles on the table with the moisture from the bottom of his frosted beer stein. "What did you say your field was, Abdul?"

"I'm in shipping," Mohammed said. "My company is interested in carrying high-grade Egyptian cotton to Durban and bringing back textiles and whatever else we can find to fill the hold. I hope you don't mind me coming along. I'll be quiet and let Fatimah do her interview. She's the journalist."

"Mind? Relieved, actually. I had no idea Miss Rashid would be so young and attractive." Nadia looked puzzled. "A good-looking light-skinned woman meeting a black man in a bar," he explained, "might have turned some heads. Could have been nasty." He frowned, momentarily glum. Then his expression turned businesslike.

"A minute ago you said you two had been involved in radical campus politics. Neither of you looks very radical to me." Hani searched their faces.

Nadia lowered her voice to a passionate whisper. "Yours isn't the only country to feel the sting of colonial rule. We know what it's like to be treated as a servant class—ignorant, lazy, unambitious, and contemptible. We've made some progress since then, but the vestiges of colonial superiority and privilege haven't disappeared, Mr. Hani."

"Call me Kenneth," he said. "It's an English name, but the heart that beats beneath is angry black African."

"You don't look like a radical yourself," Mohammed pointed out. Hani was wearing a three-piece suit.

"Don't be misled by appearances. I'm an official of the National Union of Mineworkers. Every day I have to deal with the white establishment and it helps if I wear their uniform.

"My grandfather and grandmother were lured from their village to work at Kimberley in the De Beers diamond mines. The white man paid them handsome wages, for the time, but forced them to endure unbelievable indignities.

"My grandfather was a chief. Maybe you can't understand the significance of that, coming from so different a culture. He was a man of stature and means. But at the mine he was assigned to live in a rat-infested compound. Practically next door to the whites-only village with its fine lawns and clubhouses. Every working day my grandparents had to strip naked when they came out of the digs so their hair, their mouths, even their private parts, could be inspected and probed for stolen diamonds."

Hani closed his eyes for a moment and swallowed. He seemed to be narrating a documentary. "Do you know why a chief would allow himself, his wife, and his people to be treated that way? They thought it was because he was a savage and didn't know better. But no. It was because the white man's wages provided hard cash and other white men would sell them guns for that. For that alone. So you might say my grandfather and I, in our different ways, both joined the establishment. But only if you couldn't look into our hearts."

"I'm sorry," Mohammed said. "I meant no offense." He ordered another round of beers, as if by that small sociable gesture to make amends.

But Hani got up to leave. "I must go. I have another meeting. I'll talk to others and decide if you can interview me."

*   *   *

Achmed joined Mohammed and Nadia for an after-dinner walk along Durban's waterfront. He was posing as a business rep for a Kuwaiti company specializing in portside derricks, hoists, and other equipment used to load and unload cargo. "The two sides seem to be getting complacent," he said with satisfaction. "From what I can gather, the Israeli ship docks at pier 11 the first Tuesday of every month, at first light, regular as clockwork. I witnessed the whole thing yesterday. At dawn there's very little traffic. They can unload and get on their way without attracting much notice."

"Interesting," Mohammed commented. "At dawn yesterday I thought I heard a chopper circling over the hotel. Any connection?"

"It's a French Gazelle. Powerful, heavily armed, and probably armored. It'll be a serious obstacle."

"Only one?"

Achmed nodded and pulled a small notebook from his pocket. "Four heavy containers, lead lined, were removed from the freighter and loaded aboard a single tractor trailer. The whole operation only took twenty-four minutes—six minutes for each container. These men are pros. As for security arrangements, there was one car in front, another trailing, both packed with commandos carrying Uzis. A lot of firepower, but manageable.

"But, when they pulled off the pier, two more cars that

I hadn't noticed joined the convoy, one in front as lead car, presumably to guard against ambush, the other behind to prevent anyone sneaking up from that direction."

"What were the Israelis doing all this time?" Nadia asked. She was walking between the two men, holding Mohammed's hand.

"Good question. During the unloading, I counted ten on deck with Uzis and walkie-talkies. But the instant that operation was completed, they dumped their weapons and radios into a trunk near the railing and padlocked it. They grabbed overnight bags and cameras and were off the ship and down the dock in record time. It looks like you guessed right," he admitted reluctantly to Mohammed. "They get R & R after so many days at sea and aren't going to waste a single second of it."

Mohammed stopped walking and turned toward the open sea. He inhaled the smell of brine and iodine from the docks. He didn't speak. His eyes were on the darkening slate-blue horizon, his thoughts beginning to map out a battle plan.

6

At Alfie's Fish and Chips Restaurant the dark paneling, bare tables, and gray tile floor were meant to simulate similar neighborhood establishments in London. Hani was already seated in a shadowy back booth when Mohammed and Nadia joined him. It had been several days since their first meeting.

"Who the hell are you two, anyway?" he demanded, the dim light catching the white of his eyes.

Nadia looked surprised. "What do you mean, who are we? We introduced ourselves the other—"

"Don't insult my intelligence," he said, shaking his fist. "Who do you think you're dealing with? Did you really believe I wouldn't check you out? *Al Ahram* never heard of you, and hasn't sent a correspondent to South Africa in more than three years.

"I've had you two followed since our first meeting. You have at least one other confederate who's staying at the Dolphin Hotel on the waterfront. Room 47, front. The three of you were seen together on the docks last Wednesday evening." Mohammed leaned out of the booth and glanced over his shoulder.

"Don't even think about running out," Hani warned. "I have three men inside, two more outside. Believe me, your lives depend on what you say in the next few minutes."

Mohammed looked him straight in the eye. His voice was calm, his manner unruffled. "You're quite right. Our papers are phony. We're here on a secret mission for our

61

government. I'm not at liberty to go into detail, in part to protect the operation, in part to protect you in the unlikely event of failure.

"But I assure you our mission will deal a blow to the South African regime. Indirectly it will serve your purposes as well."

An incredulous, bitter grin broke over Hani's face. "You expect me to accept what you tell me now, after admitting everything else was a lie?"

Nadia started to protest but Mohammed placed a hand on her arm. "You want an explanation? Fine, you're entitled to one. You're a rising leader of the National Union of Mineworkers, one of the most important new political forces in the country. You were born in Bloemfontein in the Orange Free State, the only male of five children. Your parents were grade-school teachers. You were an honors graduate of University College at Fort Hare, majoring in geology, minoring in philosophy."

Hani rubbed his wrist nervously.

"Failing to get a suitable job in the mines after graduation," Mohammed continued, "you got involved in labor organizing. Your union has the economic power to improve the wages and living standards of its 325,000 members and be a major force for political reform.

"South Africa depends on exports of gold, coal, diamonds, chromium, platinum, and uranium for 65 percent of its foreign exchange. You have the economic power to hit the government where its army and police can't defend it—in the pocketbook. Used intelligently, you have the capacity to demonstrate to those who support apartheid that it will only undermine and eventually rob them of their high living standards."

He leaned forward and lowered his voice. "But you must move cautiously or the government will crush the union, just as it's tried to break the back of your political movement and its militant wing."

Mohammed studied Hani's face. The man was hanging on every word now. "We sought you out, Hani," Mohammed whispered, "because you're second in command of the Durban branch of the Spear."

"You've got a lot of information," Hani stammered. "Some accurate, some not."

"It's 100 percent accurate. I said I'm on a mission for my government. My information would only be available to a sophisticated intelligence service. Incidentally, to the best of our knowledge your government doesn't know of your, let's call it, extracurricular activities."

Hani leaned against the back of the booth, silent. With a snap of his fingers he could have them killed. But he would have to assume there were unidentified others who might either take direct revenge or phone the authorities and let them do it. In which case Hani's work, and his life, would be ended. Presently the young union leader broke the silence. "You claim an Arab government sent you. Aren't you really working for the Soviets?"

"Hardly. But would that make any difference?" Mohammed had indeed picked up biographical information on Hani from the Code Orange file in Cairo. The original source was in all likelihood the KGB.

Hani hesitated, and when he spoke it was with deliberation. "At this stage in our struggle we would accept assistance from the devil. What is it you want from me?"

"Three things. To begin with, we'll need a man who can drive a tractor trailer. On the morning of the operation, my men will create a distraction on the docks. The driver will jump into the truck and race out of town on the Pietermaritzburg Highway."

Mohammed paused. Hani still seemed shaken. "Do you know the thick grove of eucalyptus trees about 20 kilometers north of town? It's just beyond the ale house." Hani nodded. "Good. The truck should be pulled off the highway and parked under the trees so it can't be seen from the highway or from the air. It'll take place at sunup when traffic won't be a problem."

Hani was noncommittal. "You said three things."

"Yes. The second, which must precede the others by

a few minutes, is a series of explosions at stores and office buildings around Durban. At least six. Eight would be better. Their aim would not be casualties but to throw the authorities off and have them chase all over town.

"Finally, we want a powerful truck bomb detonated inside the headquarters and barracks compound of the Second Commando Brigade on the southern outskirts of Durban. In this case the object would be casualties, as many as possible. You'll need explosives and antipersonnel shrapnel."

"What will be in the truck driven off the docks?"

"Nothing. That's part of the diversion."

"Diversion for what? What's your target? How would it help our cause?"

"I can't tell you explicitly, except to say our success will shake the government to its core. So much so, in fact, that they won't breathe a word of our theft. They won't want anyone to know."

"What's in it for us?" Hani asked, striking his chest. "Other than your assurance the government will be embarrassed?"

"Not embarrassed, devastated. Aware that its most secret enterprise has been compromised. And for your trouble we're prepared to give you $250,000 in U.S. currency, money I know you could put to good use."

That was enough to buy pistols and grenades for a small army. The truck driver wouldn't be a problem. Neither would the explosives, Mohammed knew. But getting past armed guards to place the truck bomb inside the base? They would probably need forged or stolen papers for that.

"If," he said, drawing a diagram on his napkin, "instead of infiltrating explosives into the garrison, your men parked a truck packed with TNT, ball bearings, broken glass, and nails on Stanton Street alongside the perimeter fence next to the main headquarters building and the camp hospital, that would produce an awful lot of wounded. And it could be set off safely with a remote-control device."

"You understand I must talk this over with some associates," Hani said finally. "They'll have a lot of questions, and you've only given me vague hints." He waited for Mohammed to fill in some of the gaps, but the Egyptian remained silent.

"Let me also point out that if this is a trap, the only men we'd expose would be low level, the driver of the truck on the docks and, possibly, the driver who parks the explosives at commando headquarters. And of course you two and your friend at the Dolphin wouldn't leave the country alive."

Mohammed and Nadia didn't have to be reminded. They had to pray the police had no informants in Spear's inner council. Hani scratched his head. "Two hundred fifty thousand American dollars?" He sighed. "We could put that to good use. If we're interested, how long would we have to get ready? When would all this take place?"

"The first Tuesday of next month. On 3 December 1979, at sunup," Mohammed said, pulling a manila envelope from under his jacket and placing it on the seat between him and Nadia. "To prove our good faith, I'll leave this with you. It contains $20,000. Earnest money. You'll get another $30,000 when you say yes, and the final $200,000 will be waiting in the cab of the truck on the dock."

The African glanced at the envelope. "What if I take your three installments without completing the mission?"

"You won't. That's why we sought you out. You, no other. Our research tells us you're a man of honor, a man whose word is his bond."

With that, the two Egyptians rose and walked out into the sunshine, hand in hand, like a pair of carefree honeymooners. They didn't look back, although they had no doubt that at least two killers were stalking them.

*   *   *

Nadia and Mohammed spent the night of 2 December in Achmed's waterfront hotel room, she on the lone bed, the two men stretched uncomfortably on the floor. They wanted to be in place with a view of piers 11 and 12 at dawn.

Mohammed was in overall command, but Achmed, streetwise and more ruthless, would be in charge on the docks. That was the key to the mission. Achmed was proud of his leading role.

Nadia argued that she wanted to be more than window dressing. She'd insisted she was as good with a gun as any of their eight-man team on the *Noorani*, the Pakistani freighter tied up at pier 12, across from the Israeli-chartered, Panamanian-flag freighter *Bolívar*. The eight had signed on to low-paying jobs as seamen on the *Noorani* in order to be in place.

"I'd like to be on the docks too," Mohammed countered, "but someone has to stay behind at a vantage point so we can improvise quickly if something goes wrong. You'll stay with me. I may need you, and I won't hear any further argument. Subject closed. Now shut up so we can all get some sleep."

Mohammed's wristwatch alarm started beeping at five in the morning. He didn't need it to wake him, just to remind him of the time. He'd only slept in snatches and welcomed the chance to get up. He roused the other two.

Outside, the light of dawn gave a rose-gold tinge to the fat cumulus clouds overhead, washing night away. The sun was due to make an appearance a little after five.

Achmed checked to see that the clip of 9mm dum-dum bullets was seated properly in his Browning, the safety off, the silencer screwed tight. He patted the four spare clips in his back pockets, two in each. Once more he laid out and inspected the contents of the flight bag he was to take with him: three stun grenades, six teargas grenades, six smoke grenades. He eyed the carton, tightly bound with hemp, that he'd been told contained $200,000 in stacks of hundreds. Just imagine, he thought, two-thousand $100 bills.

For an instant he imagined what he could do with that much money. A fortune. If the savage didn't show up to drive the truck, Achmed could take his place, ditch it at the predetermined spot, and pocket the cash. But that was daydreaming; the contingency plan if he didn't show was for another member of the Egyptian team to drive the truck. In truth, this was by far the most important mission ever entrusted to him, a mission of supreme importance, and he could hardly wait to prove himself. Any human being would be tempted by the money, of course, but he was about to go on an operation that would establish him as one of the key men in General Hazi's inner circle. His cover as a sales rep and trouble-shooter for a company selling hoists and cranes had allowed him to establish as routine his comings and goings on the docks. If his cover worked, and if everything went as it should, there was no limit to how high Hazi would rise, with Achmed, son of the slums, on his coattails. Egypt would assert its proud place in the sun once more. Achmed didn't entertain a single doubt that the plan would work—if the damn blacks carried out their part.

He had wanted to bring in more men and carry out the entire operation themselves, but Mohammed had ruled otherwise. Black fish would be invisible in a black sea, he'd said. It was just a matter of locating the right fish.

Achmed hoisted the flight bag on his shoulder, grabbed the box by the hemp handle. It was surprisingly heavy, the cord tearing into his fingers. He moved toward the door of their hotel room, put his hand on the doorknob, stopped, half turned, and threw a mock salute at Mohammed and Nadia.

"Good luck," she said.

"Allah willing," he answered.

Outside the hotel, fog rolling in from the sea engulfed him and Achmed inhaled a salty lungful. It was heavier than usual, which was good. They would have additional cover for the operation.

He walked the short distance from his hotel to the piers. His rubber soles made no sound as he stepped onto the moist wooden planks at the approach to the chain-link gate. Rolf, the skinny red-faced guard he'd made a point of befriending earlier, put a hand on his holstered gun when Achmed appeared without warning out of the mist. But he relaxed at the sound of the familiar voice.

"Morning, Rolf," Achmed said, as the guard swung the gate open for him. "Only a couple more hours and you can crawl into bed with your missus."

"If I can't find better," the guard responded and guffawed. Their shift would be over at seven and the two guards were bored and weary.

As Achmed moved past the gate onto the wharf he heard Rolf calling to his partner in the guard shed, "It's only the wog. Swarthy son of a bitch doesn't sleep."

Achmed cursed under his breath. He wished it was part of his job to snuff the two of them. Sergeant Major Samir, leader of the pack from the *Noorani*, got to do that.

The eight men who had arrived aboard the Pakistani vessel, Hazi's hand-picked former commandos, were the cream of the special operations team that the general had used so effectively in his cross-canal operation during the '73 war. They were led, trained, and disciplined by Samir, the best noncom Achmed had ever met. The squad had practiced a number of dry runs at daybreak on a little-used pier in Alexandria before signing on to the *Noorani*. The captain had not only been bribed but, after accepting a down payment, threatened with death if he failed to carry out his part. He didn't know what cargo was to be spirited aboard at Durban, and for $50,000 didn't much care. Achmed figured with that kind of nest egg the man could buy a small business when he retired from the sea.

Achmed could barely see three feet ahead. When he came to the yellow tractor trailer he'd parked alongside the *Noorani* the evening before, he silently opened the door on the driver's side and climbed in. He swung the box of money onto the seat and patted it lovingly before fishing a key from his pocket and inserting it in the ignition. Damn, he thought. Leaving all those dollars here.

Achmed climbed down from the seat and quietly eased the door closed. The plan was for his men to assemble between the tractor trailer and the Pakistani vessel so they wouldn't be visible from pier 11.

The fog was so heavy he had to call out softly in Arabic to find them. "All here? Right. You know your assignments. Where is the regular crew?"

"The captain gave them shore leave, sir," said Samir's crisp voice. He had come up silently alongside Achmed. "Except for the cook and mess boys, who are preparing breakfast in the galley. They have orders to return at 0630 sharp so the ship can pull out on schedule at 0700. He warned them that any man not here would be left behind and would never work at sea again, if he had any say in it. The captain is fulfilling his bargain."

"What's happening across the way?"

"The winches have just been turned off," Samir reported. "The cargo has been unloaded from the hold ahead of schedule. I slipped over there and counted four containers behind the lorry. They were getting the forklift to start loading."

"Sure they didn't see you?"

"In this fog? No, sir."

Achmed liked to be called sir, especially by Samir. "How many South African commandos, Sergeant Major?"

"The usual, sir. Eight. Two for the truck, three each for the front and rear escort cars. At this moment six are gathered behind the lorry ready to load."

"And the Israelis?"

"We should hear them any moment coming down the gangplank in search of black women." Samir snickered quietly.

One of the South African commandos was calling out to an Israeli coming off the ship. "Now you be careful with the dark meat, Shimon. I understand there's a new strain of syphilis that's impervious to drugs."

"Impervious? Where did you learn such big words?" the man yelled back in good humor. "Don't worry about us, we're only looking for the Christian Science reading room. That's where your sister told us to meet her."

*　　　*　　　*

69

From his hotel window Mohammed strained to see the dock through the fog. Even with binoculars he couldn't make out much beyond the guard shack with its bare bulb casting a murky light through the unlocked gate. He rubbed his eyes. As he returned to the binoculars the sound of a helicopter could be heard heavily whipping the air in its struggle to stay aloft. Nadia heard it. She rushed to the window and put an arm around his waist. "See anything, yet?"

"Nothing. No—wait. A bunch of sailors are coming through the gate. It's hard to see. About nine or ten, I believe. It must be the Israeli security contingent from the ship." He looked at his watch. The first explosions were to begin at 0545 hours. It was already 0535. The next few minutes would seem an eternity.

Fourteen minutes passed. "Don't forget," Nadia said, "their watches weren't synchronized with yours."

"I hope they have watches," Mohammed snapped.

A minute later an explosion erupted in the west, then another and another from different parts of downtown. With the heavy fog holding in the sound, the explosions reverberated widely. *Caa-ROOMF. Caa-ROOMF-ROOMF. Baa-ROOM.*

"It's going down!" Mohammed shouted. He hugged Nadia.

On the dock, Achmed and his squad waited. They had been instructed to wait for a larger blast, distinct from and following the others, before swinging into action.

The South African troops were about to use the forklift to hoist the second plutonium container onto their truck when the explosions started. "Lord, what do you suppose the ANC is up to now?" one of them yelled.

"Raise the chopper on the radio," their leader ordered, "and find out what's happening."

One of the men raced to the front seat of the black chase car and grabbed the handset. "Icarus, Icarus, this is Neptune, over."

"Read you loud and clear, Neptune," came the voice over the radio. "Attempting to raise headquarters to see if they know what in hell's going on. Will advise. No evidence of anything unusual in your vicinity. Out."

Just then a rending blast was heard and the sky to the south lit up. *Va-VROOM!*

Moments later an excited voice crackled over the radio. "The bloody bastards have hit fucking headquarters. Apparently with heavy casualties. We're going to wheel over there to see if we can eyeball anyone speeding from the scene. Cars Alpha and Gamma are going, too. Keep on your toes, lads. Be back shortly." Alpha and Gamma were the cars that had been waiting just beyond the wharf to bracket the lorry when it left the dock.

Without a word, the Egyptians inserted wax earplugs and donned gas masks. From now on all communications would be by hand signal. Achmed cast one more glance at the tractor trailer before moving out with the grenades. A young black man was sitting in the driver's seat, his hands on the steering wheel, staring straight ahead. Check, double check.

The operation was going to work, he told himself as he raced forward, adrenaline surging. He lobbed a stun grenade and then a CS tear-gas grenade at the main group to the rear of the plutonium truck. Other members of his squad tossed grenades simultaneously at the lead and chase cars. A fourth Egyptian heaved several smoke grenades between the truck and the Israeli ship to conceal what was going on.

The South Africans, caught off guard, were flattened by the ear-splitting blasts of the stun grenades. They rubbed their inflamed eyes and struggled to breathe among the searing fumes. "Christ Almighty!" one of them yelled. "Was there a bomb on the next ship?" another asked, gasping for breath and coughing. A third pulled a handkerchief from his pocket and wiped his tear-choked eyes, trying to clear his vision.

Achmed, moving into the cloud of gas, saw the flash of a white handkerchief first, then the outline of a man's head. He fired twice at point-blank range. *Spft. Spft.* The silencer masked the reports. Samir emerged from the smoke and moved swiftly behind a commando rising from the dock. There was the flash of a steel blade and the trooper slumped forward, his throat cut.

Spft. Spft. Spft. Achmed shot out one tire each on the truck and chase cars so no one could flee and bring back help. As the pall of smoke and gas started to dissipate he saw a trooper rise and race toward the gate. Before he'd gone three feet an Egyptian soldier cut him down with a burst of submachine-gun fire.

Achmed started a body count. One man was badly wounded but still alive. He shot him. Eight. Then he waved his hands to indicate to his men that they should start transferring the crates to their freighter.

Two Israelis who had dived unseen into the water with the first explosions pulled themselves up on the dock behind him and began moving in. One, armed with a knife, raised his arm to plunge it between Achmed's shoulderblades. The other was reaching for a fallen automatic weapon.

"Achmed!" Samir called, though they were still wearing earplugs. He raised his gun and fired at the Israeli poised to kill his superior. Then he swung his weapon and blew a gaping hole in the other man's head just as he was raising the automatic. A staccato of shots rang through the air as the falling Israeli clutched at the trigger, his bullets unleashed aimlessly at the sky.

Achmed jabbed his finger in the direction of the *Bolívar*, signaling Samir to put some men on guard in case anyone else came forward. Samir nodded. He grabbed two men by the pants and shoved them forward, his hand signals making clear what they were to do.

Achmed figured the rest of the *Bolívar*'s crew were merchant seamen, working for low wages and unlikely to risk their necks for anybody's cargo. After all, it was insured.

An experienced Egyptian operator climbed into the booth of the red dock crane. It sputtered two or three times before the whining motor caught. Other raiders attached cables and hooks to the first container, just as they had practiced dozens of times in Alexandria. Smoothly it was hoisted, swung over to the *Noorani*, and lowered into the hold. Again the action was repeated. One to go. The fourth would be left behind on the South African lorry on the docks.

The blood in Achmed's temples throbbed. They could have taken all four containers, but the plan was to leave one so the South Africans couldn't put all their resources into the search for the hijackers. They would have to redouble the protection of a new convoy to make sure an attempt wasn't made on the last precious plutonium container while it was being moved inland. All this as they took care of their dead and wounded at brigade headquarters and at pier 11 and tried to mount a search of roads leading from the harbor.

Mohammed had explained to Achmed and Nadia that the South Africans would probably presume the ANC had staged the explosions to cover the theft of plutonium. Why? To embarrass the government? No. To prove there was nothing they couldn't seize, despite the most rigorous protection, if they set their minds to it. Achmed had taken this in with grudging admiration. That bastard is a genius, he thought.

The plan was for Nadia to phone the police and tell them—breathless, of course—that she'd almost been run down by a big yellow truck, a tractor trailer, as it sped away from the pier. She would mention its direction before hanging up. That should keep the authorities busy for hours . . .

The third crate had been hooked up and was being hoisted when two figures started running in a crouch down the gangway of the *Bolívar*, gas masks on their faces, Uzi submachine guns in their hands. Mohammed hadn't figured on the Israelis leaving any guards behind during shore leave, Achmed thought ruefully. One of them, a small dark-haired young man in sports clothes and running shoes, squeezed off three or four rounds in Achmed's direction. A bullet creased him on the left shoulder, burning as if he'd been whipped by a hot poker.

He didn't hit the deck. Instead, calmly, he raised his automatic in both hands and fired two rounds. The nearest man was slammed backward, into the path of his partner. Before the second Israeli could recover his balance, Samir fired a single round that tore off the left side of the man's face. Blood and brains splashed across the damp brown planks of the dock.

Samir ran forward, panting, and pointed at the blood oozing from Achmed's wound. Achmed pulled the plugs from his ears and indicated that the sergeant should do likewise. "Fuck the wound!" he shouted. "The two guards you posted didn't watch the ship. Now get your ass over there and make sure the cargo loading is complete so I can get the hell out of here and you and your men can clean up and rejoin the *Noorani*. The rest of the crew should be showing up shortly."

"Yes, sir!" Samir snapped a salute and went running off.

Their tractor trailer was still parked next to the Pakistani freighter. Achmed raced to the cab, stumbling as he went. He slammed the outside of the door several times with the flat of his hand. "Get going, you stupid bastard!" he shouted. "What are you waiting for?"

The young driver, stunned and frightened, turned on the ignition and pressed the gas pedal to the floor. The truck leapt forward, its rear tires screeching. In a moment it was out the gate and careening down the street.

7

When stymied by a complex problem, Tzur found it helped his concentration to escape the city and wander through the forest of pine and fir where he was raised, at Moshav Neve Ilan in the Judean hills west of Jerusalem. Then, too, it gave him a chance to visit his parents and his girlfriend, Batya.

He adored her, had since childhood, but wasn't ready to marry. To be more accurate, he was ready but Batya refused to abandon the *moshav*. It provided cradle-to-grave security, all the basic needs of life—housing, schooling, medical care, and a regular monthly allowance. It was like a kibbutz except the children lived at home rather than in a barracks and dined at their parents' table, not in a communal dining hall. Until going off to a career in military intelligence he'd never had reason to question life at the *moshav*. Now he found the very idea of communal living stifling and unacceptable.

The two of them were strolling, arm in arm, down the sun-dappled forest trail, their footfalls cushioned by soft pine needles. The air was fragrant with pine.

"Explain to me," Batya was saying, "why it's so terrible to live here among the people we've known since we were babies? It's like a big family. When you're away on a mission I won't be frightened and alone in a tiny flat in the city. I'll be surrounded by family and friends—our family and our friends. What's wrong with that?"

He didn't answer. He was sick and tired of the same argument. It couldn't be resolved by logical debate. It was a matter of strong personal preference. She was bright and vibrant, but she had led so sheltered an existence that she was afraid of being cut from the herd. In the *moshav*, doors were never locked. Neighbors were constantly popping in during meals and at other times when he preferred privacy. The members of the community did everything but shower and procreate together. That was not for Tzur. As far as he was concerned, that was for sheep.

"Don't ignore me, Motta. I want a reason, not a bored shrug. Don't you think I'm entitled?" She was almost as tall as he, with a small straight nose, high cheekbones, fair hair, and skin tawny from much exposure to the sun. She pruned kiwi vines and cultivated tropical plants which the *moshav* grew for sale to commercial florists. The plants were an important cash crop for the community and she was proud of her role in helping expand the business.

She was wearing tight khaki shorts and a T-shirt, not to tease or excite, Tzur knew, but because light cotton clothing made sense in the heat. In another society her beauty might have drawn her into modeling or acting, not farming. The sight of her, the touch, the smell never failed to stir him.

Batya and Tzur had been lovers since thirteen. They had been picking wild berries in these same woods. They started wrestling playfully, then fell to the soft earth and thrashed around laughing in the shade of a blackberry bush. But suddenly, unexpectedly, irresistibly, their platonic horseplay turned into something else. They made love, each for the first time. It was not all that unusual in this uninhibited frontier society. In the tight community of the *moshav* it quickly became apparent their relationship had matured. People shrugged and smiled. They were well suited for each other. It was taken for granted that one day they would marry and raise a large family.

But Tzur could no longer picture himself living the regimented life in a place where every house looked the same, orangish Jerusalem stone. Each person was duty bound to turn over whatever he earned outside—in Tzur's case his air force pay—to the group. Everyone received an equal allowance, except those with children, who got a bit more. It was a sort of half-baked socialism that he found unnatural and suffocating.

But he had to admit, the setting—the forested hills, the gurgling brooks, the smell of freshly turned earth during planting and of apple blossoms in spring—was beautiful. It was usually 10 to 15 degrees cooler than the arid coastal plain where he worked and lived.

Tzur had always been precocious and something of a maverick. His parents, refugees from Poland, were religious and hoped he would become a rabbi like his maternal grandfather. But while as a child he had applied himself as diligently to his religious studies as to his lay ones, he rebelled at what he regarded as the hypocrisy of Orthodox Judaism—in fact, of all organized religions.

He thought there might be a God, or preferred to believe it, but was turned off by dogmas created by the few to control the many.

"Why should we be forbidden to eat bacon and shrimp?" he had demanded of his father one day while they were working side by side in the turkey pens, raking and shoveling droppings and bagging them for fertilizer. He was only twelve at the time, but well read and increasingly skeptical. "I understand the health reasons during biblical times; those foods could cause disease. But not today. What's the sense of blindly following hygienic rules as if they had some sort of deep religious significance?"

Avraham Tzur wiped the sweat from his face with a big plaid kerchief. The place reeked of turkey droppings and the shoveling was raising clouds of the stuff. Turkeys, those ugly, stupid, smelly birds, represented the biggest single cash crop in the *moshav*. Somebody had to do this.

A white-haired, well-muscled man, he had studied law in his hometown of Krakow but had to give it up when, having fled to escape the Nazis, he discovered that a practicing Polish lawyer wouldn't be able to feed his family in Israel. The *moshav* had been their salvation. And he'd never shied away from hard labor. He rather liked the peaceful sleep it induced.

He leaned on his shovel to bring himself closer to his

son. "Questions, Motta, always a thousand questions. Why can't you accept certain traditions on faith? It is faith that preserved our people throughout history. Had cold logic been our deity, the Jewish people would long since have vanished."

"But that's changed too," the boy persisted. "Now we have our own country, a Jewish state. I plan a military career to help defend it. Jews here are a majority, not a persecuted minority as you and Mother were in Krakow. Doesn't it follow that we can be what we want? Not follow traditions we don't believe in simply to preserve our Jewishness?"

Avraham sighed and balanced his shovel in his two hands. "You know, son, arguing with you is like shoveling after the turkeys. It's a task that must be performed endlessly. Why do I have the feeling I'll never come out ahead?"

Tzur and Batya found themselves at a rocky outcrop overlooking the *moshav* guest house. Below them lay a crowded Olympic-size swimming pool and four orange-clay tennis courts, three of them in use. The facilities attracted a lot of tourists, mostly West Germans and Scandinavians. Perhaps they valued tranquility and modest prices more than the camera-toting hyperthyroid Americans.

"You haven't been listening to a word I've said," she admonished, stepping in front of him, hands defiantly on her hips. "Except for the occasional 'uh-huh,' I might as well have been talking to the trees. Do you find me so boring?"

Trying, yes, boring, no. He pulled her into his arms, his hands working up and down her body, holding her tight against him. "You have never bored me," he said with feeling.

"Don't patronize me. You never take me seriously." She pushed him away. "I'm just your weekend mistress— when it's convenient."

"How could I not take so beautiful a woman seriously?" Again he drew her close.

"Sex. For you sex solves everything," she said, a catch

in her voice. "Sex for recreation and release. Sex without responsibility."

He knew she had a point. Maybe one day she would change. Or he would. But to get married now and live in this dull cocoon might mean a falling out and divorce, perhaps after children had been brought into the world. That made no sense, either. Things would have to drift a while longer.

He had intended to have Shabbat dinner that evening with Batya at his parents' place and then spend the night with her. It had been almost three weeks and he longed for her. But now the mood was wrong. It would only reinforce her conviction that she was nothing but a convenient vessel for him. And he didn't want to argue anymore. It would get nowhere, would only divert him from concentrating on the problem he'd come to the *moshav* to think about.

Abruptly he decided to return to base, where secure phones and computer banks would allow him to pursue some fresh conjectures.

"Batya, be patient with me. I know I can be difficult, but I adore you." He paused, searching for the words that would convey his dilemma. "What's involved here can't be settled by debating points. There's no right or wrong answer. One of us is simply going to have to change before we can marry and start a family. I'm not sure who that's going to be." He kissed her one more time, with intensity, then playfully shoved her toward the path before he changed his mind and decided to stay.

She frowned, but said nothing. He knew she prayed he would change, but she was probably beginning to lose hope. Was he outgrowing her too, becoming increasingly comfortable in the sophisticated world of the city?

"I've got to get back to Ramat David, tonight," he said. "I'm sorry. Make my excuses to Mom and Dad. They won't like it, but they'll understand."

The three people who loved him best understood from experience that when he was wrestling with a national-security problem he was a man obsessed. On the drive back to the city, he wondered what a pilot with a strange combination of language skills had been doing in the flight cabin of the disappeared Soviet aircraft. In the past he had found, with problems like this, that it helped to take scraps of intelligence and shift them around to form a number of broad hypotheses. Some could be discarded almost immediately, others used as frameworks into which missing pieces of information could later be fitted. The process often provided the approximate shape of what he was looking for.

There was one especially appealing hypothesis, that the mayday man was a KGB agent who used flying as a cover. The Russians did that sort of thing all the time. That would explain his presence in the cockpit and his flight training, despite the Moslem roots. The KGB, vouching for his loyalty, would have left the air force no choice but to allow him into flight school, even though that was normally restricted to the more politically reliable Russians and Slavs. As a pilot or copilot he could travel in and out of major cities in the Mideast without drawing undue notice. Being of Arab stock would help him move about inconspicuously. He would also have a better feel for cultural attitudes, sensing when to bargain and bribe, and when to employ harsher alternatives.

What possible use would he have for Hebrew? The hypothesis even provided a logical answer for that. If he had been assigned to intercept Israeli military transmissions or eavesdrop on phone calls from a covert location inside the West Bank, Gaza, or southern Lebanon, knowledge of Hebrew would be invaluable.

Given the recent Soviet intervention in South Yemen, he might have been returning from a mission there. Or he might have been moving to a new intelligence assignment along the flight's itinerary—in Cairo, Amman, or Damascus.

*   *   *

Dr. Petra Tewfik hadn't always wanted to pursue a scientific career. The only son of a wealthy Egyptian importer, he had

80

chosen science, for which he had a natural talent, mostly to compensate for having disappointed his father.

The boy had been called Petra to honor the name of the fortified capital of the ancient Nabataean people, whose blood he shared through his father's line. "They represented the best of Arab civilization," his father Fawzi had explained when Petra was very young. "They were fierce warriors who instead of conquering or robbing made their living protecting the wealthy caravans traveling from China and India to the Mediterranean.

"But they were natural entrepreneurs, too, and soon branched out into business for themselves. They traded spices, silks, precious metals, and jewels. They constructed a number of way stations and warehouses and established a network of agents halfway across the world. They developed their own alphabet, a code of laws, and a monetary system. And they brought some of the best Greek and Roman artisans to Petra, their fortress capital, to make it beautiful."

By extolling the virtues of the Nabataeans, Fawzi hoped his son would be inspired to excel in manly pursuits such as sports, and later on in a manly profession, perhaps as a military man or merchant baron. Three times during the boy's formative years Fawzi took him to the city for which he'd been named, in southern Jordan near the Dead Sea. They rode Arabian horses along an eight-foot-wide path through the mountains, sole access to the stronghold.

During the period from 100 B.C. to A.D. 100, when the Nabataean empire flourished, all of the city's houses, temples, theaters, tombs, offices, warehouses, and government buildings—a few of them eight stories high—had been carved out of the rose-hued sandstone walls of the valley. On their first visit Fawzi stopped the horses before the most extraordinary edifice in the valley, the treasury building. Carved from the face of the mountain, it had twelve towering Corinthian columns and five gargantuan recessed statues. Three of the chambers were spacious enough to accommodate hundreds of people at a time.

Fawzi explained that the stonecutters had worked from the top down. They would cut a foothold several feet from the top of the cliff. This acted as a scaffold for the artisans who stood on it, chipping the tops of columns, statues, and chamber openings. When the first level was finished, they would carve another scaffold and repeat the process until finally they reached ground level.

The place was breathtaking. In the early morning, shafts of sunlight fell across the roseate buildings and cobblestone roads and thousands of wild oleander bushes showed off their pink, white, and red blossoms.

Fawzi excited the boy with stories of the ancient Bedouin society that had given up nomadic life to create an empire. "They were feared, respected, and very rich," he said. "And their blood courses through my veins and yours."

While Petra was inspired by the sight and the stories, it didn't change the fact that he was too small and uncoordinated for sports and wasn't much interested in business or the military. Instead he buried himself in scientific books. His strengths were calculus, chemistry, and physics. In those subjects he pushed himself relentlessly, hoping to win his father's admiration. But while his father gave him cursory praise, it was clear he was disappointed. He wanted a man for a son, not a schoolteacher.

Petra's closest friend was Rahman Hazi, a boy who represented all that Fawzi yearned for in a son. He was the best soccer player and horseman in Petra's school and, like his father before him, was determined to make a career in the army. On his fourteenth birthday Fawzi presented Hazi with a fine Arabian stallion. A servant on the Tewfik estate had confided to young Petra that a new coal-black stallion was in the stables. The boy assumed that it was a present for him. After all, he'd won the Pharaoh's Prize as the best student in his class at the British School and was sure his father would want to reward this achievement. He was heartbroken and jealous, then, when the stallion went instead to his friend. But he never let on to a soul.

There came a point when Petra decided academic excellence was its own reward. Since he couldn't find suitably challenging educational opportunities in Egypt, he went abroad, to France, then Sweden and India. He became a first-class nuclear engineer and amassed a fine library.

The books Peter ran across in the office in Zamalek were but a small part of Tewfik's collection.

*   *   *

Peter was pleased that the political counselor at the American embassy was Tom Fentress, an old friend from his government days. Fentress had been assigned from the State Department to spend three years as an arms-control specialist in the Pentagon. He and Peter had often collaborated in policy fights with the Joint Chiefs and the National Security Council. Their arms-reduction philosophies similar, they had become intellectual allies and friends.

He wondered whether it was because of this particular expertise that Fentress had been assigned to Cairo. After seeing what lay in Tewfik's library and hearing Hazi's talk of a nuclear triggering attack, he needed an honest reading on the status and seriousness of Egypt's nuclear-weapons program. So he went to see his friend at the embassy.

They were settled on a gray tweed sofa in Fentress' spacious office. The man had lost considerable hair in just a few years but otherwise looked the same, still dressed in the foreign service uniform—blue pinstripe suit, white button-down shirt, regimental tie.

"Because we go back a long time, I'm going to be straight with you, no games," Fentress said. "That's one of the most sensitive subjects around here. Even I don't have the security clearance for certain details, only those with a clear need-to-know do. One man, our station chief, is the embassy's expert, but you're aware that under current directives the CIA won't permit its people in the field to see reporters."

Peter started to argue but Fentress cut him off. "Look, I'll give you a lead, but only on the understanding it didn't come from me. The best Western expert on the subject in Egypt is Anthony Roberts, a squadron leader in the Royal

Air Force, assistant air attaché at the British embassy. He's sharp and informed on the subject. If you can establish good chemistry, he may be forthcoming."

A visit to the press attaché at the British embassy turned up the disquieting news that Squadron Leader Roberts was on holiday at the seashore and wasn't expected back for another two weeks. Peter, unfortunately, would be long gone by then.

"Can I phone and arrange to see him at the beach?" he asked the attaché. "I wouldn't press, but it's rather important."

"Sorry, old man, there's no phone at his cottage. That's by design, of course." Then, apparently impressed with the desperation in Peter's tone and aware that he'd served in a sensitive Pentagon post, the attaché relented. "He's at Agamy Beach, west of Alexandria, at a cottage named Sea Breeze. If you're determined enough to waste a whole day you might drive up and rap on the door. If he wants to chat, he will. If not, at least you can have a day at the shore for your trouble."

Peter knew it would be rude to interrupt Roberts' vacation, but the Brit was his best shot. He would rent a car and driver and make a try on Sunday. If he had indeed stumbled into the middle of a secret Egyptian program to develop nuclear weapons for use against Israel—on the heels of a peace treaty between them—it would be one terrific story.

8

The Israeli air force, it turned out, had nothing to add to Tzur's information on the missing Soviet courier flight. But in a stroke of luck he discovered that the navy did. A Grumman Hawkeye early-warning aircraft had been on a training flight at the time of the incident. The aircraft, packed with electronics, had been orbiting over the northern reaches of the Red Sea so as not to interfere with operational flights in the eastern Mediterranean.

While it hadn't seemed important at the time, a trainee radarman who was supposed to be scanning for surface ships that might launch terrorist attacks thought he detected an unusual incident. On the edge of the radar's range, he followed a blip indicating an object the size of an airliner that displayed an emergency radar squawk as it plunged toward the sea. It continued north at very low altitude after the emergency signal was turned off. It was hard picking the plane up at that distance, but he was pretty sure it banked west over Egyptian territory, near the naval base at Ras Banas.

As soon as the Hawkeye returned to base the excited recruit reported his sighting, expecting praise. But his skeptical crew chief dismissed the report, asking sarcastically whether he'd been out partying the night before. He reminded him in harsh terms that the exercise was meant to follow ships, not flocks of seagulls, commercial aircraft, or low-flying pink elephants. But the trainee, the top man in his class, doggedly insisted he'd seen a large, slow aircraft maneuvering in a suspicious manner. It was logged in the mission report, along with his crew chief's doubts. When Tzur phoned asking for information on an aircraft emergency over the Red Sea on the day in question, a quick search produced the questionable report.

This led to a new mystery. If the trainee's account was correct, Tzur reasoned, it meant either that the explosion had not downed the plane immediately, as had been assumed, or that the whole episode had been a carefully staged charade to make people think the plane had been destroyed. If it had crashed on land, there should have been reports in the Egyptian press. After all, Russian jets didn't go down every day with the loss of scores of people. Tzur checked with the office that monitored Arab newspapers and was assured no such report had been picked up. And a call to the U.S.-Israeli intelligence liaison office determined that the Americans had no satellite photos showing a recent plane crash on Egyptian soil.

Tzur shared his suspicions with his superior and got permission to pursue the matter with a senior official at Mossad, Avraham Shavit. Shavit was a thin fidgety grasshopper of a man with thick rimless glasses that magnified his bulging eyes. He dismissed Tzur's suspicions quickly and, it seemed to Tzur, contemptuously.

"Do you really think we've been sitting on our asses? You shake your head. Thank you for your confidence. We have, in fact, obtained and studied the passenger and crew list." Shavit paused and brushed back a wispy lock of white hair, studying Tzur. "So far as we can tell, there was no one of special interest on that flight, passengers or crew. The pilot didn't have an Arab surname and neither did the copilot nor the navigator. But for the sake of argument, assuming that your conjecture about a KGB agent is correct, which I very much doubt, he'd probably be using a phony name. So that's not conclusive.

"We managed to acquire a suitcase, picked up by a Sudanese fishing boat. There's evidence of an explosion in the baggage bay. We think it might have been caused by Semtex, a Czechoslovakian-made plastic explosive. It's widely available. The name tag corresponds to one of the passengers on that flight."

Shavit took off his spectacles and rubbed his eyes wearily. "Shortly after the incident there was a step-up in radio transmissions from PVO Moscow to Egyptian air force headquarters in Cairo. They were in a low-grade code that we were able to break without much difficulty. The Russians were badgering the Egyptians to mount a search and rescue for survivors. But the Egyptians won't give the Soviets the time of day any longer. They made excuses."

"But, sir," Tzur persisted, "if the whole incident was a ruse staged by the KGB it may signal an important oper—"

"Look, Captain," Shavit said in a raspy voice, jumping to his feet and aiming a bony finger at him, "maybe you haven't been listening. We know our business. We don't appreciate a wet-nosed puppy yapping at our heels. Suppose you stick to your ivory-tower theories and leave the KGB to the experts." The elderly man's face reddened. "And may I remind you, Captain, that this has absolutely nothing to do with Junction's responsibilities, which, as I recall, are protection against military threats." He emphasized the word *military*. "We're busy enough over here without having to bother with harebrained theories. You've wasted enough of my time."

"With all due respect, Mr. Deputy Director—"

"Get the hell out of my office, Captain!"

Back at Ramat David, Tzur was summoned into the office of his boss, General Raphael Gordon. "Motta, what did you say to Shavit? I just got a call from him and he was smoldering. Told us to stick to our own business. Actually, he chose a more colorful metaphor."

Rafi Gordon was admired by subordinates for his professionalism and his fairness. And since Tzur had advance permission to discuss his concerns with Mossad, he wasn't worried about being disciplined. Not that it would have deterred him, in any case.

"Now I don't give a damn about Shavit. He sounds

like a self-important little bureaucratic shit," the general continued, drumming his fingers on the desk. "But I'm worried about you. I understand you've been putting in six- and seven-day weeks. That's fine in a crisis, Motta, but not as a steady diet. You've got a couple weeks of leave coming, why not take it now? Relax, get in some swimming and light reading, romance your girl, recharge your batteries."

*   *   *

General Hazi embraced his friend Tewfik. "Thanks for coming by. I picked up some of your favorite Havana cigars at the base this morning." He handed over the box, along with a package of wooden matches.

They were in Hazi's office at the war college. Tewfik looked around. The room was small and messy, books and papers stacked in seemingly haphazard piles against the walls, on the floor next to the battered wooden desk, on the two easy chairs. The few scatter rugs were threadbare. It was late afternoon and light was straggling through the lone window, the only respite from a drab workspace. Tewfik started to remove some papers so he could be seated.

"Careful. I want to keep those in order," Hazi warned. "It may not look organized, but I know where every single paper is that I have to lay my hands on."

Tewfik created a new pile on the floor and sat down. He pried open the cigar box with a penknife, unscrewed the cap on one of the metal tubes, and withdrew a cigar, running it lovingly under his nose. "Ah, what an aroma. There's nothing like a fresh Havana." He cut off the tip and lit it carefully. "Thank you."

Hazi nodded, filling his pipe. He didn't smoke cigars. "It's been almost three months since Durban," he said. "The South Africans still don't have a clue what happened?"

Tewfik smiled. "Everything, every blessed thing is going according to plan. Mohammed went back into the Code Orange vault yesterday and looked up the current file."

"What did he learn?"

Tewfik withdrew a roll of yellow sheets from inside his jacket. With both the cigar and pipe going the room was getting stuffy. Hazi got up and raised the window.

"I'm listening," he said.

"Immediately after the bombings and theft at the docks, the South Africans turned Durban upside down looking for the truck. Eventually they found it, but of course, it was empty. They concluded the hijackers had left one container in the truck on the docks because they were scared off."

The general tamped the tobacco deeper into the bowl of his pipe and applied another match. Leaning back, he put his boots on the desk.

"They jumped to the obvious conclusion," Tewfik went on, "that the ANC was behind the whole thing. They combed the city looking for the three missing containers, scoured the surrounding countryside, arrested known and suspected ANC leaders.

"But they were constrained by secrecy; they couldn't identify the cargo to the searchers except by physical description of the containers. And it would have been embarrassing to reveal what had happened. They had soldiers, security men, and police detectives going door to door, from the docks outward. Even embassies were inspected, on the excuse of tightened fire-safety regulations. They broke open the locks of warehouses, searched garages and private homes.

"About three weeks after the fact, through a process of elimination, they began to suspect the Pakistani freighter. But of course by then it was too late. The ship left Durban on schedule, less than an hour after the incidents at the adjacent pier."

Hazi reached over to a small refrigerator on a table behind his desk and retrieved a couple of bottles of Perrier. He uncapped them and handed one to Tewfik. "Here, my old friend, your throat sounds dry. Sorry, no icemaker. And I don't keep limes in the office."

"No scotch? Oh well, it's early. Anyway, just as you figured, the South Africans traced the path of the *Noorani* into the Mediterranean, to Valencia and Alexandria, and then through the Suez to Karachi, its home port. They broke into the shipping line's offices one night to inspect the log. Naturally, the captain didn't enter anything out of the ordinary. But the South Africans, knowing of Zia's secret weapons program, concluded he was behind the theft. They protested privately to Pakistan but were told Pakistan knew nothing. Which, of course, they didn't believe. So we're in the clear."

The general beamed. They'd started with nothing but an audacious plan—no money, no fissionable material, no weapons-manufacturing team. And now, without any official help from the Egyptian government—though to be sure a few friends such as the commander of the base at Wadi Natrun had agreed to turn their backs and ask no questions—they were on the verge of pulling off a historic coup.

*   *   *

Instead of arguing, as Gordon probably expected, Tzur had agreed to take some leave. He knew it was foolhardy— Shavit would call it harebrained—but it had occurred to him in Gordon's office that he could go to Egypt himself and nose around. Since the signing of the peace treaty tourists had been trickling from Israel to Egypt, and he'd always wanted to see the pyramids. If he could just dig up one hard fact to undermine Mossad's pat conclusion of a bomb in the baggage hold, he'd go back and rub Shavit's shriveled face in it.

A vague plan of action began to form in his mind. Tzur spoke some Arabic, but not enough to pass as an Arab, particularly not with his blue eyes and blond hair. He could rent a car and drive down to Ras Banas, where according to the navy radarman the plane had veered over land. Hundreds of people would have heard the drone of a large jet hugging the ground. Had it exploded anywhere nearby, even at sea, many would have heard it and discussed it. Disguised as a tourist with a smattering of Arabic, he could buy some oranges at a fruit stand and ask the shopkeeper about the incident in a low-key way.

90

On the other hand, if the airliner had made a safe passage over Ras Banas and he corroborated that fact, he could drive inland to Luxor, a tourist attraction, to trace the flight path there and beyond. He wouldn't need much to buttress his contention that the explosion never occurred, that it was a ruse. Perhaps on hearing his findings General Gordon himself would agree to approach someone other than Shavit to get Mossad interested in reopening the case.

It was risky. If he asked permission it would be denied. No question. But if he was right, someone had gone to a lot of trouble to convince the world that a plane had crashed. It was Junction's responsibility to investigate any potential threat to the state. His instincts screamed that this was such a case.

So he phoned an old friend in the documents section of air force intelligence. "I'm planning a sightseeing trip to Egypt," he said, "but can't travel on my official passport. Could you whip me up an Australian passport? Name? How about Ralph Langleigh. *L-a-n-g-l-e-i-g-h*. I used to know someone in grad school with that surname. Occupation? Archeologist. Oh, and I'll need an Egyptian visa for a two-week stay."

*   *   *

Peter had booked a car and driver through the hotel's concierge for six in the morning. He customarily rose at sunrise, so it was no hardship. He wanted to arrive at Squadron Leader Roberts' doorstep at breakfast time, before the man had a chance to leave his cottage. The taxi turned out to be an old four-door Chrysler, but in immaculate condition. The driver, a leathery old man who spoke pretty good English and had nicotine-stained teeth, introduced himself as Abdul.

"Where do you wish to go, sir?" he said.

"Drive toward Alexandria and I'll give you further directions from there."

The driver shrugged. It was unusual to be given so little information. But Peter didn't want to explain just yet that he wasn't sure exactly where he was going.

Abdul turned over the ignition smoothly and headed out the Delta Road, through sleepy little villages of mud huts and cinder-block shops. At this hour there was only a handful of cars on the road. Trucks were another thing. Several passed by, piled high with melons, construction materials, and crates of squawking chickens and ducks. Here and there Peter saw donkey carts hauling farm families to the fields.

Sand began whipping against the windshield like miniature hailstones, but Abdul made good time. Peter noticed that all approaching vehicles had their lights on so they would be seen through the billowing sand.

Though not normally a pushy reporter, in exceptional cases—and a secret Egyptian nuclear program would be exceptional—he could be determined and resourceful. Today he was probably going on a fool's errand. He'd have to be careful. The information he wanted and his method of seeking it, considered aggressive investigative journalism in the United States, could result in a charge of espionage by Egyptian authorities. Uncovering a nuclear-weapons program, whether or not he filed the story, could mean arrest and jail. Of course, once he left the country he could publish whatever he'd learned.

As they approached the outskirts of Alexandria, Abdul asked for further directions.

"Head toward Agamy Beach."

"Very large area, many kilometers, sir. Where, please?"

"Whatever is closest to here."

Abdul shrugged again. He was being well paid for his time, so he did as instructed and turned left at the road junction toward Agamy.

It was about eight-thirty when he announced that Agamy was dead ahead. The sun was already blazing; the day would be a scorcher.

"Stop at the nearest shop at the beach and ask for directions to the Sea Breeze cottage."

Abdul turned his palms toward the roof of the cab as if to say, Who is this crazy American? There must be several

92

places at the beach with that name. But he drove to a small grocery store and got out. When he returned he had a grin on his face. "Down this road," he announced, "third house, with red-tile roof."

What a stroke of luck, Peter thought. It was a good omen. With only the sketchiest information he'd managed to find Roberts' cottage. And it was so early the guy would probably still be home. Peter jumped out of the car, told the driver to wait, and headed for the front door. He had to knock several times before it was answered. A light-skinned Egyptian woman in a peach nightgown opened the door a crack and peered through it suspiciously. She didn't look fully awake.

"Sorry to disturb you," he said, assuming this was the children's nanny, "but I'm looking for Squadron Leader Anthony Roberts."

She shook her head. "Roberts? There's no Roberts here. Perhaps he rented the cottage two weeks ago?"

At this point a man appeared in his pajama bottoms. "What does he want at this hour? The house was sleeping!"

"Says he's looking for a Squadron Leader Roberts," she whispered.

"The nerve! He has the wrong address!" the man said, and slammed the door.

Now what? Peter wondered, heading back to the car. Why hadn't he thought to ask the British embassy guy for a street address? He didn't realize how large an area this was and that there might be more than one Sea Breeze cottage.

But he had an idea. In resort areas such as this there were usually foreign colonies, whole neighborhoods where various nationalities tended to concentrate. Diplomats, businessmen, and physicians, after all, preferred to spend their leisure with folks who spoke the same language, shared the same interests.

"Is there a British colony here at Agamy?" he asked the driver. Abdul nodded and Peter told him to head for it.

About fifteen minutes later the car stopped again. A

few multicolored Bedouin tents were pitched off the side of the road, home to the people who did odd jobs in resort areas.

"What is your wish now?" Abdul asked with a trace of scorn.

"Ask the Bedu if they know where Squadron Leader Roberts lives."

Abdul returned momentarily, smiling broadly. "That is his house," he said pointing. "But he and his family left for beach not long ago. You wait here?"

"No. Take the street nearest to the beach."

Abdul muttered something in Arabic but did as he was told. At the beach, in the cramped rear seat of the car, Peter struggled out of his limp clothes and into a bathing suit. "Do whatever you want for the next few hours," he told the driver. "Return for me at noon, at Roberts' house."

He was taking a big chance. First, that he would find the British officer among the hundreds of bathers. Second, that the man would agree to talk with an interloper and an American reporter at that. Third, that he would be allowed to stick around for about three hours until his car returned. If all else failed, he would at least have half a day at the shore.

The scorching street burned the soles of his feet. He stopped at the edge of the sand and blinked, trying to adjust his eyes to the glare. There were no refreshment stands, no hawkers of beach umbrellas, no signs of commercialization. Only hundreds of vacationers, short and tall, fat and skinny, old and infant, beautiful and repulsive, tanned and beet red. This section of beach appeared to cater mostly to family groups. Nothing topless in sight above the age of four. Children ran back and forth from the ocean with pails of sloshing water for sand castles and canals. Here and there young couples rubbed lotion lovingly on one another.

The babble of foreign voices reminded him of the delegates' lounge at the United Nations. But, of course! That was how he would find his needle in the haystack. He walked along the shoreline, ear cocked for a British accent.

When he heard one he homed in, toward a blanket with a potbellied older man and his wife.

"You wouldn't be Squadron Leader Roberts, by any chance?"

"Sorry, mate. He just headed off along the shore in that direction. If you hurry you'll catch him."

Peter flashed his most ingratiating smile. "But I don't know what he looks like."

The man inspected him for a moment, then apparently deciding he looked like a right sort said, "Tall, slender, dark-haired, wearing orange trunks. Wait a minute. His wife's nearby. I'll walk you over."

Peter followed a half step behind. "Hello," the samaritan said brightly to a woman with a long thin nose and bright eyes. She looked at Peter as if he was someone she ought to remember, a fellow she'd met once at a crowded diplomatic party perhaps but whose name she couldn't recall.

"Chap is looking for Anthony," the man said, and traipsed off. Mrs. Roberts smiled up at him, shielding her eyes from the sun. "You're a friend of Anthony's or work with him? How nice of you to stop by."

"I'm awfully sorry to bother you on your holiday," Peter said. "I don't work with your husband. My name is Peter Robbins and I'm a Washington correspondent spending a little time in Egypt. At your embassy they told me I might find your husband here. But if it's a bad time . . ."

"Heavens no," she said, moving over on the blanket to make room for him. "Come sit down. I'm sure he'll be back presently." She offered him a cup of tart lemonade.

The squadron leader, when he returned, didn't seem to mind the presence of a stranger. He had a friendly face, lean and angular. Once the introductions were made, in fact, he seemed to welcome the diversion. He chatted amiably but guardedly until Peter mentioned his recent two-year stint at the Defense Department. "What's wrong with my hospitality?" he said, getting up. "Why don't we go to the kitchen, then into the living room, where they settled into a well-worn leather couch.

"Let me get right to the point," he began, after swallowing one finger sandwich whole. "I've run into some Egyptians who seem extraordinarily interested in nuclear weapons and how they might change the balance of power in the region. It's not surprising that Egypt wants nukes, if only to deter Israel. But if Egypt is able to develop them there's no telling what sort of holocaust might be triggered."

"You wouldn't be talking about Hefez Azziz, would you?"

Peter shook his head.

"No? How about Petra Tewfik?" Peter, about to sip his drink, stopped the glass in midair and stared at Roberts.

Roberts smiled. "You needn't be startled. Egypt doesn't have many first-rank nuclear physicists, and those two are about the best. Actually, Tewfik is probably the better one. Got advanced training in Sweden and worked for a few years in India's nuclear-power program. We're not certain how far the Egyptians have gone, or even if there's a firm government commitment to a development program. But if there is, Tewfik would be one of the principals."

Roberts told him that in 1961 the Russians had built a 2-megawatt nuclear reactor at Inchass, near Cairo. Not subject to inspection by the International Atomic Energy Agency, it was considered incapable of producing sufficient weapons-grade material for a bomb. Egypt, he said, had tried to shortcut the path to nuclear weapons by trying to buy some, first from the Soviet Union, which curtly refused, and then from China, which said Egypt should rely on its own resources. So Egypt had gone on with a determined program of training nuclear physicists, engineers, and technicians. "They now are believed to number about five hundred," he said. "In addition, Egypt wants to acquire eight big nuclear-power reactors.

"After agreeing to sign the Non-Proliferation Treaty and open up to IAEA inspection, they managed to sign, in your currency, a $2 billion deal with France for two 900-

nicians. "They now are believed to number about five hundred," he said. "In addition, Egypt wants to acquire eight big nuclear-power reactors.

"After agreeing to sign the Non-Proliferation Treaty and open up to IAEA inspection, they managed to sign, in your currency, a $2 billion deal with France for two 900-megawatt pressurized-water reactors. And they're negotiating with your government for a couple of additional power reactors with an estimated price tag of $1.2 billion."

"I'm skeptical about their motives," Peter said. "As an oil-exporting country they have a much cheaper source of energy. Also, when you consider how awful the economy is and how a few billion would make an enormous difference financing social programs . . . Why squander that kind of money on nuclear power?"

"Why, indeed? We share your skepticism. But building a technical infrastructure for a nuclear option and actually deciding to make weapons secretly are two different things. We simply don't yet know which they're doing."

"The Israelis have a big head start," Peter pointed out. "Without a missile-delivery system, how could Egypt possibly expect to match them? And it's not stretching the imagination to think the Israelis would destroy any Egyptian nuclear facility they discovered before weapons were produced."

Roberts nodded. "I don't disagree. But we've heard—and I must insist that this not be published—that some Egyptian planners believe only two nuclear bombs detonated over Tel Aviv and Haifa would destroy most of Israel's economy and military industry."

"At what price?" Peter asked. "Cairo, Alexandria, Port Said, Helwan, Ismailia, and Suez City? That would be one hell of a victory. Not for Egypt but for its Arab rivals, Syria, Iraq, and Libya. It simply doesn't make sense."

Roberts shrugged. "You're using Western logic. Egypt is an ancient country with a completely different culture and value system. Human life is not treasured so much here."

9

"Do you suppose he was really just an American looking for a friend? Or was that a ruse?" Mohammed said. They were in the master bedroom of the Agamy cottage, sprawled over the rumpled sheets of a double bed.

"He wasn't Israeli intelligence," Nadia said. "The man would have been smoother, with a better story. And he wasn't KGB, because then he would have pushed past me into the house to see for himself who was inside. No. He was your typical arrogant American. Didn't even have the common courtesy to excuse himself for waking up the whole house."

Achmed, who had come in the back door of the cottage panting, peered into the bedroom. "I think he's trouble, and I say kill him."

"Have you gone trigger happy?" Mohammed said. "You know we've got to keep a low profile until it's time for the mission. Last thing we need is a murder investigation with the police buzzing around the place. Where the hell have you been, anyway?"

"Somebody around here has to be alert," Achmed retorted. "You don't just fling open the door unarmed and unprepared for anybody who knocks."

Mohammed and Nadia avoided Achmed's stare. In fact, they had been careless.

"I slipped out the back to see how he'd come and whether he had backup," Achmed said, gloating. "There was a Cairo taxi, an old man at the wheel, waiting down the road. I wrote down the license number." He grabbed a towel and flicked sand off his bare feet onto the white shag carpet.

Mohammed lit a cigarette and inhaled deeply, staring at the ceiling, arms behind his head. "Better not take any chances. Our assignment is too important. How do we find out who he is and whether he represents a threat?"

Nadia, who had moved into the kitchen to brew coffee, called over her shoulder, "He was asking for a Squadron Leader Roberts, Anthony Roberts, I believe it was. The name sounds British or Canadian. I can make some inquiries in the shops the Western community uses. If the man exists, we should be able to find out who he is and who he works for. That's a start. If it's a phony name we should get the hell out of here, fast."

Achmed tossed the towel onto an easy chair, sprinkling it with dirty sand. He noticed Mohammed wince.

So, the leader of our little band thinks he's too good to be associating with such a low caste, Achmed thought. The high and mighty Mohammed Tewfik, raised in a mansion full of servants. And now he's worried about the precious furniture in a rental cottage, some fat rich man's investment.

Mohammed was bigger but nowhere near as tough. Achmed had learned to fight in the streets and alleys of Cairo. There the prize was being able to walk away in one piece, not an engraved cup awarded for outpointing some tippy-toes in a boxing match at a wealthy sporting club. As for servants, his mother had been one, washing linens and scrubbing floors for a wealthy French family. His father had swept streets and picked up litter. They'd done whatever they had to in order to put bread and tea on the table. And Achmed, alone among four brothers and two sisters, had made something of himself. Officer. Pilot. Covert operator. Patriot. He was a man with a future.

He might have followed in his father's undistinguished footsteps had he not been grabbed by a Sunni mullah while trying to steal a Persian prayer rug from the neighborhood mosque. For some inexplicable reason the holy man had made it his personal mission to reform Achmed, sponsoring his religious and secular education. It was the mullah who pulled strings to get him a place in officers' candidate school, on the premise that firm military discipline would sand down his rough edges.

Achmed smelled the aroma of the coffee and wandered into the kitchen. He glanced furtively at Nadia, who in the excitement hadn't bothered to slip a robe over her peignoir. As she stretched to reach the sugar in the cupboard, the material turned translucent against the light from the window. Achmed sat down quickly to hide his reaction to the sight. Why doesn't she cover herself around me? he thought. Does she think I'm less a man than Mohammed? The whore flaunts herself.

"It shouldn't be all that difficult to get a name," he pointed out. "We could phone the taxi company in Cairo and ask."

"What's wrong with you?" Mohammed said, joining them in the kitchen and taking his customary seat at the head of the table. "If he picked up the taxi off the street they'd have no idea. If he booked the car at his hotel and he's an intelligence agent, our inquiry might tip him off. There has to be a less obvious way."

Achmed snapped his fingers. "Wait a minute. There are only two ways to Cairo from Alexandria, the Desert Road and the Delta Road. You take one, I'll take the other. We may have to wait all day, but when that taxi goes by we can follow it. If he stops along the way for petrol, one of us will relay a message here through Nadia so the other can proceed to Cairo. If we know where he's staying it shouldn't be too hard to find out who he is."

Mohammed smiled broadly. "Now that's a first-class plan. First class. We'd better have a big breakfast; there's no telling when we'll get our next meal."

Nadia placed the coffeepot in the middle of the table along with the sugar, cream, and cups and saucers, and took a seat between them. She wasn't going to pour their coffee.

She could be tough with men. There was the time a campus policeman had pinned her against a wall during a student riot at Cairo University, his right forearm jammed against her windpipe, cutting off her air and causing pain and terror she'd never experienced before. Then instead of herding her with the others into a police wagon he pulled her behind some thick bushes, threw her to the ground, and yanked her skirt up. When she started to scream he slammed his left hand over her mouth and waved a club over her head. She realized how helpless she was and stopped struggling then. She must think of survival.

He had a sweating pock-marked face and he grunted as he dropped his club and started to unzip. But he never finished. Nadia pulled a long hatpin from her waistband, kept there for security, and thrust it into his heart. His mouth opened with pain and disbelief, his eyes bugging out. With some difficulty she slid out from under him, straightened up, and brushed off her clothes. She was rushing away when she remembered the hatpin. The guard's pleading eyes fastened on her as she pulled it from his chest. She wiped the blood on his gray uniform. He tried to grab her, but the strength was ebbing from him rapidly. Once more she turned to leave, then stopped and bent over the slowly thrashing body as if to say something. But she didn't utter a word. Instead she spit in his face. Then she strolled toward the nearest path leading off campus like a student taking a coffee break.

Nadia was the only child of a pharmacist and a librarian. Her mother, a brilliant woman who would have loved to teach literature at the university level, had been thwarted by cultural bias. Women weren't cut out to become professors, she'd been informed coldly. Unwilling to teach nursery school, a job into which education authorities had tried to shunt her, she became a librarian instead. At least that allowed her to indulge her passion for books and ideas. Bitterly disappointed over her fate, she vowed it would be different for her only child. Times were slowly changing, faster in the West, of course, but eventually opportunities would open up for women in Egypt as well. Her daughter was going to be fully prepared.

Nadia became the embodiment of the frustrated hopes and aspirations of the mother. And of the bottled-up rage.

It was little wonder, then, that she viewed herself as an instrument of change, an activist leader on the battlefield of political and social reform.

She had met Mohammed after college, in graduate school. At twenty-three she was writing a master's thesis on the theories of Niccolò Machiavelli when out of curiosity she attended an air force recruiting lecture given by Mohammed. He captivated her, standing there at the lectern in his dark-blue uniform, a tall, muscular, distinguished-looking officer. He delivered a forceful speech but with a touch of humor, showing he didn't feel superior to his listeners. The daubs of gray in his wiry hair gave him a mature look.

Drawn like a moth to a flame, she went to talk with him afterward. What could she say? Obviously there was no place for women in the air force officer corps. She noticed the puzzled look on his face when she joined the handful of male students at the edge of the speaker's platform. After he had patiently answered them, she remained. They chatted for a moment and then she invited him for an espresso. Egyptian girls were not usually so forward; he seemed intrigued, and accepted. Coffee led a few nights later to dinner. Then more dinners and dancing. It was obvious Mohammed wanted to sleep with her, but she held back. He didn't press it, presumably figuring religious qualms kept her chaste. One night before agreeing, she wept and told him of the attempted rape. She held nothing back, not even the killing. And now a little over a year later she was part of Mohammed's team.

Nadia was skeptical about Achmed's plan to intercept the taxi. "How do you know he'll go back tonight? He may stay a night, even a week."

"With a taxi?" Achmed said. "No, if he planned to stay awhile he would have rented a car, not a taxi. If we even suspect he's an agent," he added, "we'll kill him."

She watched out of the corner of her eye as he pulled the Browning automatic from his belt and pressed it to his lips. The smell of oil and gunpowder seemed to give him a rush, a feeling of power. He gazed at the deadly weapon.

In his hands it had eliminated four Russians only a few days before and had saved his life in South Africa.

Nadia wondered if he felt remorse over the stewardess and pilots. Probably not. He rationalized that they were all enemies, that as a soldier he'd had no choice but to deal with them instantly, mercilessly. Just as he would anyone who stood in the way of their operation.

She shuddered at Achmed's coldness, at the same time comforted to know he would protect her. Mohammed was her lover and a far better man, but strangely she was drawn to Achmed too. Drawn to and repelled by . . . It confused her. She didn't like the feeling.

*   *   *

Tzur's face stared back at him from an Australian passport. The registered name was Ralph Langleigh, as he had requested. For the next couple of weeks he would have to become this man. He envisioned him as a low-key, taciturn, budget-minded archeologist making his first visit to Egypt.

The friend in air force intelligence who provided the false document told him Egyptian counterintelligence had some highly professional people but tended to be hit and miss. If he aroused serious official interest, his cover was likely to be blown. On the other hand, if he blended into the flow of tourists and businessmen, he should have no problem getting his fill of the pyramids and the Cairo museum.

Tzur had needed new clothing, books, pencils, a suitcase. There wasn't to be a single item, not even a chewing-gum wrapper, that might give away his Israeli citizenship. He'd flown to London for these purchases. Mindful that a poorly paid archeologist didn't have money to spare, he went to secondhand shops in Chelsea and bought a pair of serviceable brown brogues, two well-worn jackets, one brown, one gray, and khaki pants. Socks, shirts, and underwear he got at Marks & Spencer. Toiletries at a local chemist. He packed all the belongings he'd traveled to England with into his old flight bag and shipped them to his parents' home.

104

His precautions might have been overly fastidious in light of the Israeli-Egyptian peace treaty. But if he was caught traveling under false papers it would be presumed he was on a hostile mission. The least they would do was rough him up before turning him over to his embassy; at worst, some unreformed Israeli-baiter might see to it that he disappeared without a trace. *Finito*. Motta Tzur, boy spy, would end up in an unmarked desert grave. Batya, his parents, and General Gordon would have no idea what had happened to him. Eventually his air force friend would fess up about the false papers. An attempt would be made to retrace his footsteps. But the assignment would no doubt fall to Mossad and its agents would not give the matter high priority.

In London his excitement began to build. No wonder Mossad attracts so many free spirits, he thought. This was more exciting than anything he'd ever experienced. Danger only heightened the heady feeling of adventure. But at the airport terminal in Cairo, with police and soldiers everywhere, some of them eyeing him, the enormity of his risk began to set in. Suddenly, his decision to come seemed not only rash but quixotic, and he'd never been either before.

He would need a place to operate from, of course, and a downtown hotel seemed logical. He had left Tel Aviv without a reservation and no idea where to stay. He had thought about getting recommendations, but if he'd been noticed asking too many questions Junction or Mossad might have tumbled onto his plan. And in London he'd been so preoccupied with shopping that he never got a chance to make hotel arrangements for Cairo.

So when he handed his single bag to a taxi driver he simply said, "Hilton Hotel," assuming there must be one. In fact, there were two, the Nile Hilton and the Ramses Hilton. The driver chose to take him to the former, since he had a third cousin in reservations and got a little baksheesh for every tourist he delivered. The doorman kept a record.

At the reception desk Tzur produced his Australian passport. During the year he spent at the London School of

Economics studying statistical analysis he'd had a roommate from Canberra, so he was able to affect a reasonably decent accent. He explained that his trip was a sudden decision and he hadn't made a reservation, hoped they could scare him up a room. "Anything at all, mate."

The clerk was about to send him away, then rechecked the bookings and discovered a last-minute cancellation. "You're in luck, sir, we have a beautiful room facing the Nile." He slammed his hand on the bell. "Desk!"

*   *   *

Peter was elated on the ride back to Cairo. Squadron Leader Roberts had outlined an ambitious Egyptian nuclear-weapons effort. It would be difficult to confirm and flesh out the story, but certainly worth the effort. Tewfik and Hazi thought they were clever pumping a former Defense Department official on the Israeli nuclear program. He would play along. He could be as clever as they, and more subtle.

His cab driver Abdul said the Desert Road would be less crowded at that time of day than the Delta Road, which they'd taken on the way up. Peter agreed to the alternate route. It would give him a chance to see another slice of countryside. Neither noticed the small green banged-up Fiat that slid behind, two cars away, and followed them.

It was oppressively hot in the unair-conditioned taxi and after about an hour Abdul suggested they stop for a soft drink. Peter agreed. They could stretch their legs.

That gave Achmed an opportunity to phone Nadia. "I've got him," he announced triumphantly. "When Mohammed calls in, tell him to go to his father's place in Cairo and I'll contact him there."

As the cars passed the cutoff leading to Wadi Natrun, Achmed wished he could turn off and see for himself that the plane was being properly outfitted for their mission. To prevent mechanical difficulties Mohammed had instructed the ground crew to keep the fuel tanks topped off and to check and recheck the electronics systems, particularly any modifications. Under desert conditions, with the ever-present sand and grit, extra maintenance paid off. When they got the signal to go, everything would have to work instantly and perfectly.

Achmed decided to return to Wadi Natrun for a personal inspection at the earliest opportunity.

10

Tzur lit his pipe and settled into an easy chair to study a well-thumbed text on Egyptian archeology he had picked up at a used bookshop in London. The cavendish tobacco, purchased at a tobacconist's along with an inexpensive briar, had a pleasing aroma and little bite.

After about an hour of concentration he was distracted by a weird sound like wailing outside. He stepped onto the balcony. On the street below, in front of the Hilton, a procession was holding up traffic. Cairo drivers usually used their horns as weapons, as if by leaning on them they could blast a path through the tangle of traffic. But now they showed forbearance. A beat-up flatbed truck with a faded cab was inching through a crowd of men, women, and children, the women in black, the men in dark trousers and white short-sleeved shirts. They were beating their breasts and chanting incantations as they eddied around the vehicle. It bore a long box draped in an embroidered coverlet of crimson and gold.

He decided it must be a poor Moslem Shiite family's procession to the cemetery. They couldn't afford a hearse or carriage, so they made do with a flatbed truck. The coverlet was an opulent compensation.

In his reading he had come across the ancient origin of the name Cairo: *el-quehera umm al donia*, mother of the world. From the size of the procession, the traffic jam, the crowd spilling from the street onto the Nile, he saw what a fertile mother she was. A city built for two million was bursting with fourteen million souls and growing uncontrollably.

Tzur went back inside. He wondered whether his cover would be tested in any serious way, how much knowledge of Egyptian archeology he might be required to demonstrate. Resigned, he settled back in the chair and reopened his textbook. His life might depend on it.

It must have been about an hour later when his concentration was broken again, this time by an insistent rattling accompanied by frenzied cussing in English. It sounded like an American accent. He turned back to the chapter on the Ptolemaic period. Some time later, when he'd finished with the Roman period, he took a break. On the way to the bathroom he noticed that an envelope had been slid under his door. He snatched it up. No one can possibly know I'm here, he thought. He ripped it open. It was on hotel stationery, the kind used for telephone messages.

"General Hazi phoned while you were out," it said. "Confirming dinner at eight tonight with Dr. Tewfik." There was a phone number.

General Hazi? Dr. Tewfik? One of the names was familiar, the other vaguely so. He knew the name Hazi from the '73 war. What Israeli military analyst didn't? He was a legend, the Fox of Cairo, they called him. There had been an intercepted tactical radio message just before the onset of the conflict in which Hazi ordered a special operations force into action. Subsequent analysis suggested that one General Rahman Hazi, a top planner of the Egyptian General Staff, had masterminded a commando team that leapfrogged the Bar Lev line in a small covey of low-flying helicopters. Using authentic-sounding Hebrew messages, they reassured forward-air-defense headquarters they were part of an Israeli special ops team returning from a long-range reconnaissance mission behind Egyptian lines. Achieving total surprise, they were able to destroy three key communications links, preventing the thin force of defenders in the Bar Lev bunkers from calling in prompt air support when the Egyptian invasion was launched. It was a brilliant stratagem, opening the way to early Egyptian victo-

110

ries. How many General Hazis could there be? This had to be the Fox himself.

They know I'm here, Tzur thought. In his fear he discounted the dinner invitation and imagined a squad of counterintelligence goons coming to arrest and drag him off. Then he turned the envelope over. It was addressed to room 610. His was 612. Some careless bellhop had delivered it to the wrong room. He hadn't heard a knock on the door. Maybe it had come when he was out on the balcony. Relief descended on him like a cool shower. He went back to the chair and collapsed into it.

Tewfik? An unusual name. Nabataean? Where had he heard it, or read it? Tzur prided himself on his memory and was confident that sooner or later the answer would surface.

Then it did. Two, perhaps three years earlier, he had read a top-secret analysis of the Egyptian nuclear program. One of the scientists mentioned in that report was a Tewfik, he was almost certain. He was certain.

For the moment, he told himself, assume that the Fox of Cairo and a top nuclear scientist are having dinner nearby with the person or persons in the next room. That sounded a hell of a lot more important than the mystery of the Russian aircraft.

He rose quickly, tossed on a jacket, relit his pipe, and knocked on the door to room 610. A tall Westerner with a towel in his hand answered. "Yes? Help you?"

Tzur smiled. "A note apparently intended for you was slipped under my door by mistake. Next door in 612. Afraid I opened the bloody thing before I realized it wasn't for me. Sorry." He handed the message over.

The man read the message and seemed pleased. "Thanks," he said.

But Tzur didn't move. He held out his hand. "Name's Ralph Langleigh. I teach archeology in Sydney," he said. "Australia."

"Sorry, forgot my manners. I should have been more appreciative. Hi. I'm Peter Robbins. Newspaperman on a brief assignment here in Cairo."

"Correspondent? Fascinating. Used to think I'd like a

go at that one day. What newspaper? What sort of reporting?"

"*New York World*, based in Washington. I usually focus on foreign affairs. This time I'm writing a series on Egypt one year after the peace treaty with Israel. The Egyptian economy, domestic politics, the mood of the country, you name it."

"Spend the whole day at the hotel pool, did you?"

Peter touched his burnt forehead. "No, I was out at the shore near Alexandria. Didn't think to bring sunblock."

"In this climate you've got to be extra careful about exposure."

Tzur turned and then stopped. "Since we're next-door neighbors and since, if you don't mind my saying so, you appear a bit frazzled," he said, "why don't you come in for a tot? I picked up some lovely malt whiskey at the duty-free at Heathrow."

Peter shrugged and threw the towel back in his room. "Okay."

Back in room 612 Tzur poured a couple of generous drinks from his bottle of Glenfiddich and handed one to Peter. "On a professor's salary I don't get to drink anything near this pricey except when I pass through airports." The smooth smoky scotch rolled around in his mouth and eased down his throat.

Peter appreciated it too. "Lovely stuff," he said.

"Yes, it is. Sorry I have to serve it neat. I understand you Yanks prefer to freeze the knickers off your booze."

Peter chuckled. "Yeah, we like it with plenty of ice. Did you just get in from the airport?"

"Couple hours back. I've been wanting to come here for years. Egyptian antiquity plays a prominent part in my lectures at the university. So when I won a small lottery prize, on the spur of the moment I decided to come. What luck, getting a room with a view. The Nile across the street!"

"You don't know it, Professor, but you probably have me to thank for your room."

"How's that?"

"I asked a friend in the Egyptian embassy in Washington to book adjoining rooms for me. I was expecting our London bureau chief here. He was going to come through en route to India but had to change his plans at the last minute. So earlier I canceled the second reservation."

"I'm in your debt," Tzur said, saluting him with his glass. "Buy you dinner in the hotel dining room tonight?"

"I'll have to take a rain check. That note was a dinner invitation. But another night, so long as we go dutch."

"Dutch?"

"Dutch treat. Means each person pays for himself."

*　　　*　　　*

Achmed had parked around the corner from the Hilton and entered the lobby. There were only two clerks behind the desk. The older man disappeared into a back room, leaving a fellow who looked to be in his early twenties.

Achmed sauntered over. "Hello. Maybe you can help me. I just caught a glimpse of a man coming in, dark hair, tan slacks, and blue short-sleeved shirt, sunburned. I think it may be someone I knew at university in the United States, but I didn't get a clear enough look to be sure."

"I'm sorry, sir. We're not allowed to give out the room numbers of guests," the young clerk answered.

"It's his name I'm trying to recall. If it's the person I think, he'll be happy to know I'm back in Cairo." Achmed looked beseechingly at the clerk. "Come on, be a good fellow, he'll want to see me—if it's him."

The clerk looked over his shoulder to see whether the assistant manager had returned. Jobs in such fine hotels were hard to come by. Achmed saw him wavering. He reached into his pocket, pulled out a bill, holding it under the flat of his hand, and slid it across the counter toward the clerk. "Be a good fellow, please," he said.

The clerk glanced over his shoulder again before snatching the money and stuffing it in his pocket, not looking at the denomination. He consulted the register. "You mean the American, Mr. Peter Robbins, in 610," he said softly. "I just gave him his key. Was he the fellow you knew?"

Achmed shook his head. "Sorry, no. His name was Richardson. But thanks anyway."

Peter Robbins. So he was an American. That probably meant he wasn't interested in them or their mission. In all likelihood he was just looking for some officer, as he'd said. But Achmed had to make sure. Too much rode on this to hang back now.

He decided to wait across the street. He could be patient. If Robbins went out, he'd take a look inside room 610.

*   *   *

The three dined at a tiny place called Paprika with no more than a dozen tables, Chianti bottles with melted candles on each. It was several blocks from the Hilton on the banks of the Nile, next to the headquarters of Egyptian national television.

When Hazi asked about the sunburn Peter was tempted to say he'd got it at the hotel pool. He didn't want to be drawn into a conversation about his meeting with a British military attaché, particularly not Roberts. But long ago he'd decided it was wiser to play it as straight as possible and avoid getting caught up in conflicting stories. "I spent the day with a friend at Agamy."

"A female friend?" Hazi winked.

"A family, actually. How did you spend your day?"

"Have you forgotten so soon?" Tewfik asked. "You're in the Near East. Sunday's a workday here. We were slaving while you were ogling girls in bikinis." He and Hazi chuckled conspiratorily, as if to suggest they, too, were men of the world.

In fact, under different circumstances General Hazi could have devoted his life to women, and to drink and gambling. Although he had lacked funds as a young man, there were always rich friends who enjoyed his company and thought nothing of paying his way. He would have

114

married Lila and played around on the side, something he didn't do now but which she suspected him of. His lot would have been that of the partying sponger had it not been for an event that brought shame to his family and caused him to change the course of his life.

In many ways his father, Saad, had been a pathetic man. He had joined the rife-torn Anglo-Egyptian army during the British occupation but scrupulously steered clear of its factions. They included the Free Officers movement, which wanted to kick out the corrupt King Farouk; the Moslem Brotherhood, which was not only anti-Farouk and anti-British but wanted much stricter observance of the tenets of Islam; the Wafd party, in favor of representative government; and the bribed officers of the king who plotted to end the British occupation and extend Egyptian sovereignty to the Sudan.

Saad would rub his index finger against his nose and say to young Hazi, "See this? It's clean. Because I keep it clean and out of other people's affairs this family eats well, lives in a fine house, and walks with its head high. I am the son of a poor peasant, but I am also a man of position, a major in the army. The secret of my success is a clean nose. You avoid making enemies that way."

The secret of his success? Thirty years of army service and all he'd attained was the rank of major and a job running a supply depot. More than once Hazi had overheard uncles and cousins snickering. The major who commanded rolls of toilet tissue and cases of beans, they called him behind his back. Hazi was hurt, outraged, but kept his feelings to himself.

During the '48 war in Palestine the need for officers was so desperate that Saad was summoned from his rolltop desk at the supply depot and put in charge of a newly formed battalion of infantry. Hazi was exultant. His father was now an infantry commander who carried a riding crop as part of his uniform. That ought to put his loudmouth uncles in their place.

Early in the war word came that his father had been wounded and was recuperating in a military hospital, hit in the buttocks by an Israeli bullet. No matter; he had served with valor and would recover. As Saad told the story, he'd been leading a charge against a well-emplaced Israeli machine-gun nest near Tel Aviv when a soldier feigning death rose up and shot him from behind. "A typically cowardly act," he snorted.

But a different account which was widely believed made the rounds after the war. The night before the assault, Saad, frightened about the prospect of combat, had slipped away disguised in women's clothes. In Gaza he was discovered by a three-man patrol of elderly Israeli militiamen as he tried to board a bus for the Suez Canal. His skirt and sandals impeding him, he was felled by a single shot from a nearsighted marksman. After the war he was returned in a blanket prisoner exchange.

Hazi had vowed to atone for his father's cowardly act and make the Israelis pay heavily for his family's dishonor.

While his father had fled battle, Hazi ran recklessly into it. While his father had had no real allegiance except to his family, Hazi was a dedicated nationalist whose blood boiled at the shame Sadat's peace treaty had brought on Egypt. And while his father had avoided plotters, Hazi was always ready to play one group off against another, always shrewd enough to ensure he came out ahead.

And now he was engaged in the most audacious plot of all, to reduce Israel to nuclear ashes. If he succeeded he would change the course of history, bring great honor to his family name, and wield enormous power.

*　　　*　　　*

Tewfik lived in a palatial stucco house dating from imperial British days with large walled grounds and sculptured bushes. Nuclear engineering must be a lucrative trade in Egypt, Peter thought. They had come here after dinner to escape the heat of the restaurant.

"Let's not disturb my wife," Tewfik whispered as he turned the key in the latch. "We'll slip into my study. Hazi will show you." In the hallway he disappeared.

The study was functional and comfortable: walnut pa-

116

neling, floor to ceiling bookshelves, photos and mementos, a large teakwood desk, a camel-colored couch, and two matching wing chairs. Peter scanned the books. "Is this book yours, Hazi? *Nuclear Strategy in the Twenty-first Century?*"

"I told you he was a strategic genius," Tewfik said, returning with a tray of glasses. He poured three hefty drinks from a crystal decanter. "Ice and mineral water for the pagan from America," he announced. "Ice only for the Egyptian men of letters."

"I've written eight books on various subjects," Hazi informed Peter. "That's the most recent."

"You've obviously given a great deal of thought to the subject. Assuming Egypt could acquire an arsenal of nuclear weapons overnight, how would it employ them?"

Hazi inspected his drink against the overhead light. "Of course, you mean that as a hypothetical question, since we have a peace treaty with our neighbor."

"Purely hypothetical."

"That depends on a lot of circumstances, as we were saying the other night. How many weapons do we have? One? A hundred? What sort of delivery vehicles? Low-flying bombers only, or medium-range missiles too? What is the nature of our alliances? Theirs? Theoretically, if we were to launch a surprise attack and wipe Israel off the face of the earth, even if Israel couldn't retaliate, which I doubt, the United States would probably take drastic action. It could prove costly to us.

"Then, of course, I'd have to know how we acquired this capability, whether it was provided overnight or built up secretly by ourselves. In the latter case, we'd have to take into account the possibility—no, the certainty—that if Israel discovered what we were up to, it would launch a preemptive attack."

"So you don't think nukes would do Egypt much good?"

"I didn't say that. Not at all. Hypothetically, 'nukes' would restore us to our natural leadership role in the Arab world. If we had them and Syria didn't, Hafez Assad would have to dance to our tune. Saddam Hussein of Iraq as well."

"Nuclear capability would only be useful for inter-Arab political purposes, then, not war? Doesn't that mean if you could convince your fellow Arabs that you had the bomb, even if you didn't, you could achieve your political purposes?"

"No, I didn't say that nuclear weapons couldn't be useful in war. You'd just have to be skillful in planning the circumstances, the strategy governing their use."

As Hazi drained his glass, a floorboard creaked. A man was standing in the shadows of the doorway.

"Mohammed, is that you?" Tewfik said. "I didn't know you were in Cairo. Come in, I want you to meet someone. A journalist friend from Washington."

"Peter, this is my son, Mohammed. Mohammed, Peter Robbins."

The man walked into the light, and though he was well dressed and clean shaven, Peter had no doubt this was the same person he had seen tousled and in pajama bottoms that morning at the cottage. It was a good thing he hadn't fibbed about getting sun at the hotel pool.

And Mohammed Tewfik immediately recognized the rude man who had pounded on their door at dawn. He was glad he, and not Achmed, had discovered the identity of the man who stumbled into their hideaway. The man Achmed wanted to kill. So he wasn't an intelligence agent at all, but a friend of his father's. Only the most trusted foreigners were invited into an Arab home.

The two men smiled and exchanged a firm handshake.

11

The sun was setting across the Nile. From the back seat of the Fiat Achmed fetched a white linen sports coat that would help him blend with hotel guests moving through the lobby. Then he rode the elevator to the sixth floor and strode confidently to room 610, as if he belonged there. Pretending to fish for his key until the corridor was empty, he took out a plastic credit card and expertly slid the catch to open the door.

The first thing he noticed was a portable typewriter on the dressing table, an Italian Olivetti. That didn't tell him anything; Olivettis were sold all over the world. But a tourist on holiday didn't drag a typewriter with him. Nor did a spy unless it was part of his cover. Attached to the typewriter case, on the floor beside the dresser, was a business card:

PETER ROBBINS
Chief Diplomatic Correspondent
New York World

1975 Pennsylvania Ave., N.W.
Suite 200
Washington, D.C. 20006
(202) 555-7827

A news reporter. An American correspondent. From Washington. Or at least that was his cover. Achmed had been told that most governments found reporting a convenient cover for their agents, who could move freely across borders, ask questions without raising suspicion, take photos. By its very nature, reporting was the profession closest to spying.

In the closet he searched the pockets of every jacket and each pair of slacks, making no attempt to be neat. In training class he had been instructed that even the most careful agent might be tripped up by a seemingly insignificant scrap left in his clothes—a cash register receipt from a city that would be hard to explain, perhaps, or a dry-cleaning tag inconsistent with his identity. He inspected a pair of loafers and some tan walking shoes, turning them over and holding them to the light to see whether he'd recently walked in clay, mud, or sand. Nothing interesting there. All Achmed found were matchbooks from a couple of Washington restaurants and a cocktail lounge in a place called Bethesda, together with a small leather case with more business cards.

If he's a spook, Achmed thought, there must be something hidden away. A gun, a throwing knife, a miniature Minox camera. Frustrated, he began dumping drawers on the floor, turning them over to see if anything might be taped underneath—a list of local contacts or a safety deposit key. But again he found nothing, and concluded reluctantly that Robbins was a reporter. He could live.

*   *   *

Captain Tzur, trying to concentrate on his archeology text, was interrupted by strange noises from room 610. The walls were thin. Earlier he had heard the American reporter leave for the evening. It was too late for the chambermaid to be cleaning up, too noisy for her to be turning down the covers for the night.

Had Robbins come back to get something he forgot? Was it a thief? He inverted a thin waterglass against the wall and put his ear to it. It sounded like someone tossing drawers about. A thief, he concluded. He wondered if he should call the desk and report a robbery. By the time the hotel security man responded the thief would probably have vanished. In any case, the American reporter was nothing to him. He must not do anything that would draw attention to himself.

He sat on the bed and rested his chin on his clenched fists. His mission—self-appointed, to be sure—was to see if he could turn up anything that would force Mossad and its bastard deputy director Shavit to concede that he was right. That there was something suspicious about the disappearance of the Soviet courier flight. But his quest ought to be superseded by the discovery that a nuclear scientist and one of the cleverest planners on the Egyptian staff were consorting with an American who represented himself as a journalist. If that didn't raise enough eyebrows, this search of the American's room should.

It couldn't be an ordinary thief. Egyptian counterintelligence? Somebody who didn't like the idea of meetings between these three? Perhaps someone working for the general or the scientist was checking out the bona fides of the American when he was known to be out of his room?

Unschooled in field work, Tzur was in over his head. He would have to contact Mossad at the embassy in Cairo and turn the matter over to the experts, even though that might end his career. How could he explain coming to Egypt on false papers without the approval of his superiors? What an idiot he'd been. Ego had driven him to make a trip so he could prove himself right and Shavit wrong.

Conscientiousness would be his downfall. He couldn't consider not informing Mossad. On the other hand, what if he was wrong? There might be another General Hazi, perhaps a relative of the Fox of Cairo. And Dr. Tewfik might not be the nuclear Tewfik. In which case he'd risk blowing his career for nothing.

He reviewed the few facts he knew. Robbins didn't appear concerned that he might have read the note about dinner with Hazi and Tewfik. Tzur had given him the opportunity to make up a story, inferring he hadn't actually read the message when he invited Robbins to dine that night in the hotel. And Robbins had begged off casually, saying he was dining with a couple of Egyptian friends. They would do it another night, he'd said, so long as they went dutch treat. It didn't sound as if he was trying to hide his meeting.

The identity of the person in Robbins' room was important; it could shed light on the whole business. At the very least he should get a look at him. Tzur jumped to his feet and turned off the lights. Slowly he cracked the door and waited. After another few minutes, a man strode from 610 and firmly snap-locked the door. He was an Arab, medium height, black hair, slender, fashionably dressed in a white sports coat and faded denim jeans. He stopped at the elevator bank, his back to Tzur.

If I saw his face, the Israeli thought, I could look at mug shots or at least describe the man to Mossad operatives. Otherwise his information was almost without value.

As soon as the elevator door closed behind the Arab, Tzur raced from his room and pushed the down button. He would have to catch up with the man in the lobby and get a good glimpse of his face.

*   *   *

Achmed had to report his findings to Mohammed at his father's house. His plan had gelled. He followed the intruder to Cairo, found his room, and even cased it. Not a bad day's work. At the desk he asked directions to the pay phones, which were in the rear. He dialed the number and waited. A servant answered. He waited impatiently, anxious to tell Mohammed. But when Mohammed got on the phone he preempted him. "That stranger's a reporter from Washington, a friend of my father. As a matter of fact he's here right now, having a drink. So he's okay, false alarm. Relax. Go back to the beach cottage."

What was there to say? Achmed slammed down the receiver. Mohammed's blind luck had triumphed over his daring and cunning. Why were things so effortless for the rich?

He headed for his Fiat, intending to return to Agamy and the bitch Nadia, who would be alone for the night with Mohammed visiting his father. He drove fast, recklessly, as he usually did. But at the turnoff to Wadi Natrun he braked suddenly, going into a slight skid. The plane was only a couple of miles off the Desert Road, and the mission was unquestionably more important than Nadia. Or making a cuckold of Mohammed.

*   *   *

In the hotel lobby, the Israeli captain had seen no sign of the man in the white coat. Frantically he had inspected the crowd, then swung through the revolving door outside. Damn! he thought, I've really screwed up. He's gotten clean away and the only description I can provide would cover half the male population of Cairo. Medium build. Dark. Confident, macho walk. White jacket and jeans.

Tzur went back inside and walked slowly around the periphery of the lobby. Perhaps the Arab was huddled in a corner with a confederate. Tzur was checking out the tobacco shop when a young man dressed in a white jacket came from the rear of the lobby. He fell in behind as the man headed for the exit. No doubt about it, seeing him from the rear Tzur knew it was the same fellow. He didn't just walk, he strutted.

The man dashed across the street through traffic and headed for a green Fiat, fiddling in his pocket for his key. Tzur waited until he saw which way the Fiat was heading before he sprinted toward his own car, a rented Renault. He would try and discover the man's address, then rush to the embassy and make his report. After that, he'd be out of it. And, more than likely, out of a job. But that was not the most important thing.

He joined the heavy traffic along the Nile Corniche Road and fell in a few cars behind, remaining inconspicuous and keeping the Fiat in sight. It headed north along the Desert Road. The sign, in Arabic, said they were proceeding toward Alexandria, 225 kilometers away. The Fiat's license plate was spattered with mud and dust and Tzur couldn't make it out. He would have to wait until the man parked. Then he would jot down his address and license number.

*　　*　　*

"Let's put the shoe on your foot, Peter," Dr. Tewfik said when Mohammed returned from the phone. "Imagine you're the Egyptian Minister of Defense and you have only a single nuclear bomb, how would you use it?"

Two can play at this game, Peter thought. "Do I assume, for the sake of argument, that Egypt and Israel are no longer observing the peace treaty and war is imminent?"

Tewfik nodded. General Hazi rose and gazed out the window at his friend's gardens, absentmindedly stirring the ice in his glass with a finger.

"Okay," Peter resumed, "I suppose I might explode it far from any population center, say in the Negev Desert, and announce to the Israelis that it was a warning shot. Tell them we have several more weapons that we're capable of employing against each of their urban-industrial centers. We know they can retaliate, but we have such a large population we'll only be wounded; they'll perish. So we're ready to talk about concluding hostilities. On our terms, of course."

"No, no Peter, that would be stupid," General Hazi said, whirling around and facing him. His tone was uncharacteristically blunt. "You're applying American reasoning and capabilities to someone else's problem. First of all, we don't have medium-range missiles, only bombers. The Israelis have nuclear-armed Jericho missiles. You yourself disclosed development work on those very missiles some years ago in one of your newspaper articles. Now they're perfected.

"If we tipped our hand with a demonstration shot they would immediately destroy all our airfields, preventing further nuclear attacks from us. They might even explode a couple of nuclear weapons over Cairo. After all, according to your scenario, we fired the first shot at their territory.

"The Russians and Americans would be all over both

of us with threats if we didn't halt hostilities right away. The result—we'd suffer millions of dead and wounded, while the Israelis would prostrate the entire Arab world by their willingness to use the ultimate weapon against an Arab capital.''

Peter had spent enough time with American generals to know when a military professional was discussing what had been part of painstaking planning and when he was only offering schoolbook answers. It was plain these two had done some serious thinking about nuclear scenarios. Hazi was especially impressive. He shouldn't be underestimated.

"On reflection," Peter said, "I agree with your objections. So how would you employ a single bomb?''

This time it was Mohammed who spoke up. "You would have to be extraordinarily clever, employing the weapon in such a way that it would trigger the result you wanted to achieve, but couldn't yourself.''

"I don't understand.''

But before Mohammed could amplify, Hazi jumped up, Tewfik behind him. "What does a lowly pilot know?'' Hazi said, an edge to his voice. "You will only begin to understand grand strategy when you come to my classes at the war college.'' He looked at his watch. "Speaking of which, I had no idea how late it was. My first lecture tomorrow is at eight. May I give you a lift back to your hotel, Peter?''

12

Traffic was so heavy on the flat Desert Road that Tzur didn't have to worry about his Renault being spotted by the Arab. But he did have to drive carefully; the cars in front stirred up swirling clouds of sand and even with his headlights on he was almost blinded.

It soon became clear that the Fiat was heading not for the outskirts of Cairo, as he had assumed, but north toward Alexandria. To keep himself awake and alert, he tested his recollections of what the textbook had said about the origins of the city and its role in the evolution of modern Egypt.

The man in the Fiat turned out to be a reckless driver. Several times he veered into the left lane to pass, once almost running into a truck coming the other way. Carefully, courteously, Tzur passed a few cars. There were now a half dozen vehicles between them. No need to rush or close the gap further. In nearly two hours of travel his prey had not slowed at any of the exits; he was probably going all the way to Alexandria.

Tzur's headlights lit up another road sign. Alexandria, 100 kilometers; Wadi Natrun, 50 kilometers. He presumably had another full hour of pursuit.

What had the textbook said about Wadi Natrun? It was an ancient source of sodium carbonate deposits, *natrun* being the Arabic name for the stomach-soothing compound. It was also the site of some fourth-century Christian monasteries. And, if he remembered correctly from an old assignment when he was still in the photo-interpreting business, there was a small Egyptian air force facility in the vicinity.

The ride was boring and he started to nod off. He caught himself and jerked his head erect. Several times he pinched his thigh to stay awake.

What in the world was he doing chasing a stranger across Egypt for half the night? Even if he located the man's apartment house and recorded his license, he wouldn't get back to Cairo until the wee hours. At that time there would only be a few guards and some radio operators at the embassy. Maybe he should think about going back to the Hilton, catching a few hours' sleep, and then visiting the embassy during normal hours when he could walk into the visa section like any other tourist and then slip away to make contact with Mossad.

Distracted by his thoughts, he almost missed the Fiat's sudden left turn off the highway. He slammed on his brakes and swerved onto the road to Wadi Natrun, cursing. Now he was in trouble. No one else seemed to be turning. The Arab was bound to notice him in his rearview mirror. Thinking fast, he switched off his lights. He had no choice. He would have to inch along, veering back toward the center of the narrow roadway if he felt himself sliding onto the soft sand of the shoulder. The quarter moon cast a pale haze of illumination.

The Fiat torched a path along the rutted road. Tzur proceeded slowly, straining every sense to avoid running off the macadam and overturning in a ditch. After a few miles the Fiat slowed and stopped at a guardpost. The driver shouted something to the sentry, who was asleep, his chair tilted against the wall of the ramshackle shed.

"Eureka!" Tzur exclaimed quietly. He hadn't been on a wild goose chase after all. It wasn't likely a common thief would drive hours to a distant military post after breaking into a hotel room in Cairo. This could well be the small air base Tzur had under his photo interpreter's magnifying glass years before.

He had a quick decision to make. He could provide a general description of the man and his car, without the

128

mud-caked number. He could describe the military installation. Would that be enough for Mossad to drop other assignments and chase this one? The local station chief would probably check with Tel Aviv, where Shavit would order him to ignore the madman's ravings and ship him home without delay, under guard. Or he could slip into the base, get the license number, and note the building where the car was parked. He couldn't bluff his way past the sentry. He would have to pull off the road and see what he could discover on foot.

He pumped his brakes, slowly coming to a stop on the right shoulder, then eased out of the car and shut the door quietly. No longer devout, he prayed nonetheless that no car would light up the roadway. Crouching, he moved rapidly toward the barbed-wire fence to the right of the guardpost.

What would the Egyptians think if they spotted his car? That one of their people had run out of gas? He hoped so.

At the fence he dropped onto the cool sand and peered into the military post. The Fiat was heading in the direction of a large aircraft hangar. So he was right, it was the air base. Between the hangar and the gate there were several two-story wooden buildings, probably barracks and offices, and a parking lot.

He crawled along the base of the fence, away from the bright glare of the naked bulb at the guardpost, hoping to find a gap. It would have been handy to have his dog Ziki along. Ziki could burrow a hole under the fence in nothing flat. Well, he thought, if a big dumb mongrel can do it, so can I, and he clawed furiously at the sand and rocks.

A car door slammed in the distance, startling him. Presumably the man he'd been following had parked and gone inside the hangar. Then again, someone might have come out of the barracks to drive into town, in which case he would discover Tzur's car and probably raise an alarm.

It wasn't too late to abandon the effort. He could scramble back to the car. If the driver stopped to ask what he was doing there he could say he was lost and needed directions. Or that he'd had car trouble on the main road and headed toward the camp for assistance. If the driver wasn't curious, Tzur could simply return to Cairo and urge the Mossad chief at the embassy to check out the air base at Wadi Natrun.

What for? the man from Mossad would want to know.

Well, because he'd followed a guy who was either a sneak thief or an intelligence operative from the Nile Hilton to this place, and therefore it must be worth investigating.

On such flimsy evidence he was asking agents to risk discovery, or worse? Or was he suggesting Wadi Natrun was a secret base where the Egyptians were using a little chemistry set to build an atomic bomb? Because a well-known American journalist was having dinner with a general and a physicist who conceivably, possibly, might be involved in some sort of nuclear plot?

What he had was highly conjectural. He needed something specific that would trigger a serious investigation. He had chosen to deal himself in; he couldn't walk away when the cards were getting interesting. If he was going to find out what the fellow was up to, he had no choice but to get to that hangar.

He was fit, he was smart, he was daring, he was resourceful and, he tried to convince himself, he could pull it off.

Finally he managed to scoop out enough sand to snake under the barbed wire. He snagged his shirt and tore a hole, but he was through. He took his bearings. To get to the hangar he'd have to pass the brightly lit barracks where there were sounds of boisterous horseplay. He decided to skirt the wooden buildings, away from the parking lot and any headlights that might be turned on without warning. He wondered if they had guard dogs. He hadn't heard barking. The lassitude of the lone guard suggested this facility was not very alert.

He moved from the fence in a low, crouching run, hoping no one would come out while he was exposed. He skirted the barracks, using what little cover was available—a trash can, a toolshed, a motor pool. But the last 200 meters

130

were open ground. He threw himself down on all fours and crawled combat style.

At the beach in Tel Aviv the sand was a friend, warm to the touch, soft, inviting. Now it was an enemy—cold, gritty, salty, collecting in his mouth and under his shirt and burrowing into his shoes. It mixed with his sweat and clung to his body, turning his skin to coarse sandpaper. Small sharp rocks tore at his elbows and knees. His breathing became labored and he was fearful the whole camp would hear him. Every few meters he stopped and listened, making sure no one was near.

Finally he reached the Fiat, parked in front of the hangar door. The license plate was in shadow. He raised himself on an elbow and applied spit to the metal, rubbing it and exposing the numbers. Then he rubbed it again to be sure. Given the risk he had run, he didn't want to get the numbers wrong.

He slid back down and took several quick breaths. His face was near the exhaust pipe. He peered out from behind the car. No one seemed to be outside, no guards. It's now or never, he thought, and he dashed to the side of the hangar, chest heaving, clothes soaked with sweat. His mouth was cotton dry. His eyes burned from salty perspiration. His hands, elbows, and knees were bleeding.

There was a small dirty window from which a dull light shone. Did he dare stand up and look in? If spotted, there was no way he could fight effectively; he carried no weapons, and he could neither outrun pursuit nor explain his presence. If caught, no doubt he would be tortured for information, then shot. But he had come this far . . .

He eased himself upright against the hangar's corrugated metal siding. His back was pressed against the building, his hands against its cool undulating surface. He would have to take a chance and peer inside. His breathing seemed so loud; he feared it would give him away. He eased his body down this time so only his eyes and the top of his head were even with the base of the window. Then he looked inside. What he saw sent his head spinning and he slumped to the base of the hangar wall.

Inside was an Il-76 jet carrying the red star of the Soviet air force. Arab workmen were milling about servicing the plane. It was impossible, a mirage. No way a long-range Soviet military transport would be at a small desert airfield in Egypt.

He would have to risk a second look. No, no mirage. A Soviet Il-76. He didn't see any Russians among the maintenance crew. Only Arabs, including the fellow in the white jacket. The identification markings were CCCP-00079. As soon as he saw them he knew. Courier flight no. 79. The bird that was supposed to have crashed with all its passengers. Here it was, unscathed, in an obscure Egyptian air base southwest of Alexandria. So he had been right, Shavit wrong. He shut his eyes and a smile crossed his grimy face. Vindicated!

Just then he heard a screen door open. It squeaked and slammed shut. A uniformed officer walked out of a nearby building, joking with someone still inside as he headed for a jeep. After several tries he turned over the balky engine, snapped on the lights, and started toward the front gate.

Tzur fell to the ground again. Headlights began to sweep the hangar wall inches above him. Moments later he heard a ruckus at the gate. The officer of the guard had caught the sentry sleeping at his post and was chewing him out.

It might have been funny, under other circumstances. But now it added another danger to his line of retreat. The guard, having been castigated, would now be alert to any unusual sound or movement. He might even fire at something suspicious to prove that he was on his toes.

Tzur had toyed with the idea of looking in the parking lot for a vehicle with the key in the ignition so that he might drive slowly past the snoozing sentry. That wasn't an option now. He couldn't drive off the base unless he was ready to risk a fusillade of bullets and hot pursuit from the roused camp. No, he would have to crawl back to the barbed-wire fence, either locate the first hole or dig another with his lacerated fingers, and hike back to his car.

He couldn't wait to confront Shavit, see the bastard

132

sweat and try to explain away his failure. With that vision spurring him on he regained the fence, somehow found his entry hole, and crawled through. But at the car his exhilaration vanished. His key had fallen out of his pocket during all the crawling. It was a reflex of his always to lock a car when leaving it. What a time to be tripped up by conventional caution. He couldn't risk the noise of breaking a window to get inside and hotwire the car. Not with the chastised sentry within earshot and gunshot. Instead, he decided to hike back to the highway.

His Arabic was good enough for him to explain to a passing driver that he'd been in an auto accident and needed a ride back to Cairo. He could pay. If he made it, he would grab his passport and bag, rush to the airport, and take the first plane heading for any destination in the West. For by morning at the latest his rented car would be found and in short order traced back to him and his hotel. He couldn't wait for the Israeli embassy to open its gates in the morning. He must get out of the country as soon as possible. Tonight! What he had stumbled on had to be reported right away. Let the experts decide what it meant and what should be done.

Tzur started walking as fast as he could toward the faint headlights zipping down the Desert Road.

13

When Captain Tzur got back to the Nile Hilton it was well past midnight. He had been fortunate to catch a ride with a farmer hauling Persian melons to the capital. The honest grizzled little man, seeing that his passenger had been through an ordeal, refused an offer of payment, although it was obvious from his worn clothing that he could use the money. Tzur started to insist, then relented; he didn't want the fellow if questioned later to tell the authorities about his generous hitchhiker. Chances of the police talking to the farmer were slight, but you could never tell.

Tzur looked awful—dirty, sweaty, one trouser torn at the knee and a rip across the back of his shirt where the barbed wire had snagged it. It didn't take much to convince the night clerk he had been in an auto accident. He'd returned to Cairo, he explained, after receiving a message that his favorite uncle was desperately ill.

"No. No one else was injured. And no, I don't need to go to the hospital. Just the key to room 612, please. Also, could you prepare my bill and order a taxicab for the airport?"

Reluctantly, the clerk nodded. As Tzur started toward the elevators he called after him. "I almost forgot. There's a message in your box, sir."

It was from Robbins. "Dinner tomorrow? Please phone my room or leave message. See you, Peter."

Tzur didn't want a reporter making nosy inquiries about his absence; if things didn't work out he might still be stranded at the airport in the morning. So he asked for stationery and wrote, "Family emergency. Had to leave last night. Perhaps one day we'll meet again, under better circumstances. Ralph."

After scrubbing himself in a steamy shower he decided to wipe his fingerprints from anything he might have touched. Chances were the chambermaid would smear the prints, but there was no sense taking unnecessary risks.

The traffic jam had eased since he was last out and the ride to the airport was relatively fast and uneventful. He cursed himself for forgetting to wipe fingerprints off the rental car, then remembered that without a key he wouldn't have been able to get back into the vehicle anyway. Steady, he told himself, stay calm. Even if the authorities get a good set of prints, they'll be searching for a nonexistent Australian professor of archeology.

At Cairo International Airport he got a seat on the first flight out, a Lufthansa bound for Frankfurt. There were only two seats left, first class, in the smoking section. He hated smoke but took the ticket gratefully. The gods were smiling. He turned in his return ticket to London and paid the balance in American bills. He'd had the foresight to take a good chunk of his savings from his bank account for the trip to Egypt.

Before boarding, he sipped coffee in Lufthansa's first-class lounge and wondered about the next connection. There were a lot of flights from Frankfurt to Tel Aviv. He would not take El Al, he decided. Some sharp-eyed security man might discover his passport was fake and blow his cover. Security services watched who boarded and deplaned from El Al just as Western intelligence agencies keep an eye on Aeroflot activity. A ruckus at the El Al inspection table was bound to be witnessed by somebody's spooks, perhaps tipping Egypt off to his real nationality.

If his false papers were discovered when he got to Ben Gurion Airport, no problem. One phone call and it would be straightened out. Perhaps he'd fly TWA or Sabena in a tourist-class seat if available. He didn't want to squander his remaining savings on another first-class fare.

He noticed a passenger stealing sidelong glances at

him, a man with a stout brass-handled cane. The fellow was barrel-chested and dark-complected, had thick black eyebrows and a shiny pitted face. Turkish or Moroccan, Tzur figured. His clothing was respectable but not the quality worn by the other first-class passengers, mostly Western businessmen.

Once on board, the man did something curious. He switched from a window seat on the other side of the aisle to the lone empty seat directly behind Tzur. "Better legroom," he explained to the stewardess in accented German.

Tzur looked around the cabin, searching for an escape route. Perhaps the man worked for Egyptian counterintelligence and was only waiting for a couple of uniformed cops to come aboard to arrest him. The only exit in first class was at the front of the plane where passengers were boarding.

He was more than a little relieved, then, when the door was shut and locked and the aircraft taxied into line for takeoff. Ten minutes later it rushed forward for a smooth, powerful liftoff. But even airborne, Tzur feared the man was Egyptian security. Was he being paranoid or cautious? He wasn't sure which. Maybe the Egyptians were hoping Tzur would lead this man to his confederates.

Tzur wasn't carrying a gun, but he knew from his military training that even innocuous-looking objects like sharpened pencils or ballpoint pens could be used with lethal effect. A quick thrust through the eardrum into the brain, for instance. He hoped it wouldn't come to that. He didn't want to kill anyone. But to get his vital intelligence to Israel he would do whatever was necessary, without hesitation.

On the ground in Frankfurt, the man seemed in no rush to deplane. Tzur started down the aisle, then feigned the need to go back as if he had forgotten something in the overhead compartment. This permitted him to exit the aircraft directly behind the man. In his right hand Tzur grasped a metal-barreled ballpoint pen.

In the receiving area, he saw that he had been mistaken. The man was greeted warmly by a large family group, two older women, three children, and a fellow who could have been the twin of the traveler except for an enormous black handlebar mustache. Tzur knew that thousands of Turks came to West Germany to take menial jobs the Germans didn't want.

Relieved, Tzur slipped the pen back into his shirt pocket and patted it. For the first time since leaving Egypt he allowed himself to smile. Halfway home!

He lost no time locating a departure screen to look for a homeward flight. TWA 1172 was leaving in less than an hour for Tel Aviv. At the ticket counter, it turned out, they had plenty of room, and yes, he could have an aisle seat in the no-smoking tourist section. From his reaction, it must have looked as if he'd just won the sweepstakes.

*   *   *

As he pulled up to the beachfront cottage Mohammed was humming a tune he'd heard that morning on the car radio. Carrying a sack of oranges, black olives, flatbread, and goat's cheese from the farmers market, he went around to the kitchen door. To show consideration for Nadia and Achmed, who liked to sleep late, he walked softly on the balls of his feet.

When he peeked into the larger of the two bedrooms, the one he shared with Nadia, it didn't register immediately that there were two figures tangled in the sheets. It didn't register until he approached the bed and saw Achmed's hairy arm draped across Nadia's bare breasts. He threw the groceries to the floor, grabbed Achmed by an arm and a leg, and flung him headfirst against the wall.

"You little piece of petrified camel shit!" he shouted. "What's the meaning of this?"

Achmed was stunned. He blinked his eyes and tried to get his bearings. Roused from sleep, Nadia sat straight up, the sheet falling to her waist. She made no attempt to cover herself.

Mohammed shifted his gaze from one to the other and back again, waiting for an explanation. He clenched and unclenched his large powerful fists. Achmed, fully awake now and realizing his predicament, sprang from the floor

138

and retrieved a Browning from beneath his pillow. Propped against the bed, he aimed his gun at the center of Mohammed's chest and cocked the hammer with a sharp click, smiling thinly.

"She's a whore; what further explanation is necessary? Are you prepared to die in defense of her honor?"

Mohammed had sensed Achmed's resentment before but not given it much thought. Now he realized what the man was capable of doing. The veneer of civilized behavior that the mullah and military training had imposed on the young street punk had cracked, revealing the animal beneath. And what of Nadia? Mohammed had only physical feelings for her, not romantic ones. But he had assumed that while they were together she would be faithful. She was Arab, after all, even if she saw herself as an emancipated woman.

Achmed lowered the barrel of the Browning slightly. Mohammed took advantage of this lapse and arched a potent karate kick at his gunhand. The weapon skittered to the floor. Achmed leaped after it, but Mohammed was on him instantly, smashing his right fist into the side of the smaller man's head.

While the two thrashed around on the floor, Nadia ran to the dresser and got her pistol. Naked, she assumed the two-handed firing position she had learned in commando training. "Are you two street dogs, or what?" she demanded. The two men looked at her. She was pointing the gun menacingly, and they froze. "I don't need to explain my actions to anyone. I belong to no man, make my own choices. Do I have to remind you both we have a mission that is much more important than wounded macho vanity? When it's done you can tear one another to pieces with my blessings. I'll even rent a hall and sell tickets. But not now, not today."

For several moments Mohammed remained motionless, his right fist poised over the man under him. Slowly, he lowered it and got up. "She's right, the mission is everything."

Achmed's eyes darted toward his gun on the floor a

few feet away. Catching this, Mohammed snatched the weapon up first, slamming the back of the barrel against the younger man's teeth and drawing blood. Then he removed the clip, flung the gun onto the still-warm bed, and strode out of the room.

*   *   *

He had turned off the air conditioning so as not to wake up with a stuffy nose. The sliding-glass doors to the balcony were open and a cool breeze wafted through the room. But Peter could only toss and turn in his bed. He'd returned from his night out to a room in a shambles. Someone had broken in and tossed the contents of the dresser drawers all over the floor.

So far as he could tell there was nothing missing. Like most travelers, he ignored printed warnings from the management that valuables should be stored in the hotel safe. In any case, what was he supposed to do with his typewriter, shortwave radio, and clothes? Those were the things that had been pawed over. The Olivetti was shopworn, but the Sony was relatively new and small enough to fit in a man's pocket. There was also a fancy little travel alarm. What sort of thief was this who would run the risk of discovery, then leave without a penny for his efforts?

Peter had immediately reported the incident to the front desk, but when the night manager discovered that nothing had been taken, he lost interest. If Mr. Robbins wished to file a formal complaint, he could do it with the hotel security office in the morning. Ten o'clock. The bastard hadn't even apologized for lax security.

Even more unsettling was what Dr. Tewfik's son Mohammed had meant when he suggested that unusual guile might be necessary to accomplish what Egypt couldn't with its own resources. It was a riddle, not an explanation. Right afterward Hazi and Tewfik had cut off the discussion and hustled him out. Peter didn't have any idea why. Perhaps Mohammed was aware of his father's and the general's covert work. Perhaps he too was a physicist, working with them—although Hazi had put Mohammed down as a lowly pilot who knew nothing of grand strategy.

Since they'd agreed the discussion was only hypothetical, Peter didn't see why it mattered what Mohammed said.

The Egyptians might have drawn up a specific operational plan for the use of a nuclear weapon if and when they succeeded in building one. But the explosion of one weapon, which at most would destroy a single Israeli city, wouldn't make sense when the Israelis could destroy at least a dozen Egyptian cities in retaliation.

Peter had long since learned to trust his instincts. Now they fairly shouted that he was on the edge of something important, a development that might turn a page of history. Perhaps at his next stop, in Israel, he could find sources able to shed light on what the Egyptians were up to.

He twisted, turned, and kicked the sheets, still unable to fall asleep. His mouth was dry. Thirsty, he got up and poured himself a glass of bottled water, then stepped onto the breezy balcony. There he remained, in meditation, until the first light began to filter over the Nile's silent, muddy waters.

14

Tzur was pleased there had been no problems with his travel documents in Frankfurt. At the same time he was concerned. Neither TWA's personnel nor West German authorities had felt the bespectacled Australian archeologist fit the profile of a terrorist, and he had been cleared with perfunctory attention. No fuss at the airport meant no chance that Egypt would trace his movements home. He had successfully disappeared. But the fact that his phony passport and visa hadn't raised an eyebrow pointed to lax security. That was disquieting. A Japanese terrorist squad had shot up Lod that way. He made a note to complain when he got home. That is, after he had given his report to Junction and Mossad.

Scrutiny at Ben Gurion Airport proved incomparably tighter than at Frankfurt. The chubby pimpled girl at passport control became suspicious when he couldn't produce a business card.

"Professors of archeology don't carry them," he pointed out pleasantly.

Unconvinced, she called over a supervisor, a gaunt man about Tzur's age smoking a thin black cigar.

"According to your passport," the man said, scrutinizing the document, "you've just been to Egypt. Into Cairo one day, out two days later. Were forty-eight hours enough to satisfy your professional curiosity about the pyramids?"

Tzur smiled. "I had to arrange for publication in Arabic of one of my books," he said. "I was able to conclude my business in a day, and since I've been to Cairo a few times I decided to visit your country, which I haven't seen before."

The security man wasn't convinced. He held the passport up to the light, looking for official watermarks in the paper. Finding them, he asked for the name of Langleigh's Cairo-based publisher and the men he'd dealt with there. Tzur made up names, figuring it would be days before his story could be checked out.

The man took a long drag on his cigar, blowing the foul-smelling smoke in Tzur's direction. He was in no hurry. He wanted to know who Professor Langleigh planned to visit in Israel, if he had any friends or relatives here, how long he planned to stay, whether he had a hotel reservation.

"Don't know a soul. I plan to visit the archeology departments at Tel Aviv and Jerusalem universities to make some contacts. Who knows? Perhaps I can be published here, as well. As for a hotel room, I don't have a booking. It was a spur-of-the-moment decision to come here after my business in Cairo."

Tzur managed to keep his outward manner serene and cooperative. This spy business is pretty simple, he thought. As long as you have a reasonable story, look unthreatening, carry no weapons or incriminating material, and can think on your feet and talk glibly. He started thinking ahead to his briefing of General Gordon.

The security man's eyes narrowed and he beckoned to a couple of plainclothes policemen. "You'll come with us, Professor," he said sharply. "We have some further questions."

"Questions? Is there some problem?" Tzur said as one of the policeman grabbed his arm and pushed him forward. The security man led the way to an unmarked door to the right of the passenger-processing area.

The windowless room was small and bare—gun-metal desk, a black phone, several hard wooden chairs, and a large bare lightbulb hanging from a ceiling fan.

"Okay, let's cut the bullshit," the supervisor said, slamming the door behind them. "Who the hell are you, really?"

"What's the problem, isn't my passport in order?"

The man peered at him closely, without answering. He took a seat behind the desk and put his feet up contemptuously, all the while staring at Tzur.

While not told he could sit, Tzur pulled up a chair and did so. One of the policemen moved with his hands on his hips to block the door. The other came over to stand behind the suspect. Tzur had confidence in the quality of the forgeries by air force intelligence. He would work through this.

"So. You're determined to play games, are you? The passport's genuine, all right," the security man said slowly, his eyes never leaving Tzur's, "but that's part of the problem. Two years ago, after some blank passports were stolen from the Australian embassy in Vienna, the government changed the watermark. If your visas and airport stamps had predated the theft you might have slipped through. But your passport bears the old watermark and you're carrying a recent visa. You also have airport entry and departure stamps from London, Cairo, and Frankfurt." He leaned forward and poked his cigar in Tzur's direction. "Now, who the hell are you?"

There was no point in continuing the charade. He responded in crisp Hebrew. "Captain Mordechai Tzur, air force intelligence. If you call 320496, General Gordon or one of his aides will vouch for me. By the way," he added, "nice work. You ought to be in Frankfurt."

Still the security man wasn't convinced. He started to demand an explanation of the Frankfurt remark; then, thinking better of it, picked up the phone and dialed. "Yes, I know your number," the man said into the phone. "I just dialed it. What office have I reached?" He listened, growing red in the face.

"The operator's instructed to acknowledge only the telephone number," Tzur pointed out. "For reasons of security. Ask to speak with General Rafi Gordon."

The security man gave Tzur a disgusted look. "General Rafi Gordon, and make it quick," he barked.

When Gordon got on, the security man turned respectful. "Sorry to bother you, sir. This is Sergeant Zvi Dudick, assigned to the security detachment at Lod. We've intercepted a fellow here traveling under false papers. Claims to be Mordechai Tzur, captain in air force intelligence. He just flew in from Frankfurt en route from Cairo . . . Describe him? About five eleven, thin, blond. Looks like a goy."

Half an hour later Gordon stormed into the interrogation room. "Motta," he snapped, "you've got a lot of explaining to do."

"Just a minute; your I.D. please," Dudick said. The general wasn't in uniform. Glaring at Tzur, he pulled out his wallet and waved a laminated identification card in the direction of the security man, who insisted on taking it from him to examine. Satisfied, he handed it back. "Excuse me, General," he said.

Ignoring the sergeant, Gordon started out of the room. "Follow me," he said over his shoulder. Tzur had never seen him so angry before.

In the sedan Tzur told him everything and requested permission to repeat the full story to Mossad, preferably to Shavit's boss.

"No. Since Shavit has dealt with this thing, he's the appropriate person to hear your report and ask questions," Gordon said, reaching for the car phone. "I'll make the arrangements immediately. When this is over I'm going to kick your butt all the way to Tiberias. The work of Junction is much too sensitive to risk exposure by traveling on your own to Cairo. Without authority and on false papers, no less. How could you do such an idiotic thing? You, of all people, Motta."

Then the man's voice softened. "The ass kicking can wait till later. After the crisis you've uncovered is dealt with." Tzur sensed a little pride in his mentor's voice. Gordon himself had broken a few rules on the way up.

The general instructed the driver to take them to Mossad headquarters, then dialed the car phone and spoke a few

146

words into it. When he hung up he said, "Shavit is expecting you. Keep me informed. That's an order!"

After identifying himself at Mossad's guardpost, Tzur was whisked to the office of Deputy Director Shavit, then kept waiting in an anteroom. He leafed through dog-eared newsmagazines for forty-five minutes. No doubt Shavit was a busy man. But he was probably making a point too—that he didn't like having the director of Junction demand an immediate audience for one of his underlings.

Finally a dour middle-aged secretary informed Tzur that the deputy director would see him. She indicated the door with a sweep of her hand.

Shavit didn't look up when Tzur entered. He was studying a thick report in a black looseleaf binder. He looked scrawnier and paler than on their first encounter. Reluctantly he raised his eyes, magnified and intense behind his thick glasses, and fixed them on his visitor. "You, again," he said. "You have a new theory you can't wait to try out, I take it?"

Tzur managed to squelch the desire to gloat, keeping an even tone. "That aircraft we discussed didn't explode over the Red Sea, as we were supposed to believe. It's sitting, or at least was yesterday evening, in a hangar at an Egyptian air base at Wadi Natrun."

Shavit closed the binder on his desk and gave Tzur his full attention. With a gesture of his head he indicated that Tzur should continue.

"It's in the possession of Arabs. I'm not sure whether they're Egyptians or Palestinians. I only got a glimpse inside and the light was bad."

"Wait just a minute," Shavit interrupted. "You're telling me you traveled to Egypt? You infiltrated the Egyptian air base at Wadi Natrun? You had better start from the beginning, including who authorized your mission."

Tzur told the whole story from the start, leaving nothing out, not even the bit about the Arab in the white coat searching the room of the American journalist.

"You went alone?" Shavit asked.

Tzur nodded.

"And have you forgotten to inform me who authorized your mission?"

Tzur swallowed and croaked softly, "It was unauthorized, sir. No one knew."

Shavit rose behind his desk, quivering, his hands gripping its edge. "Idiot!" he roared. "You went without authority on a mission to Egypt? Do you realize what you put in jeopardy? We have a peace treaty that gives us a quiet western flank for the first time in our history. We're developing an exchange of intelligence with Egyptian security. They tell us all they know about the operations of Abu Nidal and Abu Musa. We tell them what we learn about Libyan plots against their leaders. There are other cooperative efforts as well, but that gives you an idea."

Shavit strode over and thrust his face into Tzur's. His breath smelled of onions and smoked kipper. "I can't believe your stupidity," he said. "You drove to the edge of an Egyptian air base without any cover story prepared in case you were discovered? Didn't it at least occur to you to raise the hood of the car? Then if you were stopped you could have claimed you'd lost your way on a side road and were looking for help to get your automobile started. But of course you wouldn't think of a cover story. You're a data shuffler, not a trained operative. That's what makes what you did so damned outrageous."

He returned to his desk and slammed his fist down. "Damn you to hell! The trouble you could have caused! You should be court-martialed and thrown into prison. But then the story would probably leak to the newspapers."

He reached into a drawer and took out a silencer-equipped Colt 357 magnum. He gazed at the gun, at Tzur, and back at the gun. "You sense what's going through my mind at this moment?" He counted to ten. At last he said, in a low, intense whisper, "At moments like this I regret I'm such a civilized man."

Tzur couldn't believe his ears. Sure, he had gone off half cocked. And if he'd failed, court martial might have been appropriate. But all that paled in light of what had been uncovered, which was of enormous importance to

Israel's security. Couldn't Shavit see the forest for the trees? "I'm sorry for my maverick behavior, Mr. Shavit. But I have some theories on what might be—"

Shavit pointed the gun unsteadily at Tzur's heart. His right hand was shaking with emotion and he needed the left to steady the weapon. "Don't you dare utter another word about your theories. I'm personally going to see to it that you get buried in a job scrubbing latrines until your air force tour is over. And then, I promise, you'll be out on your insolent ass. Maybe you can get a job as a sentry at Wadi Natrun. They could use another man of your caliber. I'll even give you references. Now get the hell out of my sight!"

No sooner had the door shut than Shavit picked up the phone and punched a three-digit number. "Avram? There's a young fellow leaving my office now. Blond, tall, looks like a Swede. He should be hitting the front gate in four or five minutes. I want a blanket investigation, from the moment he was born. Grades in school, major and minor in university, whether he was a leader or follower, his politics, all foreign trips, whether he has a drinking problem, gambles, has a weakness for the ladies, his relationship with his family. Everything. Put Dov and Avi on it."

"Yes, sir. But a domestic job?" Mossad wasn't supposed to do intelligence gathering inside Israel, only abroad.

"That's what I want. We need to walk softly on this one. He's one of Rafi Gordon's boys." He paused. "Oh, and Avram, keep it off the books."

15

Tewfik and Hazi were in the latter's dreary office at the war college. "You know," Tewfik said, "I've been thinking over that comment of Robbins' the other evening about exploding a single nuclear weapon away from a heavily populated area as a preemptive demonstration shot. With a few critical changes, that might not be such a bad idea. But instead of exploding a weapon in the Negev Desert, what if we destroyed Dimona? The population's small. What would you say, about sixty thousand? And in the same stroke we'd destroy their nuclear-weapons-manufacturing capability.

"And how would the Israelis retaliate? Not by hitting Cairo. That would be a disproportionate response. Perhaps they'd vaporize Suez City or Ismailia, or both. So what? We'd lose a million people. Our population grows by more than that every year. The canal would be out of operation for a while. Three or four months, six at the outside if they used an air burst. What do you think?"

General Hazi didn't scoff; Tewfik's feelings were easily bruised. His friend was a world-class physicist, but as a strategist he belonged in kindergarten. "Let's think it through," Hazi said. "Dimona is the best-protected city in the whole of Israel because of its nuclear-weapons production. Remember that in the '67 war one of their own pilots got disoriented and flew too close to Dimona. He was shot down by a Hawk missile.

"Even if we could get through, the result would be

temporary. Their nuclear industry would be set back and our economy would suffer, but the strategic equation wouldn't change in any fundamental way. But, on the other hand, under my plan all of Israel will be in ashes. It won't be able to threaten Egypt or anyone else for a thousand years! No, old friend, we'll stick with the plan."

Tewfik agreed reluctantly. Hazi was the strategist, he the scientist. Their strengths were complementary. "About Robbins," Tewfik said, "I don't think we should see him again while he's in Egypt. He's not as smart as he thinks, but he's not altogether dumb. He might try to follow up on the hint Mohammed let slip last night. I don't know what got into him."

General Hazi walked over and put an arm around his old friend's shoulder. "Don't worry. With the information he has Robbins couldn't even begin to put anything sensible together. And don't be too hard on Mohammed. He's under terrific pressure. I'll phone Robbins and make some excuse. He's supposed to head for the 'promised land' in a couple of days anyway." The general chuckled. "He fancies himself a great reporter. He doesn't realize he's sitting on the most important story of his life. On ground zero, you might say."

"If he lingers too long in Israel he'll be there for a firsthand report. Too bad he'll never have a chance to publish it."

"Do they award journalism prizes posthumously?" Hazi asked. The two men laughed. "By the way, how are Mohammed's Hebrew lessons coming?"

"Fine, fine. He has a great head on his shoulders. The Coptic cleric who's tutoring him lived and studied in Jerusalem as a young man. He's said to have the accent down perfectly. For our purposes, he's the ideal teacher."

"He suspects nothing?"

"Nothing. He thinks Mohammed's being trained for a mid-level diplomatic post in our embassy in Tel Aviv."

*   *   *

152

After rapping Tzur's knuckles, General Gordon couldn't help but salute his results. After all, theirs was not the prim and proper world of diplomacy but the tough, rules-be-damned realm of intelligence where it was results that counted, not how you achieved them.

That's how an experienced pro like Shavit should have reacted, Tzur thought. A reprimand, sure. But then a smile and a pat on the back. Not waving his big pistol around. Some of that had to have been theatrics, of course, to frighten off interlopers from Mossad's exclusive turf. Still Tzur couldn't shake the feeling that Shavit was angry most of all because the supposedly destroyed plane had been discovered intact. No doubt the discovery mocked Mossad's previous dismissal of Tzur's suspicions. But Shavit ought to have been overjoyed to acquire the new intelligence. Ought, in fact, to have assigned it priority attention without a moment's hesitation.

The more Tzur rolled the matter over, the more he began to suspect that the senior deputy director of Mossad had connections with whomever was behind the elaborate airplane plot. The PLO or Egypt or the Soviet Union? It was common knowledge in the intelligence community that Shavit had been devastated several months earlier when he'd been passed over for a younger, less-decorated, politically connected man to head the organization. Could someone have exploited his bitterness? Or perhaps his greed or lust?

Harboring these suspicions made Tzur uneasy. Nothing of the sort had ever happened in Israel, so far as he knew. Oh, there was the case of a Druze captain in the Israeli army who had been bribed by the Syrians into becoming a double agent. But never a senior intelligence officer. Maybe his intense dislike for the man was tainting his judgment. If he voiced his suspicions to Rafi Gordon with nothing more to substantiate them, the general could only conclude he was prompted by spite, not professionalism. No, he'd have to scratch around on his own.

On Saturday, the Sabbath, when he knew there would

only be a skeleton crew at Junction headquarters, Tzur slipped into the main computer room. Once, while hacking around to see how secure Junction's own program was, he had discovered a secret entry into Mossad's highly confidential personnel data base. Apparently it had been devised by the original programmer to allow updating of the system without going through all the elaborate blocks he'd erected to keep out unauthorized entry. Tzur was confident he could get in without tripping alarms, unless the computer trap door had been closed in the interim. What he was doing was a criminal offense. But, if his instincts were right, the national security stakes justified the risk.

The door hadn't been closed. In the deputy director's special access 201 personnel file he found that Avraham Shavit, born Sokolovsky, came from Kiev. His father had been a kosher butcher, his mother an arithmetic teacher. Both had died of heart disease within three months of one another and left four teenage children. They had emigrated at the same time; Avraham's sister went to Israel with him, his two brothers to Argentina. But his father's only sister, Sophia Zykova, and several first cousins still lived in Kiev.

Many years before, according to the records, Shavit had twice visited his aunt, once in Helsinki and once in Belgrade. What was curious was not that Shavit would want to see an aunt from the old country but that she would have been allowed to leave the Soviet Union to visit her nephew. For an ordinary Soviet citizen to be granted an exit visa even for a short trip was rare; authorities in Moscow, not known for their compassion, had to be convinced it served the state's interests. That or somebody important had to be bribed.

According to the file, when questioned by Mossad's counterintelligence department Shavit had explained that his aunt was a resource, carrying sensitive information about prominent Jewish dissidents on each visit. This made the encounters official rather than purely personal. He'd produced some supporting documentation—detailed notes of conversations recorded after each contact—and the matter was closed. Presumably Shavit's record as a water-walker was so outstanding at the time that Mossad internal security had no reason to doubt his word. But because of the mayday incident, there was now ample cause for suspicion. For one thing, the Russians must have known that Shavit was a senior member of Israeli intelligence. Various intelligence communities kept tabs on one another's top officials. Either the Soviets were allowing the meetings in order to feed information through the aunt, or they believed Shavit's fondness for his father's lone surviving sibling could be exploited at some future time.

Acting on the hypothesis that Shavit had been coopted for an operation in which the Soviet courier flight was a key element, Tzur started testing that possibility against the few facts he had. He wondered, if it was a covert Soviet operation, who those Arabs were he'd seen servicing the plane. And since the Russian armed forces had been kicked out of Egypt, how did they get the Egyptians to cooperate and allow them to hide the aircraft at an Egyptian air base?

The few pieces he had didn't seem to fit together. But notwithstanding the threats to his person and to his career, he would not be frightened off this case. It wasn't in his nature.

*   *   *

Achmed was sitting on the couch at Sea Breeze cottage oiling his disassembled pistol, perversely satisfied when several drops spilled onto the cream-colored armrest. The phone was jangling insistently. Each of the three sullen occupants waited for someone else to answer. Finally, Nadia did.

"It's for you," she said acidly, thrusting the phone at Mohammed.

"Mohammed, I'm glad I caught you in. This is Colonel Ahram at Natrun. We may have a security breech. A strange car, a tan Renault, has been sitting on the road just outside the front gate for two days. At first we assumed it belonged to the new lieutenant and that it had broken down. I'd granted him a short leave to visit his sick mother. We checked with the lieutenant and it's not his. There was nothing wrong with the car.

"We traced it through the license plate to a car-rental agency and through them to a man at the Nile Hilton, an Australian. He seems to have left suddenly. We're making inquiries at the airport to see if we can find out where he went."

Ahram paused. "Of course it may have no connection whatsoever with your project, but I thought you'd want to know. It beats me what a tourist would be doing so far off the main highway. Why wouldn't he have come into camp to ask for assistance? There may be a simple explanation, but . . ."

"You did the right thing, Colonel. The general will be pleased by your vigilance. Thank you, sir."

Mohammed hung up. "We may have a big problem," he announced, dialing a Cairo number. Then into the phone, "Hello, father? I've just had some disturbing news from the nest." He summarized it quickly. "How soon until the egg is ready to hatch?"

"We're very close now, but to be sure I must stick to the original plan. About two more weeks," Tewfik said.

"Is that American correspondent still around?"

"No, he left yesterday for Israel. Why?"

"It didn't seem important to mention earlier, but the morning of the day you entertained him in your study, he came to our door at Agamy Beach looking for a British officer."

"The officer's name?"

"Squadron Leader Anthony Roberts."

Tewfik cursed, something rare for him.

"I suggest that Uncle Hazi use his connections to triple precautions at the nest," Mohammed said. "It's too late to make alternate arrangements. The dove may have to test its wings sooner than we thought."

"I'll speed up things on this end," Dr. Tewfik said. "You'd better check out preparations on yours."

16

Tzur didn't dare go through official channels. First, because he could be mistaken. Second, some senior officers might suspect he was motivated less by national security considerations than by vindictiveness. The possibility that he had uncovered a dangerous traitor led him to Zeev Roka, one of his best friends from undergraduate days at Tel Aviv University. Zeev worked for Shin Bet, Israel's version of the FBI and a fierce rival of Mossad.

They met for a walk along the beach in Tel Aviv so they wouldn't be overheard. It was early morning. A pleasant breeze was blowing in from the Mediterranean. White seagulls wheeled over the surface of the blue-green surf, searching for food, screeching, diving into the frothy water to snatch up small, flapping fish.

"I know it sounds ridiculous, but it was almost as if I was interfering with one of Shavit's devious operations," Tzur said.

Roka stopped to retrieve an errant frisbee and sailed it back to a voluptuous dark-eyed girl in a red string bikini. "Thank you," she called out, smiling. He waved.

"Don't ask how I found out," Tzur went on, "but you should know one more thing: Shavit has an aunt living in Russia who was allowed to leave the country to visit him on at least two occasions. Once to Yugoslavia, once to Finland. He was questioned by his own counterintelligence people about that, and his answers were unconvincing, to me at least. Now, is there any way you can put him under surveillance to determine whether—"

"Whether he's a rotten fish?" Roka finished the question. "I already know the answer. Firsthand. The man's a foul-smelling son-of-a-bitch. Once I authorized an investigation into Lebanon of a drug-smuggling operation. When he found out, I almost lost my job for not turning the foreign part of the probe over to Mossad. Can you believe that? He was more concerned about jurisdiction than smashing the ring."

"That only shows he's a bureaucrat jealous of his turf. Can you mount a thorough field investigation to find out whether he's sold out?"

Roka nodded his head and grinned, showing white teeth through his dark, curly beard. "Yes, I think so. Some newly trained operatives have just been assigned to me before they go into the field on unrestricted duty. To test their skills, I can do anything with them I consider appropriate. I'll put them on Shavit. Purely as a counterintelligence exercise, you understand. Of course I'll have to supervise them closely. If Mossad should find out and complain, I'll say what better way to determine the professionalism of a new team than to target them on a high official of another intelligence agency? I'd be supported by my superiors."

Tzur grabbed him in a grateful bear hug. "You'll get back to me, either way?"

"You have to ask such a question, Motta? Of course. What are friends for?"

They parted, Roka heading in the direction of the girl in the string bikini.

*　　　*　　　*

Mohammed and Achmed approached the guardpost at Wadi Natrun in Achmed's battered Fiat. Instead of the usual lone guard there were three, a sergeant and two privates, all armed with AK-47 automatic weapons. The noncom insisted they step out and open the trunk. They complied, Achmed grumbling all the while. Instead of explaining, the sergeant ordered them to produce their IDs. Two guns were leveled at them at all times. Very efficient and professional.

"Trojan Dove," Mohammed said, satisfied that security was adequate now. Immediately on hearing the password, the sergeant saluted. The two airmen looked confused, but on seeing their sergeant salute they lowered their weapons.

Inside the hangar, workmen in overalls were finishing bolting two strange contraptions on either side of the fuselage under the swept wings of the Il-76M. In the cockpit a couple of electrical engineers were installing multicolored spaghetti wiring.

"Where are they?" Achmed asked the ground-crew supervisor. He lead them to a darkened side of the hangar. There, in the shadows, two long gray weapons had just been uncrated. They were Atolls, Soviet heat-seeking air-to-air missiles.

"Are you sure they'll work?" Achmed asked Mohammed. "I had forgotten how big they are." They were nearly 3 meters long.

"I'm told they're quite effective, yes. Especially against big lumbering aircraft. The most important question is system reliability. That's why we have two. Surely one of them will work—our mission depends on that."

Mohammed called over the crew chief. "Any trouble installing the MiG-23 radar in the forward radome?"

"Trouble? Of course. But is it accomplished and functioning? Again, of course."

Mohammed punched his shoulder playfully and waved him back to work with a big smile. "This ground crew is first class," he said.

*   *   *

General Hazi and Dr. Tewfik were in the English garden behind Tewfik's house. Carefully trimmed boxwoods and yews provided airy privacy. They sat on wrought-iron chairs with fireflies flickering around them in the darkness.

"What's taking so long?" Hazi demanded. "With the security breach at Wadi Natrun, I have to tell you I'm nervous. Time is of the essence. We ought to have left yesterday, if not sooner."

"Don't forget, my friend, we're machining highly radioactive plutonium into very precise shapes," Tewfik said. "It's not pig iron. We can't slap things together. We have to be precise in our measurements down to a fraction of a millimeter, and extremely cautious in handling the stuff. You know that." They had special tools and instruments designed for the hazardous, exacting work.

More than once Tewfik had patiently explained to his friend that while the principle of an atomic explosion was well known, putting together the elements, including the high explosive charge, the shaped components of the plutonium core, and the elaborate electronics, was not child's play. Every day new problems arose that had to be overcome.

Hazi put his lighter to his pipe. The flame illuminated his face and glinted off the gold in his teeth. "Of course you're right. It wouldn't do to go to all this trouble and end up with a dud instead of a functioning bomb. Are you sure it'll be compact enough to clear any obstructions as it leaves the aircraft?"

"Quite sure. Stop worrying. In time, we'll learn to make them small and light enough to be carried in fighter-bombers, but for now . . . In any case, we've checked and double-checked the measurements and we're certain we can get the bomb into and out of the cargo bay. It'll weigh just under a ton. And without passengers and baggage the plane should have more than enough fuel to carry out the mission." He paused. "I have a surprise for you. I've got a crew working all night. We may even be able to deliver the bomb to Wadi Natrun tomorrow, more than a week ahead of schedule."

"Allah willing. But we must tell absolutely no one until the last moment."

Tewfik threw his friend an awkward salute. This was a special moment for each of them. Hazi was on the verge of restoring his family honor, winning a historic victory over Israel, and probably catapulting himself into power once it became known to a small but powerful circle what he had masterminded. For Tewfik it would be a personal triumph

160

of another sort. He had demonstrated that brains could be as important as physical prowess or courage on the battlefield. It would have made his Nabataean ancestors proud. Pity his father wasn't alive to witness his extraordinary feat.

*   *   *

Two days after their meeting on the beach, Tzur was working in his office when Roka phoned. "Motta, this is Zeev. How are you? I'm at the air base on some routine business. How about breaking for a cup of coffee?"

"You're here? At Ramat David?"

"Yes, purely routine." Roka said it in a way that suggested it was anything but.

"Ten minutes, at the coffee shop."

Tzur found him at a table in the far corner. The adjacent tables were empty at that hour. He bought a cup of coffee and while sitting down examined Roka's expression for a clue to his news. Roka leaned forward, elbows on the table. There was no urgency in his facial expression or in his tone. They could have been talking about a soccer game or the price of gasoline. "Do you know you're being watched," Roka said in a low voice, "your apartment staked out?"

"Me? Impossible. Who by?"

"When my boys first told me, I was skeptical too. The first thing I did was check whether anyone had directed our agency to do a full field security review on you. We try to do them every five years or so for those with top-secret clearances. But your last one was less than two years ago."

Tzur ladled a heaping spoon of sugar into his mug and tried to tear open a tiny plastic container of cream. Why do these things defy opening? he wondered, and as his fingers tried again to catch the tab he felt even then that eyes were on him, that someone was watching.

"I decided to look into it personally. I went over to your apartment house early this morning to see for myself. There was a watcher parked down the street with a view of the front door and your windows. No one I recognized. So I waited. When he was relieved by the morning man, a young woman, actually, I tailed him. He went to an all-night coffee shop and met a fellow I do know, name of Avi. He's an upper-middle-level Mossad operative. Then they were joined by another senior guy called Dov."

"I thought Mossad wasn't authorized to do investigations inside the country," Tzur said.

"They're not." Roka, who was trying to quit smoking, lit a cigarette, his second in the short time Tzur had been sitting there. A busboy came to the next table to wipe it clean and empty the ashtray. Roka remained silent until he was out of earshot.

"My new team has turned out to be pretty damn good," he went on. "They followed Dov and discovered he's supervising a second stakeout, this one of an American staying at the Sheraton. Name's Robbins, Peter Robbins. Know him?"

Tzur nodded. "I didn't go into details with you the other day about my trip to Egypt, but I met Robbins there. He was in the next room at the Nile Hilton. Seems he's an American correspondent from Washington. We talked for maybe five minutes, shared a drink. That's all."

"Of course you wouldn't have hinted to him in any way about your discovery." It was a statement, but the pause suggested Roka wanted reassurance.

"Of course not. Couldn't have, the discovery came later. Never laid eyes on the man afterward. As a matter of fact, when I got back to the hotel in the middle of the night there was a message from Robbins inviting me to dinner. I was racing for the airport and didn't want questions asked, so I left him word I was called out of the country on a family emergency, back to Australia. I was traveling as an Australian professor of archeology."

Roka laughed. "Professor? Always thought you had illusions of grandeur at the university." Then he turned serious again. "Think, Motta, is there any conceivable way Mossad might draw a connection between the two of you that would cause them to break the rules, risk a blowup with Shin Bet? Anything at all?"

Tzur stirred his coffee, absentmindedly staring at the

swirls. "I told Shavit every blessed thing that happened in Cairo. Including a phone message intended for Robbins that was slipped under my door by mistake. It was an invitation to dinner. It mentioned only last names, but I told Shavit they might have been General Rahman Hazi and Dr. Petra Tewfik." The names meant nothing to Roka. Tzur explained who they were.

His friend whistled. "Could Robbins be in cahoots with the Egyptians? I haven't had a chance yet to check whether we have a dossier on him."

"I don't know much about him. I'd heard his name before, seems to be a relatively well-regarded newsman. But I didn't want to leave out the slightest detail and even recommended that Mossad check out the nuclear angle. Could be important. But on account of that Mossad includes me in its net?"

Roka breathed smoke deep into his lungs and exhaled it in two long streams through his nostrils. Then he snuffed out his cigarette with force. "The bastards know they're supposed to come to us to conduct internal counterintelligence investigations like that. It's off limits to them. But, of course, that could explain the link between you two, and Mossad's interest." He paused to collect his thoughts. "Any way you could renew your acquaintance with Robbins? Find out whether he knows something important about Egypt's nuclear effort?"

"How would that look? As far as he's concerned I'm an Australian," Tzur pointed out. "And even if I could figure out some way to run into him, why would an archeology professor be asking about a nuclear-weapons program in Egypt? He'd smell it six kilometers away."

Roka smoothed his dark beard. "And so what if he was permitted to see through your cover?" he said slowly. "Unless I know nothing about reporters, he'd smell a story, not a trap. An Israeli traveling in Cairo under cover as an Australian professor? He'd probably fall all over himself trying to pump you for information. He'd go bananas with the excitement. You, on the other hand, would act aghast at being blown, plead with him not to write about your mission. He'd be on the attack, you in retreat. In the course of your confrontation, which he'd think he initiated, you might be able to smoke out who the Hazi and Tewfik are that he met for dinner."

For several moments Tzur remained silent. Then he inclined his head respectfully toward Roka. "You counterintelligence hotshots have awfully devious minds, you know that, don't you, Zeev? But it just might work. I'd like to know why Robbins was breaking bread with those two characters too. Though how Robbins can find me out without suspecting a setup . . ."

With a look of playful disgust Roka reached for his wallet. "The things I give up for my country," he said, taking out two tickets and handing them across the table. "I planned to take my wife to the concert in Jerusalem Thursday night. You know, Mehta and Menuhin. It's been sold out for months. You take a date. I'll arrange through a friend in the prime minister's press office to scratch up a ticket for Robbins." Roka looked longingly at the two tickets. "Would you believe twelfth row center?" he sighed.

17

The soft-drink truck backed slowly onto the delivery ramp at the one-story cinder-block warehouse in Inchass, on the outskirts of Cairo. No one happening by would think anything unusual about the event, Coke and Fanta orange being delivered to a workplace. Except for the hour—four in the morning.

The driver and his helper hoisted six cases of soft drinks from the back of the truck, stacked them on a dolly, and wheeled them inside. Again, nothing out of the ordinary.

A silver Porsche, its young bearded driver apparently returning from an all-night tryst, sped past. He appeared to pay no attention to the delivery truck. When the street was deserted again, the warehouse door slid open and a forklift truck moved toward the rear of the beverage van. On its bed was a canvas tarp covering an object about the size of a large desk.

Carefully, ever so carefully, four men put the cargo aboard and tied it down. Two of them, both armed with automatic weapons, climbed in after it. The doors were slammed, secured, and padlocked.

Sergeant Major Samir held up a finger as he raced past the driver's side of the truck toward the first of the two BMWs parked at curbside. "Give me one minute. And remember," he warned, "drive carefully. We should arrive at sunup." He hopped into his vehicle and turned over the engine. The beverage truck pulled out behind his car, while the second BMW took up the rear of the small caravan.

Soon they blended into the stream of vans, tractor trailers, and market carts on the side roads of Inchass. They continued onto the Desert Road toward Alexandria, as if on a routine delivery.

But their cargo that morning was anything but routine.

* * *

Driving to the Israeli Philharmonic concert from the *moshav*, Batya was pressed against Tzur, her freshly washed hair spilling onto his shoulder, her left hand resting lightly on the inside of his thigh. He couldn't help but feel a little guilty. He was using her. Not that it was so terrible; she would hear a great concert. But she believed he had turned the world upside down to obtain the tickets and make up for recent arguments.

"Batya," he said, "I don't quite know how to tell you this . . ." She lifted her head from his shoulder, her body stiffening. "Someone may be at the concert tonight, an American. We may have to talk privately during the performance. It has to do with my work."

"Man or woman?" she asked.

"A man, a newspaper reporter."

She looked at him strangely. "Is that why you asked me to wear these clothes?" At his suggestion she had put on a scooped-neck peasant blouse and flared lavender skirt. In the past, he'd complained the blouse was too revealing.

"I'm proud of you," he said defensively. "But yes, I had another motive. Tonight I want you to draw attention. Particularly from the American."

"What is it that you want me to do?" she demanded.

"Do? Nothing. If I make contact with this man I may have to excuse myself for a while. During the concert. Or after. If it's during, just return to your seat. How often do you have a chance to experience Zubin Mehta conducting and Yehudi Menuhin as violin soloist? Once in a lifetime, right?"

She nodded, tentatively.

"If for some reason I don't make it back to my seat before the concert's over, just walk over to the Hilton

166

coffee shop next door and order a cup of tea or an orange juice and I'll join you there."

"I don't understand, Motta. I thought you wanted to be with me."

"I do, Batya, I do. But there's something I have to take of. It's a matter of national security." That would end the conversation. She knew better than to press questions when he threw up that particular shield.

They'd left early enough to beat most of the crowd to the parking lot beside the Binyenei Ha'uma concert hall. He wanted to park near an exit ramp in case they had to leave quickly. He also wanted to get to the hall early in case Robbins did. Roka had phoned with word that the American had received his ticket. The seat was a few rows back from where he and Batya would be sitting.

Once inside, Tzur insisted they stand in the lobby. Despite the studied casualness of Israel most of the men were wearing their best suits and ties, their women expensive dresses and jewels. This was a gala event. But Tzur wore brown slacks, a safari jacket, and a shirt open at the neck. He was a *sabra* and wanted the foreigner to notice that instantly.

Tzur scanned the crowd, searching for a sign of Robbins.

"Motta," Batya said, her voice rising, "didn't you hear me? I said I've made up my mind. Tonight only convinces me I'm right. I'm no longer content to just drift through life. I love you. And I suppose you love me in your own way. But in a few years I'll be thirty and I want to start a family before it's too late."

"Batya, this isn't the time or the place," Tzur said softly. He saw Peter Robbins come through the main entrance and gaze about the lobby, then at his ticket, trying to figure out the Hebrew letters and numbers; he asked an usher for help and was pointed toward the appropriate aisle. Tzur glanced at his watch. Time to go to their seats. "We'll talk it all through later," he promised her, taking hold of her elbow and propelling her toward the aisle.

"When later?"

"Over the weekend."

As they walked toward their seats, Tzur saw Robbins take his. Can you be subtle? Roka had asked. Tzur maneuvered to the other side of Batya so the reporter could get an unobstructed view of him in profile. When they passed, he turned in Robbins' direction, as if trying to locate friends. But Robbins was looking at his watch.

Tzur took his time being seated, looking back and scanning the audience again. This time he was fairly sure the American saw him, but he didn't appear to recognize him. Then the house lights dimmed as Zubin Mehta walked from the wings, bowed in response to the applause, and turned to the orchestra, baton poised.

Tzur waited. The audience waited. Then Yehudi Menuhin, a man smaller than Tzur had imagined, strode on stage and took his place among the first violins. Tzur wasn't much of a music lover. He didn't recognize the first selection, a lively number by Kaminsky. It reminded him of a fast-running mountain stream with birds circling overhead and bees touching down on flowers along the bank in search of nectar.

The instant the lights came on at intermission he stood up and nudged Batya forward so they would approach Peter's row ahead of the crowd. Then he held her back as Peter was about to move into the aisle.

The American's eyes lighted on Batya, next on Tzur.

"Please, after you," Tzur said, gesturing with his hand.

"Thanks," Robbins said, stepping into the aisle and looking back at Tzur. "Sorry," he said. "I'm lousy on names but I never forget a face. Haven't we met?" The crowd headed toward the lobby, pushing them forward.

"You must have me mistaken for someone else," Tzur said. Be subtle, he reminded himself, casual. "People always mistake me for someone else. I have a common face."

Bingo. Tzur saw something like recognition in the man's eyes. He moved with Batya away from the aisle exit, toward a potted palm in the corner.

Robbins trailed them and stood a few feet away. Then he came up and said, "This may sound crazy, but I think we

168

met a few days ago. I'm almost certain. It was in Cairo. At the Nile Hilton. We shared a drink. But you—," he raised his voice, "—you told me you were Australian, a professor of some sort. I'm right, aren't I?"

Tzur put a finger to his lips. "Not here. We'll go outside."

He apologized to Batya, then led Robbins down the front steps and to the parking lot. He didn't see a tail, but he would choose a spot where there wouldn't be listening devices and where no one could move in close enough to overhear them. They stopped not far from where he'd parked, away from the overhead arc light, between a Cadillac and a Volkswagen station wagon.

"Well? Am I right?" Robbins demanded. "You're that professor who vanished overnight, correct?"

Tzur nodded, grudgingly. "I had some business in Cairo that it wouldn't do to advertise. But since the peace treaty, Egyptians visit Israel, Israelis Egypt. It's permitted, you know."

"Business, you say. No doubt. I mentioned that I never forget a face. Another thing, I trust my instincts. I've met a good number of spooks in my day, of various nationalities, and unless I'm badly mistaken, mister, you're an Israeli spook."

"Lower your voice," Tzur said. "I'm an Israeli and I was on government business. To that extent, you're right. More than that I'm not authorized to tell you." Peter grew animated. It was working, he was taking the bait and running with it. How's that for subtle, Roka? Tzur thought.

"Look, Langford, or whatever your name is, I know exactly what you look like, when you were in Cairo, even your room number. I could sketch you with precision; I'm a pretty fair amateur artist. Either you tell me what you were doing or I'll write a cloak and dagger piece about an Israeli secret agent posing as an Australian archeologist in Cairo."

For a couple of moments Tzur didn't say anything, as if trying to decide how to respond. "I shouldn't do this," he faltered. "It's strictly against the rules."

Robbins smiled encouragingly.

"But you must promise me not to write prematurely about what I tell you. The security of the state may be involved."

Robbins said nothing.

"Well, do you agree to my condition?"

"No promises, but if you persuade me you're on the level and that lives would be at risk if I write about it now, I won't. Not until it's safe. That's pure humanity on my part."

Tzur made a show of studying the American. "All right," he agreed, "I'll trust you. Exactly who I represent is not important." Again he paused. "I was in Cairo investigating a mystery, a potentially serious threat to Israel."

Robbins looked skeptical, as if expecting a cover story. "A mystery, you say. What sort of mystery? And why did you leave so suddenly? One night you're insisting we have dinner, the next day you're gone. What happened?"

"I found the answer to part of the mystery, which put me in danger. I had to get out fast. That's the truth."

"You'll have to do better than that to convince me not to write anything."

He couldn't get away with empty dramatics about a dire security threat. This was an American, not an Israeli. And he seemed to be a smart, probing man to boot. To get something from Robbins about his Egyptian friends, Tzur was going to have to give something substantive.

"Several days ago," he said, leaning closer and lowering his voice, "a Soviet aircraft was lost over the Red Sea. Or so everyone supposed. But it didn't crash; it's being hidden in Egypt. I located it. There. That's considerably more than I should have told you."

"But why would a Soviet aircraft represent a threat to Israel? The Russians have long-range missiles and bombers; if they wanted to threaten your country they wouldn't need an airliner."

Robbins thought it was a commercial plane. Tzur decided not to correct this assumption. "Perhaps the threat doesn't come from the Russians," he proposed. "Or per-

170

haps the Russians want it to appear that someone else is behind an operation directed against us."

"How could an airliner endanger Israeli lives?"

"Hypothetically? Well, it could fly low over the sea with high explosives and crash into Tel Aviv or Haifa. Hundreds of people would be killed if our air force didn't spot it, or didn't destroy it because it was civilian. There would be hell to pay if we shot down a plane full of Russians."

"The PLO?"

"It's possible. They have a number of pilots who were trained in the Soviet bloc. We honestly don't know what the mission is or who's behind it. But we need time to investigate. A newspaper article now could be disastrous, don't you see that?"

"You don't know this," Peter assured him, "but I served for a couple of years as an official in the Pentagon. I understand your sensitivity about a premature leak."

Ah, a defense official, Tzur thought. This was getting interesting. American and Egyptian defense types putting their heads together. Maybe that's why Shavit had the American under surveillance.

Neither man spoke for a couple of minutes. Tzur looked around to see if anyone had approached. No one. Music drifted out of the concert hall.

It was Peter who broke the silence. "What if the plane carried a nuclear weapon instead of high explosives?"

"A nuclear weapon? I doubt the Russians would provide one to the PLO, or Egypt, or any third party for that matter."

"But what if Egypt developed its own?" Peter pressed. "I did some sniffing around when I was over there and British intelligence suspects the Egyptians are pursuing the bomb."

"Suspect? The British suspect? Not believe? We suspect it, too. But if Egypt exploded one atomic or thermonuclear bomb on our soil, it would mean total war. Their leaders would have to assume we'd retaliate with everything we have. They've said publicly they think we have nuclear weapons. So whether they're right or not, they'd have to assume we could blow them off the face of the map. What would they have to gain? Glory in the grave?''

Peter looked thoughtful. "I had several discussions in Cairo with a general and a nuclear engineer suspected of being part of Egypt's weapons effort. In the last conversation, the engineer's son said that if Egypt had a single weapon it would have to use it very cleverly, in such a way as to achieve what Egypt otherwise could not with its limited resources. He didn't explain himself. Does it mean anything to you?''

Tzur remained noncommittal. "It sounds like a riddle. What did you do in the Pentagon?''

"I was deputy assistant secretary in charge of policy plans in the office of International Security Affairs.''

"And were your Egyptian friends interested in your views on nuclear strategy?''

Peter hesitated. "Yes," he admitted. "Exceedingly interested.''

"I don't imagine there was any talk of using an airliner to deliver a nuclear bomb?''

"None, nothing remotely suggesting that. I only brought it up because you said a plane full of high explosives couldn't accomplish much. A plane carrying a nuclear weapon could be triggered to detonate and do enormous damage to Israel even if shot down over the Mediterranean a few miles off Haifa.''

"Food for thought," Tzur said, extending his hand. "You've given me something to mull over. Meanwhile, do I have your word you won't write about me being in Egypt or the missing plane?''

Peter grasped his hand firmly. "For the time being. You have my word.''

18

General Hazi brought his Mercedes to a screeching stop in front of Tewfik's office building, reached across the leather seat, and flung open the door. Tewfik was waiting at the curb.

"What's this all about, Hazi? You sounded so excited on the phone." In all the years they'd known each other, Tewfik had marveled at Hazi's cool under stress.

The general accelerated into traffic, cutting off a taxicab and eliciting a curse on his ancestry from the irate driver. "Excited? Excited? And why not? My friend, we are about to reshape history. I've made a decision."

"What kind of decision? Everything was decided long ago."

"I know, I know. But this is different. I'm going along on the mission. Thanks to you and your wonder workers, the bomb was delivered at Wadi Natrun this morning. All is ready. Let me be frank. If it fails—and it could—I don't want to live. I have to be at the front, leading the charge. It's my plan and if something went awry it would be my failure. But if it succeeds! Then I'll step into the pages of history. Me, the son of the commander of beans and toilet tissue. I can bury the traitor Sadat headfirst in the hot desert sand. And the army will cheer. I'll be Caesar."

Tewfik was speechless. He had never seen Hazi so possessed. Once more the general was risking everything in battle. Tewfik shuddered. Only a crazy man didn't fear death.

"I'm going, Tewfik. I phoned Mohammed and told

him to assemble the team at Wadi Natrun, but not to lift a finger until we arrive. I didn't tell him about my decision." He turned to Tewfik. "It was my plan, but without your bomb it wouldn't have come to fruition. Therefore I'm offering you the chance for immortality. You may come on the mission as well, if you choose." The general's expression was determined, intense, unsmiling. He gripped the steering wheel tightly.

Tewfik was thrown into confusion. His friend from youth, the athlete, horseman, ladies' man, brave soldier— all the things he was not, and that his father had yearned for him to be—was offering him a chance to be a man. He had long since proved to himself that the world of the mind was superior. Any dimwit with a strong back could charge the enemy, hatred in his eye, blood lust in his throat. Tewfik was different, better. If Hazi was Caesar, he was Copernicus. And yet . . . What an opportunity! He could visualize the respect in Mohammed's eyes if his father, the overweight scientist, climbed aboard the aircraft. And he could visualize the blazing eyes of his own father looking down from heaven mocking him, thinking until the last second that his feckless son would duck it.

"I'll go," Tewfik said in a weak voice.

"What was that? What did you say?"

"I said," his voice louder, "that I'll go, too. I've come this far, I'll see it through to the end." There. Finally. He was living up to his heritage as a Nabataean.

*   *   *

As ordered, they had assembled hurriedly at Wadi Natrun, Mohammed, Achmed, and Nadia. They were surprised almost to the point of shock. This was at least a week ahead of schedule. But everything was ready. The nuclear bomb was aboard, extra fuel was in the internal bladders, the two Atoll missiles were secured on either side of the fuselage, all systems checked out.

Mohammed had conducted one final inspection, alone, inside the cargo bay. Now he paced alongside the aircraft, wondering why he hadn't been informed of the accelerated plan. One more piece had to fall into place before they could go. And for that he awaited a phone call from Beirut. Surely Hazi knew that once that call came they'd have only minutes to take off, unless they were to postpone the mission until the next courier flight was scheduled, in another week. But Hazi's orders had been explicit. They weren't to take off until he arrived.

Achmed fished a pack of cigarettes from his flight suit and flipped open his lighter. Instantly Mohammed pointed at him and opened his mouth to remonstrate. Achmed snapped the lighter shut, flicking the unlit cigarette disgustedly to the floor. "Yes, I know. Petrol fumes," he said. "Why do we wait?

*   *   *

Roka phoned Tzur early in the morning. "Motta, old friend, what are you doing at home on such a glorious morning? Join me for a jog on the beach, the usual place. Say in twenty minutes?"

"You're in a good mood. Your wife finally forgive your latest fling? What you need is a cold shower, not a jog. But I'll be there."

Roka was wearing faded swimming trunks and a sweatshirt. He waved both arms and ran over as Tzur descended the worn stone steps toward the beach.

"I can see from your grin that you've learned something," said Tzur. "Out with it."

They started jogging slowly along the water's edge, shadows long from the early sun. "It's not conclusive, mind you, but Shavit has been seen three times in as many days at a little jewelry shop on Ben Yehuda Street. You may know the place, Frishman's."

"What's so unusual about that? Maybe he's buying Chanukah presents early."

Roka ignored his sarcasm. "The owner, Pinchas Jabotinsky, immigrated eight years ago in a large group from the Soviet Union. With only the clothes on his back. Then, from God knows where, he suddenly had enough money to buy the shop from old man Frishman. We have other

175

reasons to suspect he may be a deep-cover plant for the KGB."

"Have you passed the word to Mossad?"

"No. Not yet. Before we accuse one of their top officials of being in league with the Russians, we'd better have irrefutable proof.

"By the way, this is no longer a back-pocket operation run by my trainees. Shin Bet is engaged in an all-out probe. Around-the-clock coverage of Shavit and Jabotinsky. Phone and mail intercepts and bugs, the works. Even in Shavit's office. And infiltrating the enemy's command tent was no mean accomplishment."

Tzur shook his head sadly. "This may sound strange coming from me, but suddenly I'm having second thoughts. I hope we haven't started a witch hunt just because we detest the man."

"Damn, Motta, if you aren't something else. Stop worrying. The investigation won't leak. If it fails to prove he's working for the Russians, the whole thing will be buried so deep no one will ever hear of it. But I've got strong vibes on this one; and I'm not telling you everything I know. Avraham Shavit of Mossad is in bed with the Cossacks. Trust me." For emphasis, he applied a short swift karate stroke to the Adam's apple of an imaginary foe in front of him. "Under the fucking covers with the KGB."

Tzur stopped running and grabbed Roka's arm. "What did you turn up on Mossad's investigation of Robbins and me?" He scanned the beachfront, trying to spot familiar faces from previous days or anyone on the beach dressed oddly. But only a few bodies dotted the stretch of beach at this early hour.

"Not much more than I told you the other day, that a Mossad field investigation is under way. Two teams, one targeted on each of you. You were seen with your heads together at the concert. They photographed you in the parking lot using infrared. It's an illegal investigation. That was what convinced my chiefs to go after Shavit in a big way. So the scrawny runt did us a favor."

Achmed spit on the floor. "What are we waiting for? So the general and his fat aide can wave us off with a handkerchief?" Mohammed ignored the insult to his father.

Nadia went outside to look for Hazi's car. In a moment she returned, shaking her head. No sign. Finally they heard a car door slam, then another. Hazi strode into the hangar followed by Tewfik. The one looked exhilarated, the other sheepish.

"All right, hear what I have to say," Hazi announced in his commanding voice. "You have two additional passengers, Tewfik and myself. It's our plan, we'll share the risks." Then he smiled, his gold-capped teeth gleaming in the dim hangar light. "And the glory."

Mohammed was stunned. *They* were coming? His father and the general? It had all been so painstakingly planned, down to the last finite detail. "What about fuel and range?" he blurted. "You know how carefully we've calibrated our needs."

"Our weight won't make a difference," Hazi declared. "Don't worry, we'll stay out of the way." He looked at each of the young conspirators in sequence. "And if one of you should suddenly be seized with fright, I'll step in and do your job."

There was no point in arguing with General Hazi once he had made up his mind. He called the shots. Mohammed glanced at his father. The poor man looked frightened to death.

The phone rang, a loud jangling. They were all silent, even Hazi. Mohammed held his hand up. Then he picked up the receiver. He listened and jotted numbers on a notepad.

"Our man in Beirut," he said, hanging up. He called over a waiting mechanic and gave him instructions. The man proceeded to airbrush large black identification numbers on the aircraft's tail.

About fifteen minutes later, when the paint was dry, Mohammed clapped his hands together. "Let's roll it out and prepare for takeoff," he shouted to the ground crew. Then to Hazi and Tewfik he said, "Sorry we don't have flight suits for you two. The worst thing you could suffer from the high-altitude chill is a head cold."

For the first time that morning, Tewfik smiled. "Just a headcold? Allah willing."

Less than twenty minutes after the call from Beirut, the Il-76M had been pushed into position on the end of the short runway. Mohammed was at the controls, Achmed in the copilot's seat, Nadia sitting in as flight engineer. Hazi and Tewfik would ride side by side in the front end of the passenger section. Achmed completed the pretakeoff checklist, lowered the flaps, and tested the controls for free movement.

"Tower," Mohammed said into the microphone, "this is flight 001 requesting permission to take off."

"Roger, 001. Cleared for takeoff, at pilot's discretion."

Mohammed ran the four powerful jet engines up to 80 percent power. The instruments showed that all was fine. Achmed gave him a thumbs-up sign. He glanced back over his shoulder and Nadia was smiling; she too threw her right thumb into the air with bravado.

He pushed the four throttles full forward with his right hand and felt the aircraft straining against the brakes. He clamped his feet down, releasing the brakes, and the plane accelerated rapidly as clouds of sand whirled in its wake. Although the runway was too short to stop once they were past 80 knots, Achmed made a modified acceleration check anyway. At 3,000 feet he shouted, "It's a go!" Once the airspeed reached 100 knots Mohammed gently pulled the yoke toward him. The nosewheel came off the ground and the main gear skipped a bit on the runway. As expected, the extra fuel, the Atoll missiles hanging on the fuselage, and the hot day extended the takeoff roll. The plane lifted off at 121 knots, several knots above the expected takeoff speed. The corrugated-metal strips that temporarily extended the runway passed under the plane's nose.

Mohammed was relieved.

"Gear up," he said. Achmed raised the gear handle.

There were several comforting clunks as the wheel wells closed. "Gear up," he sang out.

"Flaps up," said Mohammed as he ran in some nose-up trim to compensate for the loss of lift.

"Flaps up," Achmed echoed.

Operation Trojan Dove was in its final phase.

*   *   *

The quiet Bedouin janitor hurried from the airbase on his motorbike and within minutes had arrived at his poor shanty. Wildly he yanked several packing crates and odd pieces of lumber from the corner, flinging them across the room. He turned on the exposed HF radio, made contact, and passed his message: "Trojan Dove flies, 79 or 61."

Leaving the one-room shack in a shambles, he locked the door and raced to his cousin's house to send the same message by phone. It took him more than forty minutes to get through.

*   *   *

Peter had given his word that he wouldn't write immediately about Tzur's escapade in Cairo. But he hadn't said anything about not pursuing facts. The faked crash of a Soviet airliner? A possible threat to pack it with explosives, or even a crude A-bomb, and crash it in Israel? He wasn't about to walk away from that.

A captain in the air attaché's office at the American embassy had said there was an unconfirmed report, about the time in question, of a Soviet cargo plane going down over the Red Sea. He hadn't treated it as particularly sensitive or important. "We asked the Russians, through channels, and they denied losing any aircraft. There was no spy-satellite coverage suggesting a search for a crash site. So we're not losing any sleep over it."

Contacts within the Israeli defense ministry and the French embassy had confirmed the intelligence assessment that Egypt was attempting to develop atomic weapons. But their judgment was that it would take years before the country could possibly succeed.

Peter recalled from his Pentagon days that during the '73 war the Soviets had moved what was believed to be a shipload of nuclear weapons from the Black Sea to Alexandria harbor. The Russians knew the Americans screened movements through the Dardanelles with sensitive monitoring devices and would pick up telltale radiation, tipping off the presence of nukes. They wanted the movement discovered. It had been a daring gambit to persuade Washington, and through it Tel Aviv, that Moscow was prepared to introduce the ultimate weapon into Egypt unless the Israelis stopped violating a ceasefire by clobbering the already defeated Egyptian Third Army.

If the Soviets were prepared to slip nukes into Egypt once, he thought, they might do it now for a special operation. Or Egyptian hardliners, opposed to Sadat's peace treaty with Israel, might be planning something that would force a break in relations. Or a PLO splinter group, Abu Nidal's force for instance, might be preparing a bloody and spectacular surprise.

But all this was conjecture. He must think of some way to confirm one of those scenarios or discover and flesh out another. Then he would decide—*he* would decide—what and when to write.

His only hard lead was Tzur, who no doubt would stay on the case. Finding his address in the phone book, Peter had been lucky enough to sublet a small flat across the street from Tzur's apartment house. He might get some leads watching the Israeli come and go, perhaps following him to his office. The shortest lease Peter had been able to swing was thirty days. He'd worry later about explaining that additional expense to New York. If he got the story he was chasing, there would be no recriminations. None. He didn't want to think about the flip side of that, if he failed.

19

They flew low, heading west by northwest over the desert and out over the bright azure waters of the Mediterranean. When they were well out to sea, Mohammed swung the plane to a heading of 040 degrees and flew northeast toward a point north of Nicosia, Cyprus.

"Nadia, you watch the radarscope. Your radio is set so you can only talk to us on the plane's intercom. Don't touch the radio panel.

"Achmed, you monitor the air-traffic-control frequency and check visually. The Il-76 should be taking off shortly from Beirut International. All outgoing flights from Lebanon are required to cross Nicosia."

Mohammed had given Nadia several hours of instruction on how to read the MiG-23 radar which had been specially installed for this mission. She'd probably never been so tense, or excited, except perhaps for that evening on campus when she killed the lustful cop. When she told Mohammed about it, just before they first made love, she wanted him to understand why she was acting so skittish about sex. That had changed quickly enough; their subsequent months of lovemaking had been feverish.

About fifty minutes after takeoff, the sweeping radar arc was interrupted by a small bright blip. "I have a sighting," she said over the intercom, "at 2 o'clock high, 12 miles." That checked with the position report the Soviet pilot gave and that Achmed had picked up on the appropriate frequency.

"Keep your eyes peeled," Mohammed said. "The airliner should be assuming the proper flight path any minute." He pushed the throttles forward to accelerate.

"I see the bastard," Achmed shouted. "Above us at 2 o'clock. I can see his contrails."

Hearing the excitement, Hazi and Tewfik unbuckled and ran forward to the cockpit.

Mohammed held his right hand up to warn against distractions. He had to maneuver carefully. Still flying low, he guided the aircraft astern the other plane and climbed until they were 1,000 meters behind and slightly to port. He checked the tail identification number: CCCP00061. That was the number forwarded from Beirut.

He eased back until they were dead astern and just below their prey, then flicked a red toggle switch, arming the two air-to-air missile warheads. After rechecking alignment he eased the nose up, flexed his fingers, and punched the newly installed triggering mechanism.

"Starboard missile launched," he said. When the Atoll leapt clear, the aircraft gave a gentle shudder.

As the long gray missile set out, a white finger of exhaust stretched in its wake. It was traveling true. Suddenly, abruptly, it veered left, then right, then began tumbling end over end through the air. Within seconds it fell harmlessly into the sea below and exploded.

"Damn it!" Mohammed shouted. "Damn it to hell!" Again he pressed the triggering button. This one had to work. The whole mission hung in the balance.

The second Atoll stayed true, its infrared guidance system locking onto the outboard port engine of the plane ahead and drawing toward it like a nail to a magnet. A split second later the engine exploded in a ball of flame. Immediately, the left wing flew apart, the fuselage started to break up, and the forward cabin tumbled out of sight beneath them.

The passengers and crew never even knew what hit them, Mohammed thought. To him and his cohorts it seemed to have happened in bizarre slow motion. Without turning his head he jerked his thumb toward the rear of the cockpit. Hazi and Tewfik returned to their seats.

He pushed the throttles forward so that their aircraft climbed and accelerated and in a moment had assumed the precise altitude and heading of the other plane. "We are now special courier flight no. 61, Beirut to Moscow," he announced, exultant. "As we figured, flight 61 wasn't able to make an emergency radio call, and because we hit them in the radar hole north of Nicosia, there are no witnesses."

"So that's why the tail markings were changed on the ground," Achmed said. "But why Moscow? We're supposed to be heading for Israel."

Nadia stepped forward within earshot.

"I'm sorry I wasn't free to tell you earlier. Until now, only three men knew all elements of the plan: my father, General Hazi, and myself. We couldn't risk sharing the details with anyone else. Hazi's orders.

"We're an identical sister ship of flight 61. We'll fly her exact course, making all the normal radio contacts along the way. Shortly before we make our approach to Moscow I'm going to send one uncharacteristic message. In Hebrew I'll say, 'And David slew Goliath and all the people of Israel rejoiced.' "

This brought loud objections from Achmed and Nadia. "I thought we were going to bomb Israel," Achmed protested.

"We're going to drop a bomb on Moscow?" Nadia asked incredulously. "You've got to be kidding."

"Think about it. Moments after my announcement from the crowded airspace over Moscow, before the Russians can figure out what's happening and how to react, the bomb will be on its downward path.

"They won't have time to scramble fighters and they wouldn't dare let their air-defense batteries fire with so many planes aloft. They'd have no reason to suspect an atomic bomb was about to fall on their heads. Only that one of the blips in the air above them had delivered a bewildering message in Hebrew.

"But as soon as the bomb impacts, their generals will put two and two together. A Hebrew warning followed by a nuclear explosion that obliterates a portion of the capital.

They'll have no choice but to conclude the bomb was dropped by the Israelis, and their retaliation will be swift and awesome. They won't ask polite questions through diplomatic channels—they'll fire several warheads. Not even the Americans will complain that it's a disproportionate response. Within minutes, Israel will lie in ashes. What we couldn't have accomplished with one crude bomb, Russia will accomplish for us with several thermonuclear warheads.

"And," he added with satisfaction, "Egypt will not be involved."

"What about fallout?" Nadia asked. "Won't Egypt suffer, too?"

"The prevailing winds off the Mediterranean flow west to east," Mohammed said drily. "A sudden shift could waft some fallout over the Sinai, perhaps. There might be Egyptian casualties. But not a fraction of those we've lost in every one of our wars with Israel—our losing wars."

The three of them were silent. At last Nadia commented, "Brilliant plan."

"What happens to the three of us?" Achmed asked. "I guess that's five of us now."

"In the confusion after the explosion, the last thing they'll be able to do is find out which of the scores of blips on the screen was responsible. We should be able to fly low and slip away to Finland. A team is waiting at a small field outside Helsinki to spirit us out of the country. We'll leave a navigation map with Hebrew markings, plus some Israeli food and tobacco in the cockpit. Everything has been thought out, down to the last detail."

Achmed raised the clenched fist of victory. "Allah be praised!" he exclaimed.

*　　　*　　　*

As flight 61 headed north toward the Black Sea a pair of Turkish F-4s came out of the sun to inspect the plane. They circled lazily at a respectful distance, waggled their wings, then darted into a bank of clouds and were seen no more. Achmed threw a mock salute their way.

He and Mohammed changed radio navigational aids

184

when they flew over Turkey. Achmed checked in with air traffic control. His procedure was spare and correct, with no wasted words. Flight 61 was on schedule.

"Nadia," he said suddenly, looking up from the co-pilot's controls, "go get me some coffee. Hot."

She cast a disdainful glance in Achmed's direction, then returned to her navigation chart.

"Didn't you hear me, bitch, I need something to drink!" he shouted over the aircraft noise.

"Open your pants and drink!"

Disgusted, Achmed tapped Mohammed on the shoulder and inclined his head toward the galley in the rear. Mohammed nodded and handed him the IFF settings they would need to enter the Soviet air-defense identification zone. "When you come back, reset these. In exactly six minutes," he said.

In Achmed's absence, Nadia brought the navigation chart to Mohammed. "What's this notation on the chart that says check IFF & B?"

"That means reset the radar identification friend or foe. I copied down this month's settings in operations at Cairo West Airport. If all goes well, we shouldn't have any trouble crossing the Soviet border."

"Oh."

"By the way," he went on, "I'm going to have to reassure myself about the bomb and the release mechanism. Checking the aerial-cargo drop system on the ground at Wadi Natrun wasn't enough. We ought to reach a good spot to do that in another fifteen minutes, when we're over the Soviet Union."

He glanced at his watch. Exactly fifteen minutes later he slowed the airspeed to 230 knots and threw a blue toggle switch. Nothing happened. There was no sound of gears moving or doors opening. No wind drag. Achmed returned, a cup of coffee in his hands.

"Monitor the aircraft," Mohammed said to him, and headed out of the cockpit. In the passenger section, Hazi and Tewfik were passing the general's leather-covered flask. "Already celebrating victory?" Mohammed asked, an edge in his voice.

Hazi gave him a stern look. "It's a bit nippy," he reminded him, rubbing his hands together. "What brings you back here?"

"The rear loading door doesn't seem to be operating properly. I engaged the hydraulic controls up front, but nothing happened. I'm going to go back and check. I also want to check the release mechanism on the bomb."

Hazi unbuckled and rose. "I'm going with you."

"No need to bother yourself, General," Mohammed said, but Hazi gave him a small shove, indicating that his mind was made up.

As he moved toward the rear of the plane, Mohammed squeezed past the bulging internal fuel bladders that had been added for the mission. The air was frigid, 20 to 30 degrees colder than in the cockpit and passenger cabins. In his flight jacket he was dressed for it, but Hazi wasn't. He'd refused Mohammed's earlier offer of his flight jacket. Once clear of the bladders, Hazi slipped on a grease spot and almost fell; hooking an elbow into a canvas sling on the wall he regained his balance. Grease smeared his worsted uniform.

They stopped alongside the bomb. "Looks fat and ungainly," Hazi shouted over the roar of engines and wind. But he patted the weapon affectionately. Mohammed nodded, checking the ramp door at the back. It hadn't opened at all. There was a pool of red liquid on the floor.

"What's that?" Hazi asked.

Mohammed dipped a finger into the mess. "Smells like hydraulic fluid. That seems to be our problem." Hazi pointed at a hydraulic line above Mohammed's head. Fluid was dripping from it. It looked as if it had been cut.

The general glanced around suspiciously. "Sabotage!" he yelled, as if to smoke out the culprit. "Do you have a gun?"

"Yes," Mohammed said, patting his holster. "But there's no one else here, Uncle. The traitor must have been one of the ground crew at Wadi Natrun. But no matter, we have a manual backup system. Stand clear and I'll work the crank."

Hazi nodded and retreated a couple of steps, losing his balance again as he backed into the puddle of hydraulic fluid. "Damn it!" he said, grabbing for an overhead strut so as not to lurch into the bomb and jar it.

Slowly, with great effort, Mohammed turned the balky crank. It required every ounce of his strength to buck the wind resistance. Soon, the rear ramp door started to part.

When it was fully open, Hazi grew exuberant. Grasping a handhold on some canvas webbing, he edged closer to the opening for a look at the Soviet motherland.

Mohammed moved closer to Hazi. His eyes were narrowed and his jaw was thrust outward in an expression of intensity rare for him. Hazi turned his face toward the younger man, smiling triumphantly. As he did, Mohammed closed the distance between them, put a foot on the small of the general's back, and pushed him through the yawning ramp into the rushing windstream. "Why-y-y-y?" was the last thing Mohammed heard as General Hazi hurtled, arms flailing, into space.

Closing the doors was easier, the wind helping this time. Mohammed found a rag and wiped the slippery fluid from his hands. Then he unholstered his automatic, pulled a silencer from his pocket, and screwed it on. He placed the gun not beneath the flap of the holster but inside his flight suit, hooking it on his belt before zipping the suit up partway. Then he made his way back past the fuel bladders into the passenger compartment.

There he saw his father's pale face. "Where's Hazi?"

"We had a problem with the hydraulic doors. It's fixed. But he wanted to stay down there and fondle the bomb for a while."

Tewfik looked relieved, not surprised. The bomb was their creation, and Hazi's vehicle to greatness and power.

Mohammed opened the door to the cockpit and drew alongside Nadia.

"Find the trouble?" she asked.

"Found it and fixed it. Where are we now?"

"We just entered the USSR. Over the Ukraine."

20

At the Soviet air-defense center in Sheremetyevo all was normal. That is to say, controlled chaos. Too many aircraft darted across the radarscopes to keep scrupulous track of each. Although it was a guarded secret, close calls were not uncommon. The overworked controllers were bleary-eyed as they neared the end of an eight-hour stint. Their ashtrays were overloaded, their coffee cups stained from numerous refills.

It fell to the controllers at the nearby commercial air center to exercise primary responsibility for keeping the congested air lanes functioning safely. Commercial traffic was the bulk of the work. The military airmen who sat endless hours in this dank underground command center had to monitor all traffic, but they only talked to military flights, a few light liaison aircraft carrying generals to and from the capital, now and again a large Antonov transport bringing in troops from Central Asia or a charred jet engine from a crash site that required disassembly and testing to determine the cause of failure. Most important, they controlled several wings of fighter-interceptors, mainly on routine training flights. Occasionally they checked out a suspicious aircraft. So while strictly military traffic was light, they had a full workload overseeing everything that approached Moscow. The possibility of a hostile air strike was remote, had never happened, but still . . .

The security phone rang. "Colonel," a controller called out, "it's the guardpost. A General Vasiliev demands entry. Says he's KGB. The guard won't admit him without your permission."

"Let me have the phone," Colonel Laptev said, snatching the receiver. He was a short burly man with a silver hair swept back from his forehead. "Put the general on."

He listened. "Yes, Comrade General," he said, sheepishly. "The guard was only following orders. He meant no disrespect. Yes, sir, if you'll just put the sergeant on I'll authorize your admittance." He issued the order.

What in blazes is so important, Colonel Laptev wondered, that a general of the KGB comes kicking down our door? It was unprecedented, most irregular. Should he telephone his boss at PVO headquarters? Better not. The lines would be monitored and someone might wonder if he was questioning the KGB.

General Vasiliev burst into the room. He was tall, over six feet, thin, with wavy white hair and a sallow pockmarked complexion. On his flat nose rested a pair of rectangular wire spectacles, something he had obviously bought in the West. They were not available in Moscow, not even in the special shops Laptev and his fellow senior officers were authorized to use. The general was not in uniform, but produced an identification card in a pocket-size red leather case.

"Colonel," he said, "there's a special courier flight coming in from Beirut. Due here in less than an hour, I understand. Where is it at this moment, precisely?"

Laptev referred to the board at the front of the room. "Special courier flight no. 61 is scheduled in at 1605 from Beirut," he said. He walked over to one of the radarmen. "Find out about SC 61 from Beirut. Where is it now?"

The man called the air-traffic-control center. "Should be over the Ukraine southeast of Kiev, Colonel. It's on course and on schedule."

Laptev shrugged as if to say, What's so interesting about a routine courier flight?

"Colonel," Vasiliev said, "I order you to dispatch fighters to intercept and destroy that aircraft."

190

Order? Intercept and destroy? He might be KGB but he had no authority to order a military operation and certainly not the downing of an unarmed aircraft, one of their own, no less. Laptev was a newly minted full colonel, proud of the fact that he had made it strictly on merit, not family connections. You didn't rise through the Soviet military hierarchy by being foolhardy.

"What's the reason for your concern, General?"

"I have information, very sensitive classified information from the field. I'm not at liberty to discuss it here," he said, glancing around the room. All the airmen and junior officers were listening to them.

Laptev made no move, waiting for further explanation.

"Do you defy my order, Colonel?" Vasiliev approached, hands on hips, and stared down at Laptev, who was turning scarlet.

"Standing orders, General," he said evenly, "are to exercise military prudence and scramble fighters only if there is a reasonable cause for concern or suspicion." He paused. "So far as I can tell, flight no. 61 is proceeding normally."

"Idiot!" Vasiliev screamed. "Do you think I have nothing better to do than go around ordering air intercepts because I'm bored? I've just received very reliable intelligence that this aircraft is not special courier flight no. 61, and that it presents a grave danger to the motherland. In fact, to the spot on which we now stand."

"I'll need to consult with headquarters, General."

Laptev snatched up the red phone on his desk. Immediately he got through to PVO central and asked for the officer in charge. After identifying himself and explaining the situation, he held the phone out to Vasiliev. "Colonel General Chernyayev wishes to speak with you, sir."

"Is this a secure line?" he asked, before speaking into the mouthpiece. Laptev nodded. Vasiliev lowered his voice to a whisper, glancing harshly about the room in unspoken admonishment of potential eavesdroppers.

Laptev moved discreetly out of earshot, hovering behind an air controller who was now listening to reports from outlying colleagues. "Anything out of the ordinary?" he asked.

The airman pursed his lips and shook his head. Normal all the way.

Laptev snuck a glance at the KGB man. He was growing animated, his voice rising. "Look, General, we don't have much time. The plane is carrying a bomb. Not an ordinary bomb, no. Yes, that's right. Now will you tell this dolt Laptev to shoot it down?" He held the phone out to the colonel, an imperious smile on his face.

Laptev listened a moment. "Yes, sir, I understand. Contact Kiev air control and order an intercept of flight no. 61. Force it to land well before it reaches Moscow. Do not, repeat not, destroy the aircraft until checking directly with you. I understand completely. Yes, sir."

Laptev hung up and brushed by Vasiliev, who wanted to argue. Across the room he picked up a white telephone and pressed the button. "This is Laptev in sector one, calling Kiev sector six. You are directed to scramble six fighters immediately. The mission is to force down without destroying a courier aircraft now in your airspace. Special courier flight no. 61 from Beirut. Vector 150, altitude 33."

Laptev sat down at a ground-intercept radar station.

"I demand to know what in blazes is going on," Vasiliev said, towering over him.

"PVO has directed that the aircraft be intercepted and escorted to the nearest airfield. The pilots are permitted to buzz the plane, to fire warning shots, but not to destroy it without further orders. I will personally be patched through to remain in constant touch with the pilots." Laptev wondered if he dared say more. What the hell. "General Chernyayev doesn't want to take responsibility for killing Soviet citizens until he contacts the appropriate headquarters to find out who's aboard and checks the validity of your information with your superiors."

Smirks broke out around the room. Vasiliev was outraged. Check with his superiors, would they? He grabbed the red phone.

"That's a direct line to air-defense central," Laptev pointed out. "Try the black phone if you want an outside line."

Vasiliev slammed down the red phone and picked up the black. He turned his back to the room, punched a seven-digit number, and in guarded tones spoke into the instrument. He looked at Laptev. "How long before the interceptors reach the target?"

Laptev glanced at his watch. "About fourteen minutes, General."

*　　　*　　　*

Achmed was agitated. "You'd better listen to the radio," he told Mohammed. "My Russian is rusty, but something is happening on one of the air-defense channels you listed in the aircraft flight profile. I've been trying all of them. This doesn't sound good."

Mohammed pulled on his earphones. The chatter was confusing; radio discipline seemed to have broken down. Fighters were being flushed from an airbase north of Kiev, off their portside wing in the distance.

"It's a coincidence, right?" Achmed said anxiously. "The Russians couldn't know. All the people who knew about this mission are on this plane, you said."

Mohammed shushed him. He wanted to hear the transmissions between the ground-intercept controller and the flight leader. As he strained to listen through the static and babble, he heard what he feared. Courier flight no. 61, an Il-76M, was to be located and forced to land. Somehow the Russians knew.

He pulled back the throttles and popped out the speed brakes, diving from 33,000 feet to 1,500. He had to fly below radar's line of sight. He shouted at Achmed to turn off the IFF.

"What's going on?" Nadia said, her fresh cup of coffee splashing, the spare charts skittering to the deck.

Achmed grabbed Mohammed's right sleeve. "They know? You bastards didn't trust us enough to tell us the plan, and now the whole fucking Soviet air force knows?"

Mohammed nodded, grim faced. It took all his concentration to fly the plane at this low altitude. The thermals made the wings rock and the aircraft bounced in the turbulence.

"All right," Achmed said, "they know. Why do we have to go all the way to Moscow? Why don't we drop the fucking bomb on Kiev and then scoot out to Poland? They hate the Russians." He shoved Mohammed's shoulder, attempting to wrest control of the bucking aircraft.

Mohammed let go of the controls for an instant and yanked the gun from his flight suit. He turned and fired a bullet into Achmed's forehead, just above the left eye. The impact snapped his head into a twisted angle against his chest. Blood rushed from the gaping hole onto his tailored olive-drab flight suit. The second one was dead.

He recovered control of the aircraft and engaged the autopilot. It held, despite the turbulence. He was confused. He had to think. His careful plans had been destroyed by Hazi's last-minute decision to launch the mission early. Forced by that to improvise, and before he knew Hazi and Tewfik were coming along, Mohammed had severed the hydraulic line, figuring it would prevent operation of the rear door and be excuse enough for scrubbing the mission. Then he had planned to slip over to Finland and scuttle the plane offshore, with the bomb, Achmed, and Nadia aboard. His story to Hazi would have been that they had almost made it out, but were intercepted by fighters at the border and shot down over the sea.

The bomb was designed not to detonate unless armed. Operation Trojan Dove, as far as Hazi and Tewfik were concerned, would have been dealt a setback, but not an irreparable one. They would have had to build another weapon and find either another aircraft or an alternate strategy. And he, Mohammed, would have remained at the center of their scheme.

But then Hazi and Tewfik had decided to join the mission and somehow the Russians had learned about it. Now Hazi was dead, searching the netherworld for Caesar's ghost. Achmed was dead, no doubt trying to cuckold Satan in hell. Now what?

Nadia was standing just behind him. He turned and glanced up at her. She looked wary, suspicious, uncomprehending. She stared at Achmed, then at Mohammed, her eyes demanding an explanation. The sunlight glinted off something long and sharp in her right hand.

"Achmed went berserk," he said. "He wanted to scrub the mission."

"You didn't have to kill him."

"You're wrong," he said, whipping the gun from his belt. The shot hit her full in the chest and drove her sprawling against the wall. When she hit it, her back rebounded slightly and her arms and legs flopped. Her face actually looked innocent at that moment. Then her body slid onto the cabin floor. A hatpin fell from her hand.

The chatter over the radio indicated that the MiG pilots were having difficulty locating him. His low altitude temporarily masked him from ground radar, but he knew it wouldn't take long for other overlapping radars to find him and fix him for the interceptors. And the interceptors had at least a limited radar capability that would allow them to shoot down.

Maybe he should follow Achmed's suggestion, veer northwest toward Warsaw, and then if he eluded Soviet and Polish interceptors, head north toward Finland. If he made it to the Baltic he could ditch and might stand a chance. The aircraft was equipped with life vests and a raft. Was there enough fuel? Flying low burned about twice as much. Perhaps he'd have enough to get out. It would be close.

He changed course again to confound his pursuers. As he did, his father stumbled forward into the flight cabin and surveyed the carnage.

"Why, Mohammed? Why, my son? Were they traitors?" He said this in a soft, sad voice. It struck Mohammed that his father was in his own way as innocent and vulnerable as Nadia had appeared at the moment of her death. No, not at that moment only. With a surge of pity Mohammed

195

realized he had been vulnerable, if not innocent, all his life.

Reluctantly he swung the Browning automatic around and aimed dead center at his father's heart, not wanting him to suffer. He paused, studying Tewfik's confused, pained expression. Then he lowered the pistol.

"I, I can't do it," he said, his voice breaking.

And at that moment the aircraft was ripped apart by a tremendous explosion as two air-to-air missiles, fired by a pair of MiGs, slammed into the plane simultaneously.

21

Caught in the grip of a nightmare, Captain Tzur twisted and thrashed and kicked the sweat-drenched sheet off his bed. Shavit was chasing him over scorching desert dunes waving a razor-sharp scimitar. It was hard to run in the soft sand, which gave way under his bare feet and impeded his flight. Tzur was young and strong, Shavit old and scrawny, but the pursuer pressed on relentlessly, gradually closing the gap between them. Perhaps because the old man was light, he didn't sink as deep into the sand and could make better time.

Suddenly, Tzur became aware of a pounding noise. He tossed his head to the left and right, seeking to identify the source of this new threat. Shavit was still chasing him through the desert, there was no one else. Then it occurred to him where the insistent noise was coming from. He sat up in bed, getting his bearings. It was the front door.

Bang, bang, bang, bang! Whoever it was didn't give a fig if he woke the whole building. "I'm coming, I'm coming," he shouted as he grabbed a pair of trousers. It was five-thirty in the morning.

The pounding continued. Angered, Tzur rushed to the door and threw it open, then blanched at what he saw. There stood Shavit, pale and dressed in funereal black. Behind him, in the hall, were two muscular young men in similarly somber clothes.

Shavit looked troubled. He strode inside without invitation or explanation, offering no excuses. "Get dressed and come with me," he said. Then, as an afterthought, "Please."

He must have found out about the Shin Bet investigation, Tzur thought. The madman is here for retribution.

Tzur kept a loaded Beretta in a dresser drawer under his shirts. No, he'd never make it. There were three of them. The younger goons must be armed. Better to act submissive and see if an opportunity arose to make a break for it.

Outside they led him to a bronze Mercedes. With a wave of his arm, Shavit indicated that Tzur should get in back. He joined him there, the other two men taking the front seat. The slamming doors sounded like pistol shots shattering the early-morning calm of the seaside neighborhood.

"Where are you taking me?"

"Be patient. In good time I'll answer your questions," Shavit said, and the car careened from the curb, kicking up a cloud of sand and diesel exhaust.

From his kitchen window, across the street, Peter was watching. Always an early riser, he had been drinking a cup of coffee when the three men accompanied Tzur to the car. The American threw on some clothes and grabbed his car keys.

Not a word was spoken as the Mercedes picked up speed, heading south along the coast. Tzur grasped at a comforting thought: surely a carload of Shin Bet men was following, prepared to intercede in the nick of time. After all, Roka had put Shavit under round-the-clock surveillance.

The car started to climb uphill, the driver ignoring the speed limit. There were no police on the road at that hour. Off to the left, Tzur saw the tall stone clock tower of Jaffa. Finally the car slowed down and braked.

"We're here," Shavit announced. The driver jumped out and opened Tzur's door, the other man, Shavit's.

Before them were rows and rows of sun-bleached tombstones. Here and there a few scraggly flowers stood as silent testimony to love and grief. They were at a very old cemetery. Tzur shuddered. Was he to be executed and interred? Was this how Mossad disposed of its enemies? It couldn't be. There were laws. Israel was a democracy.

Shavit said nothing as he led the way to an open grave site on a rise overlooking the sea. Six men were waiting there. Tzur recognized only one, Moshe Rabinowitz from Mossad. The fat jolly linguistics expert, whose startling analysis had started Tzur on his quest, wasn't laughing now. Like the others, he wore a dark suit.

"Where's the other one, Avi?" Shavit said.

"Ten kilometers away, being neutralized, as ordered."

Shavit nodded his approval and gestured for Tzur to join him at the lip of the open grave. Alongside it stood an unvarnished wooden coffin. Silently Tzur started to recite prayers he hadn't said since his bar mitzvah. He was about to be shot and buried in that plain coffin, in that open grave. Too late for intercession by Shin Bet, if indeed its operatives were anywhere near.

Roka, he thought, where the hell are you and your men? We were the closest of friends in school. I saved you from flunking out. Tutored you before that geometry exam so you wouldn't have to join your father at the fruit stand. If ever I needed a favor, just ask, you said. Well, this is it, I'm calling in the favor. Where in heaven's name are you when I need you?

*   *   *

Peter tried to contain his excitement as he followed the bronze Mercedes at what he hoped was a discreet distance. There was very little traffic at that hour of the morning and he feared detection. The sedan was traveling well over the speed limit, about 70 miles an hour. He, too, had to break the limit, or risk losing them. He kept an eye on the rear-view mirror, watching for a police car.

He wondered who the three men in formal clothes were and where they were heading in such a rush. Two of them looked as if they could be agents. Strong and stocky, in cheap suits. Of course he had caught only a glimpse. He hoped they were going to their headquarters. Once he found out what intelligence service they worked for . . .

He didn't know what he would do with the information. He might look up David Poretz, an Israeli reporter he'd gotten to know in Washington. Poretz was back home now as national security correspondent for *Davar*. In the tight and inbred society of national security Poretz would probably know most of the key guys in the intelligence community.

Peter looked again in the rearview mirror. A taxicab that had fallen in behind him several blocks earlier was still with him. At first he hadn't paid it much attention, thinking it might be making an early pickup for the long ride to Ben Gurion Airport. But it was still there and seemed to be closing the distance.

Without warning, a panel truck pulled out of an alley and halted broadside in front of his car. Peter slammed to a stop, narrowly avoiding a collision. He cursed the driver. Three men jumped out of the back of the truck and rushed toward his car. They were carrying pistols. A robbery? Peter yanked the stickshift into reverse, then saw that his path had been blocked by the taxi behind him.

He rolled down the window. A tall thin young man was smiling incongruously at him. "Look," he said, "if you want my wallet, it's yours. Not much, but it's yours."

"Out of the car," the man ordered.

Peter sized up his situation. There were five men now, two from the taxi, all with drawn guns. "Yeah, sure, you bet." He got out quickly and closed the door. As he was reaching for his wallet, the lanky man thrust his gun hard under Peter's chin.

"I was only getting my wallet," he said. "I'm not armed. What's this all about?"

"I'll take your wallet now," the man said, motioning with his fingers. "Remove it carefully and hand it to me."

Peter complied, relieved. They would take his money and let him go. It was only a couple hundred dollars. He'd

200

report it to the police and put it on his expense account. If only he hadn't lost Tzur.

"Your name Peter Robbins?" the tall man asked.

"Yes, that's right."

"Have your passport with you?"

That was a strange question for a stickup. "No," Peter said, confused, "it's back at my flat on Reuben Street."

"Where were you rushing so early in the morning, Mr. Robbins?"

"Just a drive along the coast. I couldn't sleep. I needed some fresh air."

"Couldn't get fresh air walking along the beach? You Americans have to drive everywhere?"

"Now, look here, if this is a stickup, take my money and let me go."

"The only place you're going is into the rear compartment of our truck," the man said, waving his revolver. "Leave your keys in the car. One of my men will drive it."

"But I'm an American newsman. I was driving on a public street. Maybe I was traveling over the speed limit, but—"

"Into the truck," the man said, jabbing him painfully in the ribs with his gun.

*   *   *

Standing not more than a few feet from Tzur, Shavit reached into his back pocket. Tzur closed his eyes as he did when the dentist was about to start drilling. This was it. He was about to die. But why? What had he done? Maybe it wouldn't seem like such a waste if at least he understood.

When after a moment nothing happened, Tzur opened his eyes and saw that instead of a gun, Shavit had pulled out a big white handkerchief. He removed his thick glasses and wiped his eyes and his mouth before starting to speak. Beneath his dark suit his chest seemed to be shaking. "Captain Tzur, you wanted to know about a pilot. I believe you called him Mayday Man that first time you came to my office. Your curiosity is about to be satisfied.

"Shortly after the war of independence, two Jews, father and son, immigrated to Israel from Morocco. The family name was Tal. The boy, Amrom, was only eight; he'd lost his mother to cancer two years earlier. Ismael, his father, was a strong, dark, imposing man with a good Jewish heart. He looked like an Arab and spoke the language of his youth fluently.

"Ismael was recruited into our secret service. He was a natural. Smart, smooth, fearless. His missions kept him away much of the time and he worried about his son back in Eretz Yisrael. My wife took a liking to the little boy. We couldn't have children of our own and he came to live with us. We raised him like a son."

He stopped, swallowed, blew his nose. From the distance came the sound of shovels digging into sandy earth. A new grave was being dug. "To make a long story short, Ismael was part of a team that discovered the earliest stages of an Egyptian effort to develop atomic weapons. He helped identify the principal participants. A central figure was a brilliant young nuclear engineer, Dr. Petra Tewfik.

"After that, Ismael spent a lot of time in Egypt. He managed to get a job as gardener on the grounds at the Tewfik estate. But trimming hedges and pulling weeds wouldn't get us the sort of intelligence we needed. So he came up with a bold plan. His own son would be placed in Tewfik's house and would become a deep-cover agent.

"Ismael located a poor distant cousin of Tewfik's who lived in a village near Luxor. Husband, wife, and son, age thirteen, the same age as Amrom. An accident was arranged. A leaking fuel line, a spark, an explosion that killed all three members of the family. But police records will show that only two bodies were recovered, father and mother. We took three innocent lives, in order to avoid a holocaust.

"Amrom, posing as the son, appeared at the Tewfik home in Cairo, told his story, and begged for a roof, a crust of bread. He was a dark, handsome young man with an appealing manner. Petra and his wife were charmed by him

202

from the start. They were childless too. Before long, they adopted the boy."

The sun was coming up fast now, heating the still air. Shavit's wasted body was perspiring heavily but he didn't loosen his tie or remove his jacket. Instead he looked into the sun for an instant, blinked, and continued his narrative. "Mohammed Tewfik, born Amrom Tal, was a fine student and athlete. At eighteen he entered the Egyptian war college and gravitated toward the air force. He wanted to be a pilot. He was good enough that the Russians picked him out as a potential future military leader and gave him eighteen months' advanced flight training in the Soviet Union. Six months each on fighters, bombers, and transports."

In the distance several car doors slammed, followed moments later by the appearance of six Shin Bet men, Roka in the lead. They fanned out around the grave site and Roka moved swiftly to Tzur's side.

"What the hell's going on?" he whispered. "We would've been here sooner if it hadn't been for that American, Robbins. Can you believe he was following you and Shavit? The Mossad boys carted him off somewhere. We had to hang back so we wouldn't be spotted and get mixed up in that encounter. You all right?"

Tzur nodded and signaled Roka to listen. The Shin Betniks were outnumbered by the Mossadniks. Roka looked uneasy.

"You come at a propitious moment," Shavit said to the men from the rival agency. "I've been telling Tzur about something you seem to have been drawn into, one way or another.

"You, Tzur, suspected the Soviet aircraft incident was a fake, which is true. It was an Egyptian operation from its inception, run by a General Hazi. You know, the Fox of Cairo. But we were on the inside all the time. Amrom— Mohammed—reported to me every step of the way. That's why I was so angry at your meddling. You were right, your instincts remarkable. But you could have destroyed years of painstaking effort, don't you see?"

Tzur nodded his head. His throat felt parched.

"The coffin before you doesn't contain a body," Shavit said. "It contains all the worldly effects of Amrom Tal. He was a great hero, one of the bravest and smartest Israel ever had. And except for you gentlemen—," he waved his arm to encompass them all, "—no one will ever know what he did, what he gave, what it cost.

"If only his real father were still alive to share the triumph!" He stopped, shaken, and took a few moments to regain his composure. "You see, gentlemen—Tzur, Roka—you were right. I was consorting with the Russians. When it became clear that the bomb would in fact be built and that the Soviet transport could carry it to Moscow, I alerted a KGB contact I'd been cultivating in Tel Aviv. I told him I had urgent information to pass at the right moment and that he should open up a special shortwave channel to be monitored in Moscow night and day.

"That was the backup plan. I hoped it would not be necessary. We had two men at the air base where the plane was kept, a janitor and a truck driver who could come and go. Plus Amrom. The idea was to blow up the aircraft shortly before the mission. That would have kept our deep-cover agent in the heart of their program. But then the bomb was loaded ahead of time and Hazi joined the flight unexpectedly. Our man at Wadi Natrun got the message to me."

The old man took his glasses off and rubbed his eyes. "When the general and Tewfik joined the flight, that raised a suspicion in my mind that Amrom's cover had been blown. If so, the mission might have succeeded. I couldn't gamble on Amrom outwitting and overpowering four people who might be onto him. So—s-s-so," he stammered, "I told the Russians that what they believed to be special courier flight no. 61 was carrying an atomic bomb targeted on Moscow. I told them enough so they could find it and shoot it down."

The men murmured and exchanged disbelieving glances. Moshe Rabinowitz started to speak, but Shavit held up his hands for silence and continued. "Amrom understood we would have to do something to prevent the mission from being completed. We felt we had covered all possible contingencies. But we never dreamed General Hazi would decide at the last moment to join the mission."

Shavit's voice broke, and he fell silent again. Presently he clasped his hands together and looking toward the heavens called out in anguish in a high, quavering voice, "May the good Lord forgive me, may his dead father Ismael forgive me, may my dear departed Sarah forgive me. I killed the fine young man we regarded as our son, Amrom Tal, the Mayday Man. I sacrificed him. To save Israel."

22

After a short bouncy ride in the back of the panel truck, made more uncomfortable by hard wooden benches, the journey ended. The tall man holding Peter's wallet motioned with a jerk of his head for his two compatriots to get out. They slammed the doors behind them, leaving the captive and captor alone.

"Tell me again, Mr. Robbins, but honestly this time, what were you doing out so early in the morning?"

"Fresh air, I was getting some fresh air. I couldn't sleep. I thought I'd drive south along the coast and stop somewhere for a stroll. Any law against that?"

A sardonic grin appeared on the Israeli's face. He was middle-aged, about thirty-five, trim, with a five-o'clock shadow and a thin hawklike nose. "No, no laws against driving along a public road. But we do have laws in this country, as you do in yours, against espionage."

"Espionage?" Peter said, throwing his head back and laughing. "You're kidding. If I've broken any law in Israel it was for driving over the speed limit. Guilty. Give me a ticket and let me go on about my business."

"What exactly is your business, Mr. Robbins?"

"I told you. Newsman. I work for the *New York World*, based in Washington. I wonder if our readers would enjoy a feature story about how Israel enforces its traffic laws. What did you say your name was?"

"Very good. The best defense is a strong offense. You threaten to write a story embarrassing our law enforcement.

And will your story include why you were following four of our government employees this morning?"

"Following? I wasn't following anyone. You can't prove anything of the sort."

"Then I take it you didn't know one of the passengers in the Mercedes you were following was Mordechai Tzur?"

"Who's he?"

"Indeed, who is this Tzur you've never heard of? Tell me, Peter—may I call you Peter?—do you play chess?"

It was stifling hot in the back of the van. Peter took out a handkerchief and mopped his face. The interrogator, noticing his discomfort, called out something in Hebrew and one of the men outside opened the doors wide. The two remained within sight, smoking and talking.

"I learned chess as a kid, at summer camp. But I haven't played in years. Why do you ask?"

"Just curious. We're very curious about you. For instance, why would a well-known Washington correspondent on a brief reporting assignment in Israel suddenly move out of a five-star hotel into a poorly furnished apartment? An apartment that just happens to be across the street from one occupied by this man Tzur. With a one-month lease, no less."

"There are lots of interesting stories to report in your country. I decided to extend my visit and save my paper a little money in the process. Hotels peg their charges on businessmen and tourists and are quite expensive, as I'm sure you're aware."

"You know, espionage is a serious charge."

"You keep saying that. What do you base your accusations on?"

"Mr. Robbins. Peter. You insult my intelligence. Not long ago you visited with this fellow Tzur in Cairo, at the Nile Hilton."

"But he said his name was Langleigh."

"Ah, so you do know this Tzur, alias Langleigh. As a matter of fact you had adjoining rooms in Egypt."

"I talked with him for maybe five or ten minutes. He

said he was an Australian archeologist. I didn't know he was an Israeli."

"Didn't know he worked for the Israeli government?" The man reached under his seat and pulled out a battered attaché case. He withdrew a black and white photo and handed it to Robbins. "And how do you explain this animated conversation the other night in a parking lot outside a Jerusalem concert hall? With a man you don't know to be Israeli."

A wave of fear swept over Peter. He felt weak. He had to admit his story must look pretty fishy to Israeli authorities. The photo was grainy but the two of them could be made out clearly. Peter was pointing a finger at Tzur as if threatening him. "I met this guy in Cairo by chance," he croaked. "Briefly. I ran into him again at the Menuhin concert and demanded an explanation of who he was and why he'd lied to me. He insisted we go outside to talk. That's all there is to it. It's all purely coincidental. You can't prove espionage. There's nothing remotely resembling espionage."

Peter took his handkerchief out again and wiped his face and neck.

"Coincidence. Proof. Appearance. All very interesting questions you raise, Peter. But let me remind you that your success as a reporter traveling abroad comes from access. You obtain access based on your credibility as an honest journalist. Now imagine, for the sake of discussion, that Israel had a strong circumstantial case suggesting espionage activity, that charges were brought and the details leaked, say to your competition at the *New York Times*. Even if the charges were never proved, what would the effect be on your career, on your ability to earn a livelihood?"

Peter's expression was sufficient answer. If he was perceived as an intelligence agent rather than what he was, an aggressive journalist, his career would be shot. At least his reporting abroad.

The man retrieved the photograph and handed Peter's wallet back. "Your car is parked nearby, the keys inside. I suggest—and it's only a friendly suggestion—that you vacate your flat on Reuben Street and check back into a hotel. I suggest that you forget about Tzur and whatever he may have told you. It's a security matter that doesn't involve you or your country."

Peter rose and stuffed the wallet into his back pocket. His lips were tightly compressed. He was angry, but even more than that, worried. He had certainly violated no laws. They could never prove a case of espionage. Still, the *New York Times* would love to skewer a rival reporter with a story about his having been charged with espionage. Foreign officials would forever suspect there might be some truth to the charges. His career would be a shambles.

He didn't trust himself to say anything to the Israeli intelligence operative. But as he climbed down the man had a parting remark. "Earlier you asked my name. Call me Checkmate."

*   *   *

Tzur, in his parents' home at Moshav Neve Ilan, rose early and slipped downstairs. He had a lot of serious thinking to do. After a hurried breakfast of orange juice, tea, hard cheese, and pumpernickel, he wrote a note to Batya, went and slipped it under her front door, then headed for the promontory overlooking the guest house. For years it had been a favorite place to gather his thoughts, nurse a slight, savor a victory, or stargaze with her.

His dog, Ziki, bushy tail sweeping from side to side like a windshield wiper, fell in beside him as he climbed through the crisp mountain air. Ziki was twelve and had developed cataracts in both eyes, but he still acted like a frisky pup. Somewhere ahead, in a tall fir, a whippoorwill was calling.

Tzur had always been self-assured, had always thought he had a special knack for overcoming any problem, however difficult, by working through it with a combination of knowledge, logic, and intuition. It was a gift. But now, after all that had happened over the last several days, he wasn't so sure. What arrogance, venturing to Egypt without a clear

210

plan, without authorization or backup. Even if he *had* stumbled onto the missing aircraft.

Even more arrogant was his conclusion that because Shavit hadn't responded as Tzur thought he should, the man had to be investigated. He could have shared his suspicions with his boss, General Gordon, and let an experienced, dispassionate professional consider the facts. But instead he had struck out on his own and roped Roka into his scheme.

Another mistake was telling the American reporter about the missing Soviet plane. Sure, it had bought some time; Robbins had promised not to write anything for now. And it had added a crumb of confirmation about Egypt's nuclear program. But, as it turned out, at a time when Israel already had a man planted with access to every minute detail. Unfortunately a fellow like Robbins, enterprising enough to follow a car from Tzur's place at sunrise, was not about to dust off his hands and walk away. No doubt he would keep on digging. If the nosy American caught on to the larger dimensions of the case, it could screw up everything. There were still loose strands to be cut in Egypt, some nuclear scientists to be bought off or disposed of, perhaps some secret labs to be destroyed in contrived accidents. But that was for others, pros working under the strict control of higher-ups.

He could have no further contact with the newsman. He would see Shavit, fill him in on what Robbins knew, and leave the matter up to him. No more freelance interference on his part; he'd learned his lesson.

He sat down on a flat smooth rock, tucked his arms around his knees. Down below, a thin curl of smoke rose from the chimney in the guest-house kitchen. Even though it was Shabbat, the one morning when most of the *moshavniks* could sleep late, those who had the misfortune to draw weekend duty had to prepare a whopping big breakfast for the tourists.

Ziki nuzzled against his arm, inviting the scratching he knew he would get. Ziki, you grungy old mutt, Tzur thought, scratching him behind the ears.

What had his father once said long ago? Logic is not a deity; faith must also be an important component of life. And what did he, Mordechai Tzur, have faith in, besides himself? What was he doing with his life? Nearly thirty years old and all he thought about was his career in military intelligence. Did he love himself, his freedom to do whatever moved him, more than wonderful, beautiful, patient Batya? He didn't know why he had resisted so long. The love of this woman and the chance to raise a family were more important than life in the city. He'd grown up on the *moshav*; it wasn't so bad.

He could no longer delay a decision about Batya. He had been stringing her along for years without wanting to recognize it, rationalizing his indecision but not being honest with himself or with her. Her best childbearing years were almost gone. If she wasn't going to be his wife, she should choose another.

He would talk it all through with her, thoroughly, thoughtfully, compassionately. They would weigh all the pros and cons and together decide what was best for them both.

Ziki, his sense of hearing still keen, heard Batya coming up the trail and, barking happily, bounded off to greet her. She stood in the clearing to catch her breath after the steep climb. Tzur appreciated the fact that she hadn't pressed him to explain himself before. She knew when he was ready he would share what he could.

The early morning sun, behind her, cast a golden haze around her face and figure. She reminded him of a fawn stopping in the forest to sniff the air, deciding whether it was safe to proceed. At the sight of such elemental grace and beauty his heart quickened and he dismissed his plan to talk out the future of their relationship. That was the old, cold, logical Tzur. He rose and held open his arms to her.

"Good morning, Mrs. Tzur," he said with feeling, "and how would you like to spend the next forty or fifty years?"

She hesitated, a questioning look on her face. Then she broke into a radiant smile. "First," she said, walking slowly to him, "you'll have to ask me properly. Get down on your knee."

Instantly he sank to both knees, throwing his arms around her waist and pressing his face against her body. They both wept, quietly, happily. Ziki barked, trying to press his wet nose between them.

The Author

A Washington-based correspondent for 30 years, Harvard- and Columbia-educated William Beecher is also a former assistant secretary of defense. Now Washington bureau chief of the *Minneapolis Star Tribune*, he has reported in Washington for the *Boston Globe*, the *Wall Street Journal*, and the *New York Times*, where he broke the story of the secret bombing of Cambodia. In 1983 Beecher shared a Pulitzer Prize for his coverage of U.S.-Soviet relations and arms control negotiations. He and his wife, the parents of four daughters, live in Bethesda, Maryland.